A KID WITH A GUN

Flashes of gunfire spewed from the muzzles of their guns, but the shots went wild as the gang was caught up in the excitement of a sudden firefight. The Kid duckwalked to the nearest body and snatched the pistol from the dead man's belt but was having trouble firing it.

Suddenly it was as though they'd figured out where the killing was coming from and the ground around me exploded with their shots. I rolled behind a fallen blackjack tree and the lead from their pistols chewed up bark. The Kid was fumbling with the bandit's pistol, when one of the riders closed ground on him.

The rider had the hooves of his pony thrashing the Kid, and when I drew a bead on him, I saw the man take aim and fire three quick shots into the Kid. Three white flashes that lit up the Kid's frozen features. I took aim and pulled the trigger. . . .

ALSO BY BILL BROOKS

Quint McCannon Westerns
Deadwood
Dust on the Wind

LEAVING
CHEYENNE

Bill Brooks

A DELL BOOK

Published by
Dell Publishing
a division of
Bantam Doubleday Dell Publishing Group, Inc.
1540 Broadway
New York, New York 10036

ISBN: 0-440-22652-X

Printed in the United States of America

Published simultaneously in Canada

February 1999

10 9 8 7 6 5 4 3 2 1

WCD

For Gary and Laurie Davis
who keep a light in the window
and a pallet on the floor for me

CHAPTER 1

All the horses froze that winter. All the cattle. They froze to death where they stood, caught in the teeth of a seven-day storm that rattled windows and doors and killed every living thing that stood in its path. The snow and wind closed all the roads leading into and out of Cheyenne. You could have shot a pistol in any direction and not hit a living soul. Temperatures plunged to sixty below and the cold was so bone-deep, even whiskey couldn't fight it. Men went crazy and women wept with fear because it was like a white death that had descended on that place. Children stared wide-eyed as if they were frozen, too.

Nothing moved among the drifts of snow, and the wind howled like mourning women. Horses and cattle weren't the only creatures who died that winter.

They found Persimmon Bill frozen to death in a snowbank; the only thing exposed was his head, the eyes a milky glaze of white. And when they dug him out, they found the neck of a shattered whiskey bottle in one hand, the snow stained brown around him. Someone said his craving for liquor finally killed him. He was the first one the winter killed.

Little Dick's wife, Cleopatra, grew sick and took to her bed, and Dick wrapped her in blankets and a mangy buffalo robe and placed warmed bricks at her feet, trying to save her. She cried in her delirium that the angel of death rode a pale horse and was coming for her. Against good sense, Little Dick went out in the midst of the storm to fetch the town's only doctor. When he slammed the door behind him, an icicle rattled loose from an overhang and pierced Little Dick's neck and bled him out; his blood froze to an irregular pool of crimson ice beneath him.

Jonas Fly, performing his duty as city marshal, braved the killer storm to go and quell a fight between two prostitutes who were fighting over a miner caught on his way to the goldfields in the Black Hills. The whores had gone into a rage from opium and greed to get the miner's poke, and that, along with the storm that had them locked together, had turned them crazy. One of the whores had a straight razor and slashed the other, cutting the miner in the doing. Jonas made the mistake of getting between them just as the miner pulled a belly-gun to kill the whore. Jonas was felled with a bullet through his eye and a razor cut to his throat. His dying finger squeezed off a shot and killed the other whore.

I was three miles away on my small ranch waiting out the storm that was quickly killing my cattle and horses, and starting to feel a little crazy myself. Everything I owned was dying before my eyes and there wasn't anything that I could do about it. There wasn't anything I could do about my friends, either. I might as well have been a thousand miles away.

When the storm finally blew itself out and the chinooks came again, I surveyed the losses and knew there was nothing left for me in Cheyenne. Every dime I had had gone into buying the ranch and a herd of longhorns whose bodies lay facing south in dark clumps amid the dissipating drifts. My dreams of a settled life were as dead as everything else. The winter had killed us all in one way or another. I knew it was time to move on.

I put the ranch up for sale and watched as the gray wolves and coyotes came and made short work of the carcasses of my cattle and horses. I watched the ice dripping from the eaves and drank bitter black coffee and weighed my options. I was down to thin pockets and no future, a situation I was well accustomed to most of my life. I knew one thing, though: Cheyenne and me were quits. Every reason I had to stay was gone. When finally the weather grew warm enough, I took one last walk up the hill to the cemetery with Cleopatra because she'd asked me if I would. The warm winds tugged at our clothes and the sun lay at low angles across the winter landscape and made the slopes of ice look blue in places. As we climbed the grade to the little boot hill, we could look back and see snow on the roofs of the town and black wisps of smoke curling from stovepipes. It was a peaceful scene if you didn't know better. Death was surely as among the living as it was that little cemetery ridge.

"I'd as soon it had been me that died than him," Cleo said, her voice quavering like wire in the wind. She coughed into a small silk hankie and it tinged red.

"All these years, I waited for a good man to come along. . . ." Her voice lost its strength and she coughed again and knuckled the dampness from her eyes. Her pale features stood in stark contrast to the black mourning dress she wore. I understood what it felt like to be willing to trade places with the dead.

I counted the graves of my friends and it was like ticking off time, each one representing a memory, a good time, a shared glass of liquor, a laugh, a sense of indescribable loss.

"I know he loved me," Cleo said, standing before the rock cairn of Little Dick's final resting place. The ground was still frozen and the dead had to be buried under rocks until the thaw, when graves could be dug. Little Dick, Persimmon Bill, Jonas Fly. Three good men come to a bad end.

"I know he loved you, too," I said to Cleo.

"He left me the café," she said. "But I don't know that I'll stay. I was thinking of selling it and moving East—Boston, maybe." Cleo had been a prostitute that Little Dick had met and married only a few short months before. Maybe she thought she needed to run it past me, her plans to leave Cheyenne, since Little Dick and I had been friends for the better part of twenty years.

"You don't need my permission," I said. "Little Dick would want you to be happy. Slinging hash for cowboys and living up here in this high lonesome country isn't much of a future for a woman."

She put her hand through the crook of my arm.

"Thank you for saying that, Quinten," she said. "Walk me back down the hill to town and I'll fix you a good breakfast before you go off to wherever it is you're planning on going."

I was staring at my reflection in the mirror of the Arbuckle while Cleo was in the kitchen fixing up what she called a "hellacious" breakfast, when the door to the café rattled opened before closing hard against the hard wind. A man wearing a greatcoat and a bowler stood there looking about.

"We're not open for business yet, mister," Cleo said, popping her head out from the kitchen. "There's been a death in the family."

"I didn't come here to eat," he said. Then, looking directly at me with dark, feral eyes under a massive brow, he said, "You McCannon?"

"Who's asking?"

I noticed he had a slight limp as he approached the table.

"Teddy Blue," he said. He looked at Cleo just long enough to make an appraisal, but it wasn't the usual sort of look a man gives a woman; there was nothing to indicate he had that sort of hunger in him.

"I don't know you," I said, taking my makings from my waistcoat to roll a shuck.

His gaze switched back to me.

"You've heard of me, though," he said.

I had. Teddy Blue had a legendary reputation as a cowboy, lawman, buffalo hunter, and Indian fighter.

"Yes, I've heard of you, Mr. Blue."

"You mind?" he said, indicating the empty chair across from me. I nodded and he took the seat, setting his bowler atop the table. I noted the rings he wore:

silver and gold, one on each of his pinky fingers. He unbuttoned the greatcoat and I saw the butt of a pistol in a shoulder rig under his left arm. Walnut grips and a brass strap hung in well-oiled leather.

"I saw a lot of dead cattle and horses on the way up," he said. "Saw the same thing once before in the winter of '68. You could walk clear across Montana on the backs of dead beeves and never once set foot on the ground."

"I know you didn't come here to talk weather," I said.

He twisted his mouth like maybe he had a tooth that was aching. He had a face like granite that had stood the weather for some time.

"I'm looking for a woman," he said.

"A lot of men are."

"I'm looking for a *particular* woman," he said. His eyes lacked amusement, but then, it wasn't an amusing time.

"What does that have to do with me?" I asked.

Cleo came out of the kitchen carrying a plate of eggs, salted slabs of ham, hot biscuits, and a jar of sorghum and set it down without taking her eyes off Teddy Blue.

"We met somewhere before?" she said.

He looked at her again, those dark eyes registering everything about her, every curve and wisp of hair and the way she stood there with her fists balled on her broad hips.

"I think I would have remembered," he said.

"Kansas, maybe," she said. "Perhaps Dodge City."

"No. Least not whenever I was there."

"I have a good memory for faces," Cleo said. "And you sure look like someone I met once."

"Got me confused, sister. Sorry to say."

That seemed to satisfy her curiosity. I was splitting open those warm biscuits and drowning them in sorghum. Seven days waiting out the storm and doing my own cooking had left me famished for a regular meal, something that wasn't burnt black or whang leather–tough.

"She looks sickly, that woman," Teddy Blue said after Cleo retreated to the kitchen.

"It's been a hard winter," I said. "Her man died and now she's got lung fever."

Teddy Blue smoothed the sides of his hair with the palms of his hands, then lightly rested them atop the table next to his bowler. They were hands that had seen hard work, but none lately. The lining of the hat was white silk.

"I never liked it this far north," he said. "Hard country to carve out a living."

"Then why did you come?"

He watched me cut into the biscuits with my fork, watched the sorghum run to the edges of the plate and soak into the eggs.

"Like I said, I'm looking for a woman."

I put the fork down.

"You want to tell me what this has to do with me, Mr. Blue? I'd like to have at this meal before it grows cold."

"I'd like to hire you to help me find her," he said.

"You believe it takes two men?"

"Two men with grit and a reason to find her. I know she came here, know about the two of you. Figured you could lead me to her." He had a rather sure way of speaking, as though he'd done it a lot—used his voice to command attention and to strike bargains.

"This woman," I said, "what's her name?"

I waited for him to tell me the name and when he did, something the size of a fist caught in my chest.

"Etta Landrow," he said. "That's the woman I'm looking for. Least that's the name she was using from what information I've been able to gather."

"You want to tell me why you're looking for her?"

"You knew her, didn't you, McCannon?"

"If you already know that, why ask?"

He cocked his head slightly, twisted his mouth again. He was clean-shaven but the shadow of a beard darkened his chin and cheeks. A small scar cut through his left eyebrow and another the shape of a quarter-moon welted his right cheek.

"She's not who you think she is, McCannon. So if you think you're protecting her from me, you've got it wrong."

"Why don't you tell me what I don't know, Mr. Blue?"

"She's wanted for murder. That's why I'm looking for her."

He pulled back the flap of his greatcoat to reveal a Texas Ranger badge pinned to his waistcoat. I could also see the pistol hanging from the shoulder rig was a double-action .44, a Colt Frontier model.

"You're a little out of your territory," I said, and went back to concentrating on my breakfast.

"I go where I need to go," he said.

"Well, good luck in your search." I made an effort to keep my voice level, to act unaffected by the news he'd brought, but my mind was turning over the information fast.

"You haven't heard me out," he said.

"I've heard enough."

"If you fell in love with her," he said, "you wouldn't be the first. Etta's an easy woman to love."

"How would you know that?"

"I know because she's my wife," he said. Suddenly the eggs and everything else seemed as cold and uninviting as the waning winter. A light rain began to peck at the window.

"Her married name is Etta Jane Blue," he said. "Has sort of a nice ring to it, doesn't it?"

I wasn't buying it. You share the intimacies with a woman the way I had with Etta, you don't just throw all away because of a stranger's accusations.

"Look, I've run out of trail. I'm willing to pay for your help to find her. Five hundred for the information, or your gun to back me up, depending on what you know."

"Five hundred or five thousand, it won't buy anything from me," I said.

"I'm not the only one looking for her, Mr. McCannon. I find her first, she'll get safe transportation back to Denver and a fair trial. The others looking for her find her first, they'll make sure she doesn't make it back to Denver."

Suddenly he had my full attention.

"Who are these others and why do they want her?" I said.

"She was involved in the killing of the son of an important man."

"Who is the man?"

"A federal judge by the name of Thaddeus Beam."

"What does Etta have to do with it?"

"She was reportedly in the escort of another man at the time, a real wild wind. They both knew the dead man and had been seen in his company the night of the killing."

"For being married to her," I said, "it doesn't sound like you kept a tight rein on her."

He shifted his weight in the chair, touched the brim of his upturned bowler, and seemed to study it for a moment.

"We were married a long time ago, Mr. McCannon. It didn't work out. She went her way, I went mine. Trouble is, we never actually got around to a divorce." His gaze fell into the hat like he was looking inside it for something, a lost marriage perhaps.

"So this judge hired you to find her?" I said.

"No. He hired others to do that. I got word of it and decided I'd better round her up before his hired men did."

"Why trouble yourself?"

"Because she's still my wife and I know the assassin the judge hired to find her."

I waited for him to give a name.

"You ever hear of Colorado Charlie Utter?"

All I knew of Colorado Charlie Utter was that he'd paid for Wild Bill Hickok's funeral and a grave marker to have the notorious gunfighter buried in Deadwood, that they'd been pals for a short time, and that right after the funeral, Colorado Charlie Utter disappeared. Not much to know about the man.

"What about him?" I said.

"He's deadly, and intolerant of wayward women.

Rumor has it"—Blue leaned a little over the table—
"that he doesn't like any kind of women."

"You seem to know a lot about him," I said.

"I ran into him and Wild Bill in Kansas one time.
Bill was the law there before they fired him for shooting his deputy. Charlie was there and there was some
talk about his unnatural desires."

"You get around," I said.

"I was a lot of things and been to a lot of places
before I turned to rangering. I know most of the worst
of humanity that roam this frontier. I've put my share
of men in the ground or in prison. I'm good at what I
do, McCannon, make no mistake about it."

He stood then, took up his bowler, and replaced it
atop his head and tapped it lightly.

"I'll be staying the night at the Inter-Ocean and
leaving first thing in the morning. I could stand your
help in finding Etta," he said. "And you look like a
man who could use a stake. And in case you know
where she is and are thinking about getting a jump to
warn her, just remember, McCannon, these others that
are after her—they're all professional gun artists. If
they weren't, they wouldn't be riding with Colorado
Charlie. You'll not want to go them alone. You care at
all about her safety and welfare, you'll throw in with
me. Two of us might stand a chance, least a better
chance than if we go it alone."

"Wish I could help," I said.

He turned as he reached the door.

"Another thing you ought to know," he said.
"That man I told you Etta was involved with, the one I
believe had a hand in the killing of the judge's boy—his
name is Gypsy Davy and he broke jail before they

could hang him. My suspicion is, he's also looking for Etta, probably to make sure she keeps her mouth shut about what happened the night of the murder."

He left and I sat there staring after him through the window, watched as he crossed the street with that slight hitch to his gait and headed for the hotel. Cleo came out of the kitchen and said, "You look like a ghost has jumped into your hide. What did that man want?"

"His wife," I said.

"Good Lord, don't men know that when a woman disappears on them, she's not looking to be found?"

I stared out the window onto a half-frozen world that was as forbidding as a bitter heart, and I knew I'd have to find Etta and learn the truth no matter where that truth led me. I was leaving Cheyenne, but not in the way I'd planned.

If I knew anything at all about her, Etta Landrow wasn't the kind of woman to commit murder no matter what the circumstances. But if I didn't find her before the others did, there would be no way to prove it. I knew Teddy Blue was right about our chances of going it alone as opposed to throwing in together, but I'd learned a long time ago, you didn't buy a pig in a poke. I had to make sure Teddy Blue's story wasn't a pig.

Every time I thought the dance had ended, the old grim fiddler started it up again.

CHAPTER 2

I walked to the telegraph office and sent a wire to a man I knew in Denver—a one-armed old puncher from my droving days who'd ended up striking it rich by marrying a wealthy widow twice his size. Now, instead of sleeping in his soogan on a muddy trail somewhere along that thousand-mile stretch between San Antonio and the Kansas boomtowns, he was sleeping in a canopy bed on satin sheets. His name was Harve Sweetwater. He'd lost his arm while serving as a city constable in Rock Creek, Wyoming, chopped nearly off by a madwoman with a hoe after her man shot him through the jaw. Harve told me later it had been a bad day all the way around and had satisfied himself that he wasn't cut out to be a peace officer. He'd gone to Denver to a hospital to recover and it was there that he had met the rich widow who was volunteering as a nurse. Her name was Zerelda Beechcomb and she took to Harve like a preacher to whiskey. Harve called it a case of mad love.

I knew all this because the last time I was in Denver with Billy Cody, we ran into Harve Sweetwater in an outlandishly opulent restaurant Cody insisted we eat in—they had an oyster bar and Cody liked to be seen by the blue bloods. Cody's surprise was such that when he saw Harve leaning against the bar wearing a fancy black suit and a cravat with a ruby stickpin, he dropped an oyster into his lap. Cody called Harve over and asked him what bank he'd robbed. Harve brayed like a mule and bought us a round of drinks and told us the story of his good fortune.

"I fell into it, boys, like a mud cat into a two-holer. I was lost, and now I'm found."

He looked blissful. Cody looked envious. I figured if a man lost something as dear as his arm, he had a right to whatever good fortune came his way after that. The three of us got as hammered as a keg of roofing nails. Every time Harve tossed back a tumbler of gin rickeys, he would flap his empty sleeve and crow for the waitress to bring us another round.

I thought about that night now, as I waited for the telegrapher to send the telegram, the stuttering clack of his key of small comfort to me. I was grasping at straws trying to find out what I could about Etta's life in Denver. I needed to learn what I could about the killing and Harve Sweetwater was my only source of hope. My mind still wasn't accepting the things Teddy Blue had told me about Etta. Part of me wanted to believe he was a man with a mission but not necessarily the one he claimed. If it was true that he'd been married to her, maybe she was running from him, and maybe she had a reason. I needed to get to the truth and find out what I could. And if anyone knew anything about the sins of the high and mighty in Denver, I figured it to be Harve Sweetwater. He was married into it. I was counting that he could tell me something I didn't already know about the murder and the players involved.

"Make sure and tell the operator at the other end to send someone to deliver that message pronto," I said. The telegrapher peered at me from under his green eyeshade, then tapped out some more code and sat back and waited.

"May take awhile to get a reply back," he said.

"I'll check in with you later," I told him, and headed up the street to the rail station. I needed to buy a ticket on the next flyer to Ogalala. From there, I'd rent a horse and ride out to the ranch that Etta's aunt owned. That was the last place I'd seen Etta, the place I left her while I went off to find Ben Beadle's killer. I'd wanted to go back long before now, but the winter came and killed everything. When I'd left her last, whatever future we had talked about was hanging by a thin string. She had told me when I left that she wouldn't wait forever for me to make up my mind. Now I was sorry as hell I'd taken so long.

I was halfway to the station when I ran into Claude Klingbill, the town's undertaker. He'd buried some of my enemies and most of my friends, and as soon as the ground thawed, he was going to bury a few more. His features were more gaunt than usual and his stovepipe hat was battered and muddy and angled to one side. His gait was unsteady and he smelled like a saloon.

"Awful early to hit the juice, ain't it, Claude?"

His eyes tried to focus on me but were having a devil of a time doing so.

"Mac?"

He started to topple and I caught him before he landed in the mud.

"Easy, Claude."

Through the broadcloth coat, I could feel bones; he seemed like a man without flesh, his frame as starved as a lobo after a hard winter. He hadn't shaved or had a haircut in some time and had the odor of the unwashed mixed with the stink of liquor. That stench caused me to shift downwind of him. I knew Claude as a man who normally took fastidious care about his person, and certainly not a man given to displays of public drunkenness.

He gripped my shoulder with one claw of a hand and steadied himself. "I'll buy you a whiskey if you'll drink it with me," he said.

"It's nine o'clock in the morning, Claude."

"Oh," he said. "Well, hell then, we better get started before they close up the saloons."

"It's none of my business," I said. "But if you fall down in the street and don't get up, a wagon might run over you, or you could suffocate in all this mud."

He swayed slightly, looked about, then settled his gaze on me again. "Hardly would make a difference if I did, Mac." His eyes welled with tears and his hands began to shake.

"Jessie?" I said.

He nodded. The kid he'd been taking care of, the one Long Bill Longly had shot through the spine and crippled, had apparently also been claimed by the harsh winter.

"When?" I said.

"This morning," Claude said, his voice quavering.

"I went in his room and found him staring at the ceiling."

"You did what you could for the boy, Claude. Maybe it's for the best. His suffering is over, we still got ours."

"I know," Claude said. "I know to hell it is and he is in a better place than this crap-hole. But it don't stop me from wanting to get drunk and go dig up Long Bill and shoot him in the goddamn face for what he did to Jesse!"

"Well, hell. If it will make you feel better," I said, "let's go get some shovels and do just that."

Claude looked at me for a moment, saw that I wasn't making fun of him, then smiled at me like a proud father.

"You'd do it, wouldn't you?" he said. "Go dig him up with me so I could shoot him in the face?"

"Hell, yes. I've got nothing better to do right now anyway except buy a train ticket."

"I'm glad they hanged that son of a bitch," Claude said. "But I'd still like to shoot him in the face." He seemed to be talking more to himself now than to me. He muttered something I couldn't make out, then looked at me again like it was the first time he knew I was standing there.

"Ticket?" he said. "You leaving?"

"For good this time, Claude. The winter took all my livestock and killed off all my friends but you. I've got no reason to stay. I guess I wasn't cut out to be a rancher. What I know about raising cows you could stick in your hat. A man ought to stick to what he does best. Besides, there's some business I have to go take care of."

"Hell," Claude said, looking all around him. "We all got reasons to leave this godforsaken place!"

"You going to be okay?" I asked. "If I turn loose of you, you won't fall down in the street and get run over by a wagon or smother in the mud, will you?"

He straightened himself mightily and I felt the bones go stiff in his arm.

"I may be miserable and drunk," he said. "But I am too dignified to fall down and let some damn ignorant teamster run over me or drown with my face in the mud."

"Good," I said. "I don't need to lose any more friends."

"None of us do," he said. "By the way, where you taking the train to?"

"Nebraska," I said.

He blinked, staggered a step, caught himself, and said, "Pitiful choice, Mac, pitiful choice."

I waited until he made it across the street and into the Blue Star before going to the station to buy my ticket. The next train to Ogalala wasn't for another two days. When I came out of the station, I saw Teddy Blue standing across the street smoking a cigar. He'd just cupped the flame to the tip and was snapping out the match, the gems of his pinky rings catching the sunlight. He nodded and I kept walking.

CHAPTER 3

My horse was hitched to the rail in front of Little Dick's Café, but my gear was stowed in a back room of Kung Chow's Laundry just across the street. I'd thought last year when I'd bought the ranch that I'd never have to sleep in a room the size of a jail cell again, that I'd have plenty of space to sprawl my lanky frame and let fly my elbows and lots of windows to look out of. And for a time on the ranch I did. Now I was right back where I started the first day I set foot in Cheyenne. Texas was beginning to look good to me again, and that was a bad sign.

The old Celestial was spooning some soup into his puckered mouth, drops of it glistening on his chin whiskers, when I walked in and closed the door behind me.

"Mistah Quint, you back already," he said. "You want me to fix you some soup, it's got some chicken in it?"

"No thanks," I said. The soup was a thin yellow

water and I sure didn't see any chicken floating around in it.

"That must have been a pretty small chicken, Kung," I said. He grinned until his eyes disappeared behind the waxy folds of his skin.

"Most the chicken gone now, just some of the feet all that's left. But still pretty good."

Chicken feet soup had never been a favorite of mine. Kung couldn't have weighed more than ninety pounds with lead in his pockets. It wasn't surprising; all the man ever consumed was soup and tea.

"I'll be leaving in the morning," I said. "You can rent out my room after I'm gone."

He looked up from his bowl. It was a glass bowl with little blue fat-bellied figures painted on it, the same as the ones on his teacup.

"You leave for good, Mistah Quint? You not coming back?"

"First train out," I said. "I'd like to settle up with you for the room."

He slurped down more of the soup and watched me with the curious gaze of a cat.

"Three dollah," he said. "Should be enough."

I took the money from my waistcoat pocket and set it on the table next to his teacup.

He eyed it for a moment, then went back to eating his soup.

"Sorry to see you go, Mistah Quint. You a funny man, always make Kung laugh. Ha ha."

I never understood why he thought I was a funny man, but then there was a whole lot I'd never understand about Kung. You look into his eyes and you knew that they've seen some strange and mysterious events, things you'd like to ask him about. But like me, or like any man, Kung's private world was better left undisturbed.

"You'll have to give me the recipe for that chicken feet soup," I said.

His laughter sounded like rice paper being ripped apart.

I packed what few possessions I owned, but my mind was still turning over the events of the story Teddy Blue had told me. It didn't seem possible that Etta could or would be involved in murder. And it seemed even less likely she'd be running with the likes of Gypsy Davy, a notorious individual, according to Teddy Blue. Question was, who was he and why was she in his company?

I made a shuck and smoked it slow and stared out the one lone window that looked onto an alley. The snow lay in dirty clumps, but above the roof lines I could see a triangle of flawless blue sky, the world in contrast between its beauty and its ugliness.

I wondered how I could have been so wrong about Etta, then realized that, the truth be told, I'd known the woman for a total of only six days—plenty of time for a man to let himself be fooled, especially if the object of his foolishness was a russet-haired beauty with soft hands and a warm smile.

But I also remembered looking into her eyes and knew that whatever we'd shared couldn't have been a total lie. Somewhere between the idea and the reality stood the truth, and I aimed to find out what it was. Regardless of what secrets or sins there were, I'd be damned before I allowed any harm to come to her.

There was a knock at the door and when I opened

it, a kid stood there with a telegram in his hand. He was a waif with dirty cheeks and rolled down socks who I'd recognized from around town running odd jobs and errands. I'd heard his folks died of diphtheria and he was an orphan, twelve, maybe thirteen years old. The West was full of orphan kids and they were forced to grow up fast or perish. This one had the eyes of an old man, tired and distrustful.

"Telegram, mister. Old Man Kersaw told me to bring it to you."

He stood there after handing me the telegram and I gave him half a buck. He looked at it, then put it in his shirt pocket and thanked me.

"Hey, kid. What's your name?"

"Eli, mister. Why you asking?"

My own son would have been about this boy's age had he not died of the milk sickness as an infant. "No reason, kid," I said. "Thanks for bringing me the telegram."

I waited until he left, then read the wire.

GODDAMN AND JESUS! I HEARD YOU WAS DEAD, KILT AND BURIED IN THAT HELLHOLE TEXAS! STOP I GUESS YOU AIN'T STOP I GOT INFORMATION YOU REQUESTED BUT JUST AS SOON DELIVER IT TO YOU IN THE LIVING FLESH STOP CATCHING THE AFTERNOON FLYER WILL BE IN CHEYENNE TONIGHT STOP DON'T LEAVE UNTIL I ARRIVE STOP LOADED FOR BEAR AND READY FOR ADVENTURE STOP YOURS H SWEETWATER ESQ

I read the telegram again, disbelieving the message. What the hell was that crazy fool up to? I hadn't requested that he come to Cheyenne, nor did I want him there. My plan was to travel fast and light. Unless I was wrong, Teddy Blue would be on the morning flyer to Ogalala dogging my steps. That was fine, because I planned on renting the fastest horse in Nebraska and shaking him off my tail once mounted.

I went directly to the telegraph office and sent a wire to Denver.

"Just two words?" Kersaw asked when he looked at what I'd written.

"Send them!" I said.

He nodded and tapped out the words "Don't Come" then charged me a nickel.

"You could have gotten a full line for the same price," he said, but I was already halfway out the door. Last thing I needed was a Texas Ranger and a one-armed puncher riding my heels while I looked for Etta.

CHAPTER 4

Strange things happen when men are left with too much idle time on their hands.

The chinooks were easing the cold and warming the air enough that icicles dripped steadily from the overhangs, turning the main drag into a slop of mud. But even warm winds weren't enough to relieve some of the madness the killing winter had wrought.

I'd walked across the street to Little Dick's Café to get a cup of coffee and tell Cleopatra I was leaving on the next flyer and that if she was smart, she would sell the café and leave, too. The place was full and she was busy. I had to stand around until a pair of bachelors vacated a table near the window.

Cleo had hired one of the local prostitutes to help her in the café after Little Dick's death. The whoring business had nearly died along with everything else that winter. It was an arrangement that suited both women.

The younger woman's name was Katy O'Brian. She had copper hair, green eyes, and a brogue that spoke of shanty Irish. The way I heard it was she'd come from Brooklyn, New York, and worked her way West with a theatrical troupe. How she ended up in Cheyenne was just a matter of misfortune, like most everybody else who'd ended up here, myself included among the lot.

She wasn't unpleasant to look at and after I took my seat, she came to my table. She wore a prim but simple calico dress and a white apron; her hair was bunched atop her head and held with Spanish combs.

"Marnin', sar," she said, and offered me a half-hearted smile.

I ordered coffee and she poured me a cup from the pot she carried and asked if there would be anything else. For a full moment our gaze met, then I nodded that the coffee would be all and she left and I forced myself not to let my gaze follow the swing of her hips. The winter had been long and lonely and Katy O'Brian was the only other woman in the place besides Cleo. But my mind was on another woman and I needed to keep it there.

That's when I looked out the window and saw more of what the winter madness had wrought.

Two men were rapidly approaching each other from opposite directions—one from the east end of town, the other from the west. They had their pistols drawn and aimed. One of the men was Charlie Harrison, the other Jim Levy, and both had reputations as shootists. I knew them slightly but couldn't attest to their abilities with a side arm, for I'd never seen either of them shoot so much as a prairie dog. I couldn't hear what they were shouting as they closed the distance between them, but about forty paces apart, they began firing at each other.

The sudden eruption of gunshots made the diners drop their forks and dive for shelter under their tables. I counted seven shots before I saw Harrison fall. He tumbled to the mud and lay there for a moment, then struggled to rise. Then I watched as Levy hurried to the wounded man, stopped a foot from him, aimed his pistol, and fired a final round into Harrison's skull. Levy did this as casually as if it had been a turkey shoot. He then knocked the spent rounds from his revolver, reloaded, and sauntered off toward the Blue Star, leaving Harrison sprawled in the muddy street. I didn't know what their differences were and it really wasn't any of my concern, but it angered me that one man would kill another in such an indefensible position, as Levy had done.

Several patrons rushed outside once the shooting subsided and pretty quickly a crowd had gathered around the body of the slain man.

"Well, isn't somebody going to do something?" a woman said. She was holding the hand of a child who stared wide-eyed at the dead man. "Doesn't any of you have a sense of decency?"

"Don't know what you'd have us do, Emma. We ain't got no law since Jonas was murdered," a man in a brocade vest said. " 'Sides, the way I saw it, it was a fair fight. Charlie just wasn't as good a shot as ole Jim was."

"Pick this man up and take him to Claude Klingbill's," I said. "The woman's right—decent people don't leave dead men lying on the street!"

It took a moment before several of the bystanders grabbed up the corpse and carted him off to Klingbill's.

I guess the woman was mistaken about my intentions, for she approached me and said, "I'm glad that somebody is willing to do something! Will you go and arrest the killer of that poor man?"

"They were both armed," I said. "No judge or jury would convict him."

She glared at me for a moment, then turned sharply and pulled the child after her.

I walked to the Blue Star, entered, and approached the bar where Jim Levy stood drinking with several men who were talking about the gunfight and buying him drinks. He didn't seem to mind all the attention. I took my place along the oak. It wasn't any of my business, that's what I told myself.

"Hell of a piece of gun work out there," I said.

Jim Levy turned toward me, his gaze taking me in. "What say?"

"The way you walked up and shot that man in the head once he was down—hell of a piece of gun work."

He stiffened.

"I never shot two men in one day, mister. Don't push your luck."

"No, Levy, you haven't shot two men in one day and you won't today, either, unless you're a hell of a lot luckier with me than you were with Harrison."

His eyes narrowed.

"I know you," he said. "You was one of Ben Beadle's men. McCannon, that's it."

"Yeah," I said. "That's who I was."

"You looking to mix it up?" he said. Some of the men surrounding him looked eager to see Levy kill his second man that day. Like I said, it had been a damn long, boring winter.

"No. Just saying it doesn't take a lot to walk up and shoot a wounded man."

"Well maybe I ought to shoot you," he said.

"Yeah, maybe you ought to," I said. "But I won't miss like Harrison did, so you better not, either."

His features slackened and I knew the starch had gone out of him.

Somebody standing to his right whispered to him that I was the one who'd killed Dave Beltrain, the previous city marshal, and sent Bill Longly to the gallows. That took some more of the starch out of him.

"It was a fair fight, McCannon," Levy's crony said. "We all saw it."

"Yeah, it was a fair fight," Levy said. "The son of a bitch stole a shirt of mine and I called him out on it."

"You killed a man over a shirt?"

He nodded.

"It was wool," he said, as if that justified it.

"Jesus Christ," I said and walked away.

I spent the rest of the day buying a new mackinaw and a pair of boots for my trip to Nebraska and generally trying to kill time that was crawling slower than a mud turtle. I knew if I let myself, I could get drunk as sin just to forget why things were the way they were. At one time in my wild days, I'd known the bottle a lot better than I knew my own name. Two years of fighting for a losing cause in the Civil War then losing a wife and a son to milk sickness had left me adrift in a world where only Tennessee sipping whiskey and the hollow affections of whores could come anywhere close to easing the pain and keeping the nightmares at bay.

Forty-one years old and I'd already outlived most of my contemporaries. I felt like a man alone in the world and the hand of desire for old escapes kept knocking at my door—all I had to do was answer. And I almost did answer it that night when Katy O'Brian showed up at my room in the back of Kung Chow's Laundry.

"I saw the look you gave me this marnin'," she said. "I know when a man is interested."

I felt ashamed of myself because she'd been right; I had looked at her like a man who was interested.

I'd been lying on the bed in the darkness when I heard the knock. Out of habit, I had slid the self-cocker from its holster and told whoever it was to enter. The dim light from the hall behind her was enough to make me ease the hammer down on the pistol and lay it aside. That's when she told me that she noticed the way I'd looked at her.

"I won't lie to you," I said. "But I'm not looking for any company tonight."

"I am," she said, closing the door behind her. I sat up on the side of the bed and lit the oil lamp and watched the flame climb up the glass chimney and spread a soft yellow glow in that corner of the room.

"I've brought a bottle of whiskey," she said. "For us."

She set a three-quarters-full bottle of Red Thunder—a busthead liquor made of alcohol, plug tobacco, and snake heads—next to the lamp, then I watched her remove her black wool capote and scarf and toss them on the foot of the bed. She still wore the calico dress I'd seen her in at the café. It rustled when she moved.

"Will you pour me a glass?" she said.

I excused myself and went out to the laundry and found a pair of teacups in a cupboard where I knew Kung kept his plates and bowls. I had no intention of involving myself with Katy O'Brian, but I knew the look of loneliness when I saw it and understood the need for company on a desolate night, so I didn't turn her out like I probably should have.

"I sometimes think of killing myself," she said, sitting on the edge of the bed next to me. The glass cup in her hands probably cost more than a whole barrel of the cheap whiskey held inside it. "Life, you know, it gets hard lots of times." I watched her drink from the cup, putting it to her lips and taking a deep swallow before holding it out for me to refill.

"I came all this way for a man only to discover that the man I came all this way for didn't want me after a few months of having me. Strange creatures, men are. They hound you and hound you until they get what they want, then when you give it to them, they don't want it anymore. Like little boys, really."

Her Irish brogue was tinged with deep bitterness.

"After that, I quit trying to figure it out," she said. "I had to eat, to live, you know? And there's only one thing a man will pay a girl for way out here—anywhere, for that matter. So when Garrity left me, I figured why should I give myself to the next man who wants me, only to wind up in the same boat?

"Why should I do that now?" she said, turning her face toward me.

"I can't think of any reason," I said, and poured myself half a cup of her whiskey.

"You are damn right," she said. "So I began charging for it and I defy anyone to tell me it's wrong to want to survive."

I didn't know what Katy O'Brian wanted, so I just listened.

"Thing is, a garl can kid herself for only so long. And after a time, after she's got herself enough of a reputation, you know, ain't no man going to want to take her for his wife—not when he can get what he wants for a dollar or two and not be troubled with the rest of it."

I tossed back my drink and reached for my makings.

"Would you mind rolling me a cigarette, too?" she said.

I rolled us each one and we smoked in silence, the slow burn of the paper replacing whatever words we might have shared for that time. She drank her whiskey and asked for more and I filled her cup again and she drank that. Then she leaned over to set her cup down next to the bottle and as she did, she kissed me. Her mouth was soft and wet and her inexperience at such an intimacy proved itself in the awkwardness of the kiss. I didn't kiss her back and I didn't pull away. I was torn between my own loneliness and hers, knowing for her, at least, it didn't matter who or what I was, just as long as I was willing to drink with her and listen to her and share the empty hours with her.

The kiss lingered but a moment, then she pulled away and looked at me.

"You saying you don't want me?" she asked. "Am I not woman enough for you, or is it because I'm a prostitute?"

"You're young enough to be my daughter," I said.

"I thought men liked that," she said. "Men are always telling me how much they like it that I'm young."

"Maybe some men, Katy, but not all of us are like that."

"You don't have any desire for me?" she said, her hand resting on my knee.

"Yes, I have some desire for you, and for that I'm ashamed. I'll drink with you, and I'll sit here and talk with you and listen to you, but I won't sleep with you."

She looked duly disappointed.

"I've come to that," she said. "Where a decent man won't have me even for free."

"How much is passage to New York?" I said.

"What?"

"I'll be happy to buy you passage back to New York if that will help."

"Do you think a garl like me will fare any better in New York than out here on the frontier?" she said. "Ha, the only thing different would be that back in New York I'd have a pimp to see I worked and gave him every dime!"

"Then what's the answer for you, child?" I said.

She lowered her gaze and let her hand slide from my knee.

"Answer," she said. "There is none. I am what I am, what the fates have made me. I'm a young whore who will soon be an old one and we all know what happens to them, eh?"

"It doesn't have to be like that," I said.

"Oh surely it does, sar. How else can it be?"

I took twenty dollars from my saddle pockets and placed it in her hand.

"You can do with this what you want, Katy. You can spend it on liquor or opium, or buy yourself passage back to New York. It's not much, but it could be a start."

She stared at the money for a long time.

"I don't want it," she said, and tried to give it back to me.

I curled her fingers into a fist. "Keep it," I said.

"I'd like to do something for you," she said.

"Maybe someday you can."

She kissed me again, then stood and put on her capote and scarf and took what was left of her whiskey and said, "I thought it would surely be a cold day in hell before a man ever gave me money without me giving him something in return."

"Judging by the sound of that wind outside," I said, "it surely is."

"Cheyenne and hell," she said. "It's all like the same place, ain't it?"

"One and the same."

"Yes, exactly." She laughed and waved her bottle and slipped away.

I lay on the bed for a long time and stared at the darkness and listened to the wind chattering against the glass, and it sounded like the teeth of hunger gnawing at my soul.

CHAPTER 5

A hard knocking and a loud feminine voice shattered the dream I was having. I opened my eyes to the dull pearlescent light of morning that angled its way through the window of my room. It took me a few moments to get my bearings straight. The dream had been about a woman and a moonlit river that ran red.

"Quint! Quint!" The voice was Cleopatra's.

I pulled on a pair of drawers and opened the door.

"You've got to come," she said. "It's Claude!"

"What's happened?" I asked as I put on my shirt and boots.

"You won't believe," she said. "Come quick!"

When I emerged from Kung's, I could see a crowd gathered at the far end of the street and directly in front of the Blue Star Saloon.

In my rush I grabbed up the self-cocker but left without my hat. A man on the streets of Cheyenne without his hat wasn't considered fully dressed.

Cleo hurried ahead of me toward the crowd holding her skirts and high-stepping through the mud.

For a crowd, it was a quiet bunch. I pushed my way through and that's when I saw Claude and Long Bill Longly—well, the corpse of Long Bill Longly, stiff as a board and trussed to a hitch-rail with baling wire. Claude had himself a mean-looking shotgun that he was aiming at the dead man.

"You killed that boy, you evil son of a bitch!" Claude cursed. There was a dried rose in the lapel of Long Bill's black suit that looked fresher than its owner and all in all, it was a real strange scene.

"Claude," I said.

The undertaker looked around and I could see he was, if anything, drunker this morning than he had been the day before.

"I dug the bastard up, Mac, just like I said I was going to. Now I'm going to give him some of his own medicine, going to cash in his chips for what he did to Jesse."

"Looks to me like Long Bill's chips have already been cashed in, Claude. You really think this will make you feel better—blasting him with that scattergun?"

"Goddamn, it took me half the night to dig him up, but I did it! Want the whole town to see what happens to trash that kills innocent boys!"

Claude's clothes were splattered with mud, even the seat of his pants. Tears ran down his cheeks and his hair stuck out wildly. He was a sorry and pathetic sight.

I looked around at the crowd but no one said a word.

From the far end of town, the engineer on the morning flyer from Denver cut loose the whistle as he approached the station and the sharp blast caused several people to jump.

"Claude, this would be unseemly if you were to shoot a dead man," I said. "Folks around here would find a thing like that hard to forget."

"I don't want them to forget!" he shouted. He had a hard time maintaining his balance and staggered about like he was stepping in postholes, trying hard not to topple over. I was worried that he'd fall and accidently shoot himself.

"Why don't we go have a drink and talk about this," I said.

He blinked, looked around, looked at Long Bill, whose eyes were closed and oblivious to Claude's rancor, then back at me.

"Soon as I fry his hash!" Claude said, trying to steady the twin barrels on the stony figure of Long Bill. Death had not been kind to Bill; some of the skin was sloughing off his hands and cheeks. His color had turned an ash-gray and his hair was stringy.

"Maybe you should use this," I said, offering him my self-cocker. "Makes less of a mess."

Claude started to protest the offer of the pistol until I reminded him that there were women and children in the crowd. "You don't want to leave those little ones with nightmares all the rest of their days, do you, Claude? That's no way for people to remember you. Besides, some of those pellets might miss their mark, hit someone innocent."

He looked sheepish and a bit contrite.

"You're right," he said, and started to trade his shotgun for the pistol.

Just then a voice like the sound of gravel in a bucket stirred from the crowd.

"Jesus H. Christ! I've seen about everything now!"

A voice like that you don't forget in a lifetime.

Parting the crowd of gawkers like Moses parting the Red Sea came Harve Sweetwater, Esq., formerly of Texas and lately of Denver high society, fully decked out in a beaver hat, buckskin jacket, and striped trousers tucked down inside a pair of fancy hand-tooled boots; he had a hogleg with a twelve-inch barrel strapped to his hip in a silver-encrusted holster shoved in his waistband. The gun was a Ned Buntline Special. He even wore a checkered cape like the one Wild Bill Hickok used to wear. He looked for all the world like he'd just stepped off the front cover of one of Dewitt's Ten Cent Romances, an actor about to give his greatest performance. Wild Bill and Billy Cody would have laughed their arses off.

"Claude Klingbill, when the hell did you start supplying your own business?" Harve cawed. "Why, that man looks deader'n Stonewall Jackson, God rest his soul."

It took Claude several seconds to recognize Harve, but as soon as he did, tears formed in his eyes.

"Harve, is it really you?" Then seeing the empty sleeve, Claude said, "Where's your arm?"

"Left it up in Rock Creek to a woman with a hoe, nothing but a bone by now, I suspect, all the meat chewed off by the coyotes and wolves. I aim to go back there someday and see if I can find it, take it and have it bronzed now that I can afford to. Now let me ask you something, why the hell you getting ready to plug a dead man?"

Claude looked at the shotgun in his hands as though seeing it for the first time. Harve looked at me and said, "Quint, how you been?"

"You didn't get my wire not to come?" I said.

"What wire?" he said with a mischievous grin.

I knew it was pointless to say anything more about his arrival.

"I was just going to shoot Long Bill," Claude said.

"Why?" Harve asked, as he took a closer gander at Long Bill, then wrinkled his nose and added, "This feller's putrid."

By now, the crowd was beginning to grow restless, unsure of whether there was going to be a show or not. Some had disappointed looks on their faces, realizing that they might not get a good story to tell their grandkids about how a drunken undertaker dug up a dead man and shot him right there on the streets of Cheyenne. They would say it was the result of the terrible winter, how it turned men crazy, even men like Claude Klingbill, who was a paragon of propriety. There would be lots of stories to tell about that winter, but none would be quite so interesting as that of seeing a dead man shotgunned. So they were growing a little restless waiting for Claude to fill Long Bill full of buckshot.

"Of course he's putrid," Claude said. "He's been dead since last autumn."

Harve shook his head as he continued to inspect the corpse. "I heard you had a bad winter up here," he said. "Just never knew how bad until now. Did he pop up out of the ground himself, or did someone dig him up?"

"What difference does it make?" Claude said.

"None that I can see," Harve said, then looked at the pistol in my hand. "He must have been a bad piece of work for you to have dug him out of the ground so you could both shoot him."

"This is foolish," I said. "Claude, give me that shotgun before you shoot your feet off!"

Without so much as a word, he handed me the shotgun. I asked some of the men to get a wagon and take Long Bill back up to boot hill, then said to Harve, "If you came here to help, you can start by helping me get Claude sober."

"Hell, I knew the minute you sent that wire," Harve said, "you were ass-deep in trouble of some sort or other." He took an arm and I took an arm and together we marched Claude to his house where we tried to pump him full of hot black coffee.

Claude sputtered and cursed and carried on, then passed out on the bed from exhaustion.

Harve looked at him a long minute, then said, "Do you think he has passed over?" He put his ear to Claude's chest and listened, then added, "Nope, he ain't dead."

"Why'd you come, Harve?" I said. "I sent you a wire telling you not to."

He produced a silver flask, unscrewed the cap and took a pull, then handed it to me. I declined. "I've not had my breakfast yet."

"This is breakfast, son. A cowboy's breakfast, or have you forgot?"

"It's been forever since we were drovers, Harve."

"It ain't been that long, son. We ain't that far removed from what we was. Look at me: I'm a rich man, but I still spit in the street. And look at you, you ain't changed a lick. Still tall in the saddle, restless as tumbleweed. Why ain't you married and settled down with a bunch of ankle biters?"

"You look like you're doing okay for yourself, Harve—that fancy jacket and new boots," I said. "And that hat had to cost you thirty dollars. And if you came here to talk old times, you've wasted a trip."

Harve took another pull, looked at the flask, which had *HHS, Esq* engraved on it, then said, "That's twenty-dollars-a-bottle firewater, son. Sweet as honey, smooth as a woman's teat, but it'll sneak up on you and kick you like a mule." Then he smacked his lips and flapped his good arm and the empty sleeve that held his stump, crowing like a rooster.

"Look here at this piece of iron ole Ned Buntline gave me. Sumbitch will shoot the eye out of a gnat at a hundred paces! I came loaded for bear, son. Came to help you do some killing!"

"Who said anything about killing?" I said.

He looked at Claude passed out on the bed, then at me, his whiskey flask in one hand, his Buntline Special poking down along the leg of his trousers and said, "I know anything at all about you, I know we're going to do some killing!"

CHAPTER 6

A strong wind blew out of the north and Harve said, "Jesus Christ, this is cold country," and pulled his flask.

"Twenty-dollar whiskey," he said with a shudder. "Goddamn, never thought I'd be drinking twenty-dollar whiskey."

"You want to tell me what you learned that made you hop a northbound freight and come all this way?" I said.

We'd left Claude stretched out on his bed snoring peacefully and walked over to Little Dick's Café. Cleopatra was hustling flapjacks and slabs of bacon to some of the same faces I'd seen in the crowd a few minutes earlier who had been waiting to see a dead man get shotgunned.

"That's a fine-looking woman," Harve said, watching Cleo hustle tables. "Lot's of hip and thigh to her."

"You mind?" I said.

"Soirees, Mac."

"What the hell is that supposed to mean?"

"It's what the rich people do in their free time—attend soirees. Zerelda, God rest her soul, loved nothing better than to throw a soiree and she threw lots of them."

"Harve, if you caught the flyer up here just to tell me about Denver social life, I'm not interested."

Cleo ventured over and Harve ran his gaze over her like she was a piece of grazing land he had in mind for a thousand head of hungry longhorns. She eyed him askance and shook her head.

"You boys want coffee?"

"Just enough to spill some of this sipping whiskey into, sis," Harve said.

I glanced across the room and saw Katy O'Brian waiting on a fat man and several of his cronies, one of which was Jim Levy, who had his back to me. I saw Levy reach out and take her by the wrist and pull her toward him, then say something to her before losing his grip.

"Why dilute good whiskey?" Cleo said, referring to Harve's admiration of his liquor.

He snorted and lifted the flask in a salute and said, "Sis, you're just the ticket."

"You'd not be the first one to come along and try and charm the bloomers off me, mister."

He found that humorous. I found it distracting.

"Bring us coffee, Cleo, and don't turn your back on this one-armed reprobate."

"Cut off my other arm," Harve said, "and I'd still have eyes."

"Tell me what you found out about the murder," I said. "Before you wear my ears out."

He snuffled and leaned forward.

"Those soirees I was trying to tell you about," he said, "are where the rich and powerful let their hair down, and sometimes their drawers. A man can learn a lot of dirt by just listening."

"You know, Harve, listening to you get the facts out on the table is like riding to Austin backward on a bony mule. Spit out what you're getting at."

"You've gotten irritable in your old age," he said.

I leaned back and rolled myself a shuck while waiting for my coffee and Harve to tell me what he knew about the murder.

"Judge Beam and Chief of Police Tommy Murphy was among the regulars who attended Zerelda's soirees, so I knew them about as well as I cared to. And it was Murphy who led the investigation into the judge's boy's murder. The kid's name was Tyron and he was just the opposite of the judge in every respect when it came to his morals and reputation. They say he liked to beat up whores, for one thing. Maybe that had something to do with them finding his body in the red-light district."

I felt a dull throbbing just behind my eyes.

"And there was something else, too," Harve said. "His ears was missing."

"Missing?"

"Somebody cut them off and took them." Harve had a vacant look in his bloodshot eyes like he was trying to see a dead man without any ears.

"You ever hear of a wild hair called Gypsy Davy?" he said.

I told him about Teddy Blue and how he had dropped the same name on me.

"Seven shades of humanity," Harve said, spilling

some of his whiskey into his coffee cup then adding three spoonfuls of sugar.

"What's this man have to do with the killing?"

"Gypsy Davy is a breed, but worse than that: he's an educated breed—went to Harvard, which is somewhere back East. The boy has himself a law degree and they say he was also some sort of a doctor, too. Dark-haired and dark-eyed, handsome devil and women fall all over themselves at the very sight of him."

"This doesn't sound like the same man Teddy Blue told me about," I said.

"He tell you Gypsy Davy is a stone killer?"

I nodded.

"Well, he is that, too."

"How do you come by this information, Harve?"

"Gypsy Davy was, until the murder, the most popular feller in Denver. Hell, Zerelda and all the other rich matrons in the city couldn't wait to invite him to a soiree, that's how I come to know him."

"So the thinking is, he killed the judge's boy, this Tyron?"

Harve shrugged his shoulders. "Well, he was arrested for the killing, then broke jail. Word has it he said this woman was to blame, that he was innocent."

"Tell me about her," I said, feeling a coldness trickle through my blood.

"She was a looker," Harve said, smacking his lips after sipping his coffee.

"What was her name?"

He squinted the name into memory. "Etta, I believe it was," Harve said. "That's all the name I got on her. She was seen in his company at one of Zerelda's soirees and between the pair of them, you didn't need no gas light to see by. They lit up the room."

Harve described her to me and I was having a hard time denying that it was Etta Landrow, the same woman I'd fallen in love with.

"What about this business with the ears?" I said.

Harve shifted his weight in his chair.

"They say Gypsy Davy keeps himself a necklace of ears from the men he's killed. I think that's what put Chief Murphy onto him as a suspect—the kid's missing ears and that necklace."

"Tell me you're pulling my leg on this one, Harve."

Harve shook his head.

"Wore 'em once to one of Zerelda's soirees. Looked like black prunes. Only he claimed he'd bought them from some natives in Borneo when he was traveling the world."

"How the hell does such a man get invited to rich folks' parties?" I said.

"The rich are easily bored, Mac. Anything out of the ordinary, they're interested in. And a fellow like Gypsy Davy with his handsome looks, fancy talk, and educated ways fits right in. That string of ears helped make him a curiosity. Sorta like a big rattler, dangerous and fascinating as hell all at once, if you know what I mean."

"Tell me something," I said. "Why isn't a man like that swinging from the end of a rope instead of drinking champagne and rubbing elbows with the wealthy?"

Harve looked at me, then said, " 'At's a good goddamn question and I don't know, except to say that wealth brings its own perversity to the table."

There was a commotion and a shattering of glass

and I looked around in time to see Katy O'Brian stumbling backward and Jim Levy rising out of his chair, his face flushed red.

He didn't have time to push her again before I hammered him over the head with the barrel of my pistol and dragged him outside.

He sputtered and struggled like a man hell-bent on getting himself killed will do, but I had a good grip on him and when I turned him loose, he landed in the mud. He managed to struggle to his knees and feel around for the knot on the back of his skull before recognizing who it was that had done the damage to him.

"McCannon! You son of a bitch!" His fingers came away smeared with blood and this incensed him even more. He managed to rise halfway before I hit him again, cracking the barrel atop his collarbone and that put an end to his cursing me. He howled like a scalded dog.

"Next time you want to get rough with somebody, Jim, come see me," I said, and turned to go back inside the café. Several diners had followed us out and stood there with napkins stuffed in the collars of their shirts. If they weren't going to get to see a dead man get killed, maybe they could at least see one or two live ones end up dead.

Somebody yelled something and before I could turn around, two pistol shots cracked the air almost at the same time. The plate glass window behind me shattered into a rain of broken glass and I was still drawing my piece when I saw Jim lying facedown in the mud, smoke curling from the barrel of a pistol in his left hand. Ten feet away stood Teddy Blue with a policeman's model Colt still aimed at the back of Jim Levy's spine.

I watched as Teddy Blue slipped the revolver back into the shoulder rig under his greatcoat, then tipped his plug hat in my direction.

"You should have killed that man when you had him down," Teddy Blue said. "Lucky thing I came along or it'd be you in the soup, and I'd be out a man to help me find those people I'm looking for."

Those people, I thought.

Harve was right, there was going to be killing and it had already begun.

CHAPTER 7

That night I drank a whiskey alone in the Blue Star and thought about the train ride to Ogalala the next morning. I had a lot of questions to ask Etta Landrow, or was it Etta Blue? Whoever she really was, she'd done a damn good job on capturing my heart. And I wondered if it wasn't a case now that I'd just been too lonely for too long and had let myself be blinded by a pretty lady with a soft voice and a warm bed. I hated myself for even thinking that way about her. The whiskey tasted good but it wasn't doing its job of making me forget.

Earlier, Harve had gotten drunk by noon and I let him pass out on the bed in my room behind Kung Chow's Laundry. It was just as well, I didn't crave company, his or anyone else's. I thought about the men who were after Etta, thought about what Teddy Blue said about Colorado Charlie Utter and the assassins the judge had sent to find Etta and make sure his own brand of justice was carried out. I thought about Gypsy

Davy and wondered how it was she came to be involved with a man who would wear a necklace of dead men's ears.

I'd kicked around for a lot of years and never heard or came across anything to match the things I was hearing now.

I thought of Texas and the old friend I'd shot down there near the border over a woman; thought about my late wife and son. I was a man with no home and no place to go and the last good thing I'd found in life was a woman named Etta Landrow who people were now telling me was involved in an ugly murder with some really bad company.

I didn't want to believe it and I wasn't going to believe it until I heard it from Etta. That was if I could find her before Judge Beam's assassins did. Teddy Blue sat at a table in the far corner by himself and I knew he was dogging my every move, but unless I walked up and shot him, there wasn't much I could do about it. I grabbed the neck of the Jack Daniel's and walked over to his table.

He didn't say anything.

I poured out two whiskeys and set one before him.

"It's not much for saving my hide out there on the street today," I said.

He nodded and tossed the liquor back before swiping off his mustache.

"You were the law down in Del Rio at one time," he said.

"How'd you know?"

"I heard about the killing. You did the state a favor by putting that hombre in a deep hole."

He was talking about Pancho Vega, the old amigo and border bandit I'd killed over a faithless woman.

"We ever met before?" I said.

"No, but word gets around. I was with Company A of the Texas Rangers back then, running down the last few wild Comanches that still had enough fire in them to raise hell."

"And now?" I asked.

"I'm still a Ranger, but I'm not chasing down Comanches any longer. Rounded up the last of them in Palo Duro Canyon. They went home to roost and we caught them there."

"Just chasing women these days," I said.

"One woman," he said.

He eyed the bottle in my hand and I poured him another drink, the liquor like amber oil under the yellow light, and watched as he washed his throat with it.

"If you don't mind my prying into your business," I said, "what happened between you and Etta that she would leave you?"

He offered a tight smile.

"I was off chasing wild Comanches, remember."

I nodded, tossed back a glass of Mr. Daniel's sipping whiskey and rolled myself a shuck.

"We were young," he said. "Put a young woman out alone on the Texas frontier, you can't expect much good to happen." His eyes crinkled in the corners, the skin permanently burned by wind and sun. He stared off into the past, seeing old memories flame to life again. A spot just below his right eye ticked.

"We were married less than a year," he said, his voice a rough whisper. "I'd been gone on a long campaign and when I came home, she told me she was leaving. I helped her pack, bought her passage to Denver. She always wanted to live in Denver. I reckon that's where she must have first met this Gypsy Davy."

He found a cigar in the pocket of his greatcoat and bit off the end and held it between his fingers awhile before lighting it.

"She wrote me a couple of letters," he said. "But then they stopped coming and I never heard from her again or anything about her until I was up in Dallas and read about the killing in the *Dallas Herald,* saw her name." He shifted the cigar in his mouth from one side to the other.

"I learned she ran a hat shop here in Cheyenne but it burned down. I wondered maybe if the fire had something to do with the killing in Denver."

I nodded, told him the story about how I'd come to Cheyenne to work for my old friend Ben Beadle who had operated a detective agency; how Ben had been murdered, his office set on fire with him in it; and how the fire had burned down Etta's hat shop in the process.

"That's how we met," I said. "Etta and me, the first time. I questioned her about the fire, what she saw that night. We went from there. It didn't have anything to do with Denver."

"I'm relieved to know that," he said.

"What connected you to me?" I said.

"I didn't know her long," Teddy Blue said. "So I didn't know that much about her, about her past. But I learned recently she had an aunt in Ogalala and I sent a wire inquiring about Etta, stated that there had been some serious trouble and that I was looking for her. The aunt wired back and said Etta had been there but had left. She also mentioned that Etta had a visitor while there and gave me your name. It's the only lead I have. I came here to find you, hoping you could tell me where she was."

He must have seen the look of surprise for he said, "You don't know where she is, do you?"

"I figured she was still in Nebraska," I said.

He shook his head.

"Not according to the aunt. The trail runs out right here in Cheyenne with you. The aunt figured maybe she'd come back here looking for you."

I ran the possibilities through my mind and came up with nothing.

"I guess I'll cash in my ticket to Ogalala," I said. "If she's not there, I don't know where she is. It's a big country, Mr. Blue."

"Unless the aunt is lying," he said.

"She didn't strike me as a dishonest woman," I told him.

He shrugged his shoulders, stood up, and buttoned his coat.

"What would you do to protect someone you loved?" he said. "Ogalala is all we've got, McCannon. You want to take the chance the aunt's telling us everything she knows? And if she does know something more than she's telling, better we find her before Colorado Charlie Utter and his boys, or Gypsy Davy."

It wasn't what I had in mind, I thought, throwing in with Teddy Blue.

"Train leaves eight-fifteen," he said. "I could use the help."

"Tell me something," I said.

"What's that?"

"Do you still love her?"

He twisted his mouth and removed the cigar stub, examined the ash and finally said, "You don't love a woman like Etta then just stop because she left you. You ever been hard in love, you know that much, Mr. McCannon."

Yeah, I thought, I knew exactly what he meant.

CHAPTER 8

A cold rain driven by a hard wind had the three of us
huddled around the potbelly stove at the train depot
the next morning. I'd tried to talk Harve out of coming
with us, but he'd simply waved that Ned Buntline Special of his in the air and declared he was up for excitement.

"You don't have an investment in this," I had ar-
gued as I packed my saddlebags.

"Seems to me you are trying to look a gift-horse in
the mouth," he said. "I only got this one arm left, but I
can shoot like a sumbitch."

"You can get shot, too," I said.

"Looky here," he said, pushing the beaver hat
down squarely on his head. "I've lived all the life one
man can stand. I've been down to hardtack and river
water coffee and I've et fish eggs on crackers. Had me
ugly women, tall women, fat women, skinny women.
I've ridden behind the ass of cows and slept in the
saddle and I've slept in beds with satin sheets, too.

Drank horse piss from a boot and champagne from a slipper. I guess I ain't missed a thing if'n I was to get shot before breakfast. I'm willing and you need guns if you run up against Colorado Charlie Utter and his bunch, or that ear-wearing Gypsy Davy. 'Sides, I'm a freeborn man and can go where I damn well please. So finish up packing, Mac, and let's stop jawing."

"Okay," I said, "but you ought to know I've not had much luck with friends lately—most of them are up there on boot hill taking a long siesta."

He winked and said, "But not me."

Teddy Blue was already at the depot waiting on us when we came in. He looked at Harve, looked at the flap of his coat sleeve, then at me. I introduced them and Harve said, "Teddy Blue. Hell, I've heard of you."

"I'm from Texas as of late," Teddy Blue said. "But I was a lot of places before Texas."

"Seems to me I recall you killed the Harris brothers in a barn in Missouri," Harve said. "All three of them on the same day."

Teddy Blue warmed his palms over the potbelly.

"Killed the ones that was there, yes sir."

"Never did hear why you killed 'em," Harve said, trying not to act overly inquisitive but primed for some juicy conversation. "But I'd read plenty about their exploits as bank robbers. Those boys claimed they robbed more banks then Frank and Jesse James."

"They robbed a few."

"I see," Harve said, and warmed his own hand over the stove.

Teddy Blue pulled a big silver pocket watch from his waistcoat, snapped open the face, read the time until he was satisfied, then closed it and slipped it back in his pocket.

"You were with the Pinkertons as I recall," Harve said, not content to let a potentially good story go by the boards, now that his curiosity was up. "On the scout for Jesse and Frank when you come up on them Harris boys. Leastways that's the way I read it in the *Police Gazette*."

"Yes, sir, I was with the Pinkertons at the time."

"You just catch them boys in that barn, or was you waiting for them?"

Teddy Blue leaned forward a bit, arched his back, and said, "The beds at the hotel are pretty soft. I prefer a hard bed, keeps my back from aching."

Harve took the hint that Teddy Blue wasn't much interested in talking about the Harris brothers of Missouri and tugged his flask from inside his coat and held it forth.

"Anybody care to have a nip of ole Tose?"

We heard the train's whistle and gathered up our gear in preparation of boarding. The cold rain pecked at our necks as we stood on the platform and Harve finally turned to me and said, "Don't the weather ever grow pleasant in these parts? I ain't seen the sun but once and that was in my dreams."

It was a six-hour ride from Cheyenne to Ogalala and when we finally unlimbered ourselves, the rain had stopped but the sky was flushed gray and a strong wind was blowing up from the Platte. A few waddies with nothing better to do than hang about watching the comings and goings of strangers gave the three of us a careful once-over.

"We'll need to rent saddle horses for the trip out to the aunt's place," I said.

One of the waddies leaned and spat from a plug in his cheek and called out to Harve: "Hey there, old timer, you lose your arm in the war?"

They were just slothful youths, ragtag boys without enough to keep their minds occupied. Harve was content to let the comment pass, conceding that they were ignorant and disrespectful street trash.

We hied up to the livery stables but found the old man there had only one horse to rent at the time.

"Have more in the morning," he said. "All the others I got is let out at the present." Then he started to tell us the names of those that had rented his other horses and why they'd rented them, but we turned and headed back up the street to find a place to eat our dinner.

"That feller must be dang lonely to tell us his business," Harve said. "But from what I've seen of Nebraska so far, I can understand why. This looks like one of the loneliest places I've ever been."

The last time I'd been to this territory, it wasn't Colorado Charlie Utter or Gypsy Davy that troubled my mind, it was a man by the name of Tom Feathers, the son of a rich man who wanted Etta's attention, and more than just that. I'd figured that once I was out of the scene, Tom Feathers would move in and stake his claim. He might be a good man to look up if I couldn't find Etta, a piece of information I kept under my hat.

We found the rooms at the Big Muddy Hotel; they had a bar downstairs and a dining room that served oysters and freshwater mussels and Harve insisted on treating us all to some oysters and steaks the size of elephant butts.

We ate until we could barely push ourselves away from the table, then went to the bar where Harve further insisted that he treat us to a few after-dinner drinks, which turned out to be gin rickeys. I didn't care much for anything but good Tennessee sipping whiskey and so after the first gin rickey, I ordered some mash and stayed with that.

Teddy Blue said that he wasn't a drinking man by nature and turned in his drink for some black coffee. I saw his gaze take in everything and everyone. It was the gaze of a born lawman. In a far corner sat a group of men playing poker with a circle of other men standing around them so that you could barely see who the cardplayers were.

"Must be a high-stakes game going on," Teddy Blue said. Then I caught a glimpse of one of the cardplayers and knew why there was such a crowd.

Billy Cody was wearing a beaded buckskin jacket and under the yellow light above the table, his finely trimmed mustache and Vandyke gave him the appearance of an actor, which he had been—him and Texas Jack and Wild Bill before Bill jumped a train back to Kansas. Once there, Hickok promptly got married and headed for the goldfields in the Black Hills, where he was murdered and had left a widow that hardly knew him.

Cody had told me my last trip to Nebraska how damned scared Wild Bill had been in front of Eastern audiences. His fear of making a fool of himself, Cody said, was what got him killed. If Hickok had been more like Cody and Texas Jack, he'd probably still be alive and living well from his fame. As it was, the only ones living well from Wild Bill's fame were the dime novelists who wrote about him. Men like Ned Buntline, who was also sitting at the table to Cody's left.

"You met Billy Cody?" I said to Teddy Blue.

"That him?" he said, pointing with his chin toward the table.

"That's him."

Harve said, "Goddamn, he ain't aged a lick!"

"He's a lot smaller than I imagined him," Teddy Blue said.

"Bigger than life," I said.

"I heard he met the queen of England, Victoria," Teddy Blue said.

"He gave her a pair of silver spurs," I replied.

"Heard he killed a Cheyenne war chief name of Yellow Hand." Teddy Blue's interest bordered on disdain, as though Cody's fame didn't scratch much dirt with him.

"What would the queen of England want with a pair of silver spurs?" Harve said, two steps behind the conversation because of the number of gin rickeys he'd put away.

Billy Cody was holding court more than he was playing a simple game of stud poker. He enjoyed the attention and was in his element when surrounded by admirers. I imagined that the long winter had made him as restless as everyone else to leave the confines of his big house up near North Platte and come to town and do a little celebrating and give folks a chance to have a look at him. From what I knew the last time I'd visited him at his ranch, Cody felt like the prophet who was honored everywhere but in his own home. He loved his wife and daughters, but they saw him only as a husband and father and provider, not quite the way he saw himself or the way he preferred to be seen.

"We could have used him down in Texas fighting Comanches," Teddy Blue said, turning his back and leaning his elbows atop the bar. I wasn't sure how Teddy Blue meant his comment; with Teddy Blue, it wasn't easy to tell what he was thinking.

"Comanches are a fearsome bunch," Harve said, hoisting his gin rickey. "Here's to them poor sumbitches!"

Teddy Blue nodded and said, "Don't toast them too hardily, Mr. Sweetwater, they killed plenty of Texas Rangers and a lot of other folks as well, before accepting their medicine."

"Yes, sir," Harve said. "They were a *fearsome* bunch."

Harve left us standing at the bar and went over and plowed through the knot of spectators around Billy's table and began slapping him on the back and calling him Cuz; it took Billy by surprise, then he recognized the old drover and whooped and cleared a place for him at the table, ordering a fresh round of drinks.

"You want to join your friends," Teddy Blue said, "go ahead. I'm thinking of taking a walk, getting some fresh air."

"No," I said, "I think I'll grab some shut-eye. I'd like to get an early start in the morning."

Teddy Blue nodded, shifted his weight within his greatcoat and walked out the front door. I headed for my room, knowing that Harve and Billy Cody would be up most of the night drinking and telling grandiose stories, each of them slightly envious of the other's position—Harve wanting to be widely known, and Billy wanting to be wealthy.

As for me, I just wanted to find one woman. It didn't seem like a lot to want in a world full of wanting.

I was asleep when Harve pounded on my door and shouted, "Teddy Blue's just killed a preacher!"

Rain hit the window and I thought, Good Goddamn, what else can go wrong?

CHAPTER 9

⁂

I followed Harve to the "bad" part of town—the red-light district of cribs and bagnios. Every town had a bad side and Ogalala was no exception. Whores and pimps and dope fiends lurked in the shadows, men who would crack your skull with a lead sap while their women would pluck you like a chicken.

"What the hell was Teddy Blue doing in this end of town?" I asked Harve, who only shrugged and said, "Same as any man I expect, looking for some comfort." The odd thing was, Teddy Blue didn't strike me as the sort of man who would find his comfort in a red-light district.

A sizable crowd had gathered outside a false-fronted building, torches flared and sputtered under a soft rain. There on the porch, looking as dead as a Nebraska winter, was sure enough a man dressed like a preacher, half his jaw shot away, blood staining his white collar. He was staring at the rain, but he wasn't feeling any of it.

Teddy Blue was there and so were three deputies with shotguns aimed at him.

"Man, Creek ain't gonna like it you shot a preacher in his town," one of the deputies said to Teddy Blue just as me and Harve walked up. "Specially *this* preacher."

Teddy Blue's shoulder rig hung empty. I saw his pistol in the belt of one of the deputies.

He shot me a glance when we parted the crowd and stopped just shy of the porch where the dead preacher lay.

"He's a preacher, then I'm Abe Lincoln," Teddy Blue said to the deputy.

"You don't understand, mister," the deputy said. "That feller ain't only a preacher, he's the city marshal's son-in-law."

"What happened here, Blue?" I said.

"That man," Teddy Blue said, pointing at the dead man, "is no preacher; or if he is, he wasn't when I knew him. He's wanted in San Antonio for murder and robbery."

"What in hell you talking about?" the deputy said. He seemed to be the only one of the three that could, or would talk. They were all three, jug-eared and slackjawed with their hats tugged down low. "That there is the Reverend Elihue Morral, Bittercreek Newcomb's daughter's husband."

Harve Sweetwater started to ask a question when a stir swept through the crowd and a man well over three hundred pounds pushed his way to the forefront.

He stopped just short of the body, looked at it, and spat.

"This the sumbitch that did it?" he said to the talking deputy while nodding at Teddy Blue.

"Yes, sir. 'At's him. Me and Hedge and Roy were just next door when we heard the shooting. Saw this man standing over Elihue with a smoking pistol in his hand, Elihue's jaw blowed off. That's some of it over there in the mud puddle."

The big man turned and saw the chunk of bloody flesh and bone floating greasy in the rainwater, then turned back to Teddy Blue.

"That there's my baby's husband, mister. And he's a goddamn preacher to boot! You double-sinned tonight!"

"He's a wanted man in Texas for murder and rape," Teddy Blue said flatly.

"Well you know something, you dandified sumbitch? This here ain't Texas and you ain't the law! I am. And what we do with murdering sonsabitches is hang 'em from the hanging tree." He pointed off toward a large cottonwood a hundred paces distant that stood like a lone sentinel, like a tree that was waiting to hang its next man.

"Get a rope!"

I knew Bittercreek Newcomb from down in Oklahoma Territory when I spent a year working out of Judge Parker's court in Ft. Smith. How a man like him ever went from illegal whiskey peddling and petty thievery in the territories to city marshal of Ogalala was something of a mean trick—big tall bastard with a dark face and curly black hair who looked like he wouldn't know what it was to crack a smile. Maybe all that whiskey peddling and crime he pulled down in the territories had made him a sour and bitter man, like his name.

"No rope," I said, and that spun Bittercreek half-way round on his heels. I already had the self-cocker drawn and aimed at the center button on his shirt.

"This man's a Texas Ranger," I said, nodding toward Teddy Blue. "And if he says that dead preacher was wanted down in San Antone for crimes, then I believe him. You best, too."

Harve Sweetwater had slipped up on the porch behind the talking deputy and had placed the long barrel of his Buntline Special just behind the deputy's ear and thumbed the hammer back.

"I believe him, too, boys. Don't make this into a bloody mess!" Harve said. He was a nervy yahoo for a one-armed man who'd spent the last ten years of his life sleeping between satin sheets with a big fat wife.

"What the hell business is this of yours?" Bitter-creek bellowed like a bull; but all the bellering in the world wasn't worth a wooden nickel against an ounce of lead.

"Blue's with me," I said. "And there will be no hanging."

"He goddamned killed my sweet baby's husband and I won't stand for it!"

"You'll stand for it or join him," I said.

He gave me a hard eye and said, "I know you from somewheres?"

"I arrested you and Emmett Dalton once in the Nations for selling snake-head liquor to the Indians."

He shook his head; he didn't remember because it had probably been more than once some federal marshal had hauled his bacon into court.

His recourse was to blink like he had a cinder in his eye.

He turned back toward Teddy Blue.

"What proof you got that Elihue is wanted in Texas?"

"These," Teddy Blue said, pointing to his eyes. "I never forget the face of a wanted man. Got a memory as long as the hind leg of a dog. When he was in Texas, that fellow went by the name of Dirty Bob Braddock."

Bittercreek Newcomb was breathing hard now without having done anything; his chest heaved and fell beneath the greasy duster he wore, his sombrero was battered and mud-stained; his face was as red as beets.

"Looks like what we got here is a Mexican stand-off!" he declared.

"No, sir," I said. "What we have here is a bunch of dead men if you don't release this man and back away."

"Well, you'll be just as dead as the rest of us," Bittercreek sputtered.

"Maybe so, but so will you and that deputy with the Buntline Special behind his ear—that's a fact."

There was a long moment when the only sound was the patter of the soft rain on the tin roofs of the whorehouses and into the puddles where it collected, then Bittercreek Newcomb let out his breath and said, "Alright, goddammit. Hedge, Roy, you help Pat here get my son-in-law up to the funeral parlor—take his jawbone, too."

The deputies didn't move right away and Bittercreek had to tell them again before they lowered their shotguns. I nodded to the one who had Teddy Blue's pistol in his waistband and the deputy handed it back to him, his eyes full of regret but full of relief, too; he would get to go home and see his wife and children this night.

"I'm gonna wire the police down in San Antone," Bittercreek said. "And if I find out they ain't never heard of no Dirty Bob Braddock, then I'm coming to arrest you for the murder."

"You won't arrest me," Teddy Blue said.

"Why not?"

"This job can't pay enough to get yourself killed over a murderer and rapist, even if he was married to your daughter."

"Who says *I'd* be the one getting killed if I was to come looking for you?" the fat lawman said.

"Don't come looking for me, mister." Teddy Blue said it as calmly as if he were ordering a dog to sit and not move, then turned and walked away into the descending rain.

"Let it go," I said to Newcomb. "That feller may have been a good husband to your little girl, but he sure as hell isn't worth getting killed for."

Bittercreek Newcomb leaned to the side and spat and didn't bother to wipe his chin.

"I can round up a hundred men if I have to," he said.

"A hundred won't be enough," I said. "Leastways not where you are concerned. Let it go."

"I still don't remember you from down in the Nations," he said, as though that was still troubling his mind. "What are you doing up here?"

"Just passing through, Marshal. Just passing through."

―――――

We got halfway back to the good side of town before Harve said, "Hot damn, but we come close to shooting the ribbons out of those yahoos, didn't we, Mac?"

"We came close to dying, Harve, that's the way I saw it."

"Hell, dying, living, it's all the same thing in the end, ain't none of us getting out of this world alive."

"I'd just as soon die in my sleep than out here on these muddy streets, if you don't mind," I said.

"Hell, I'm ready for a drink, how about you, Mac?"

"We better just sit tight and stay off the streets," I said. "Bittercreek Newcomb might still want revenge for Teddy Blue killing his son-in-law."

Harve grumbled his ascent and didn't say anything until we'd reached our hotel.

"You know what I saw back there?" he said.

"No, what?"

"The prettiest Chinese whore I ever laid eyes on, and I've been to San Francisco."

"You better lie low, Harve."

"Cause of Bittercreek?" he said.

"No, I think maybe Cleopatra has her eye on you."

He looked dumbstruck for a moment, then grinned like a beaver.

"You think?"

"Well, I think she was at least warming to you by the time we left Cheyenne."

"Well, then, I'd best be careful and get me safe on back to that sweet woman when this is all over."

"You can go now, if you want," I said.

"No, sir—we ain't finished the job yet and I intend to be there at the end. 'Sides, I ain't killed nobody yet."

"You have a one-track mind, Harve."

"Well, sir, my daddy raised me right. He said, 'Don't try to ride a horse and a woman at the same time.'"

"I don't know what that means," I said.

Harve smiled and said, "Neither do I, but it means something."

We reached the hotel and I started to head for my room when I caught a glimpse of a man in a bowler hat and a greatcoat sitting in the shadows of the bar. I told Harve I'd see him first light and went over to where Teddy Blue was sipping coffee.

"Did you have to kill that man?" I said, taking a seat across from him.

"I never kill anyone I don't have to," he said.

"You try and arrest everyone you see that's wanted for a crime in Texas, we might be a long time finding Etta."

His gaze held steady over the rim of his cup.

"It's not likely I'll run into that many," he said.

"That's not the point."

"It couldn't be helped," he said.

"What were you doing that end of town?"

He lowered the cup and embraced it with both hands.

"I thought maybe I might find her there."

"Etta?"

He twisted his mouth and looked at his reflection in the cup. "It's a long story," he said.

"I'm listening."

"Maybe another time. It's late, I'll see you in the morning."

He didn't move and I knew our conversation was over, at least for the moment. I didn't want to even guess about the reference to finding Etta in the bad part of town. Hell, right then I needed a whiskey, some time alone—I guess, we all did. But the questions kept running through my mind like wild horses across the high sage flats: *Where was Etta? What was her involvement with Gypsy Davy and the murder? What did Teddy Blue know about her that would make him seek her out in the red-light district?*

The only way I'd find the answers was to find Etta, but the real question was, did I want to know the answers? I still loved her and maybe the truth wasn't what I really wanted to hear. When the bar dog asked me what I was having, I told him to bring me a bottle, then took it to my room. It had been a long time since I felt the urge to drink hard enough to forget, but this seemed like the right occasion.

CHAPTER 10

The next morning we rode out of Ogalala on three rented horses heading west to the aunt's house under a stormy sky. Harve complained that he hadn't seen the sun shine since he'd left Denver and wondered openly if Nebraska was good for anything other than boredom until we spooked up some sandhill cranes near the river. When the big birds lifted into the air, Harve said, "Good God Almighty, them's big chickens." Of course he knew what they were, he was just trying to lift the somber mood that had overtaken us. Nobody laughed but Harve.

The aunt's house was about ten miles outside of Ogalala and every mile seemed like twenty. Then it commenced to rain hard and something made me think that even the gods were going to be against us this time around.

The place was just as I'd remembered it, a two-story white clapboard with black shutters and a porch on three sides with the summer kitchen out back. The memory brought with it the scent of stored apples and the long kiss Etta and I had shared there in that small room with the spring sun coming through the windows.

We reined in and I said that since I knew the woman, I'd knock on the door. Harve shifted under the stiff wind coming out of the northeast and drew up the collar of his coat while Teddy Blue sat on his horse, stoically taking in his surroundings; he seemed immune to the conditions, the rain beading on the crown of his bowler.

My knock brought no reply, but I'd seen the hack near the rear of the house under a lean-to and the piebald mare in the corral, so it seemed likely that the aunt would be home. I knocked again and this time my eye caught a glimpse of women's shoes through the tatted curtains of the parlor window. The shoes had feet in them and my heart skipped a beat.

I tried the door but it was bolted. I went around back and saw the broken window to the summer kitchen and the door ajar. I found the aunt there on the floor of the parlor, strangled, her eyes staring at the wainscoting, a harness strap knotted around her neck. There was something else I noticed, too.

I unbolted the front door and motioned Harve and Teddy Blue to come inside. I wanted them to see the dead woman.

"Jesus Christ," Harve said when he looked down at her.

"Gypsy Davy," Teddy Blue muttered as he squatted next to the aunt.

"He's cut off her ears," Harve muttered.

"If she knew where Etta was," Teddy Blue said, "you can bet she told him."

"Now what?" Harve said. "The trail looks like it ends here."

I'm no expert on dying, but it looked to me as though the aunt had died a hard death. Teddy Blue was undoubtedly right; if she had known anything about Etta's whereabouts, the aunt would have told him.

"I've got one card left to play," I said. "It's not much, but it's something."

Harve pulled his flask and took a pull, then offered it around, Teddy Blue and I both declined.

"We'll need to let someone in town know," I said.

"Play your card," Teddy Blue said.

We rode to the Feathers' spread. It was a thin chance that Etta would have gone to Tom Feathers's for refuge, but then how well did I really know her in the first place? The rain had stopped but the wind had increased and dark clouds scudded so low it seemed we rode right through them.

The main house lay in a valley between swelling mounds of brown winter grass and when we topped a ridge, we could see it there, quiet and seemingly undisturbed except for a wisp of black smoke curling out of the chimney before that got swept away by the stiff wind. It was a raw day in every respect and none of us, I was sure, had gotten the picture of the dead woman out of our mind.

"Seems awful quiet for a cattle operation," Teddy Blue said.

We'd ridden through a large herd of the new Shorthorn cattle a mile from the main house. Harve hawked and spat his disdain when seeing them.

"A cow without long horns ain't much in my book," he said.

It was true, there was no activity surrounding the house as you might expect.

We saw the blood trail from the front porch leading to the barn just as we rode up.

Teddy Blue jerked the pistol from his shoulder rig and said, "We've ridden into some bad business here, McCannon."

We found three men hanging from a rafter; the cold gray light silting through the roof shone muted on their twisted faces. They were dressed like drovers and their tongues lolled out of their mouths black and thick. And like the aunt, their ears had been sliced off.

"Sumbitch," Harve muttered.

"You know any of these men, McCannon?" Teddy Blue said.

I didn't. They were no doubt hired hands who had gotten caught unawares.

Teddy Blue's gaze took in the scene, then his eyes trailed toward the back of the barn where a door swung in the wind.

"The blood trail continues out that way," he said.

The trail led to a well twenty yards beyond the barn.

We heard a strange sound from the depths of the well, but it didn't take a professor to figure out it was the labored breathing of a person. Something the size of a fist knotted in my stomach. The only person I cared about might be lying in the bottom of the well dying.

"We'll get a lantern and tie it to a rope and lower it down," Teddy Blue said. And that's what we did.

We didn't have to lower the lantern far, for there about ten feet down was Jake Feathers, Tom's rich daddy, the one whose watch Calamity Jane had stolen that night in North Platte that I'd had to return to keep her out of jail. He'd proven to be a very unlikable bastard, but right now that was besides the point.

His face was bloody and when the light neared his eyes, they grew stark and wide with fright. He uttered something unintelligible and screamed.

"Feathers, if we lower you a rope can you get it tied around you so we can haul you out of there?" I said.

He moaned and I asked him again, then he said in a weak voice, "I'll . . . try."

It took a good half hour before Feathers got the rope knotted around himself well enough that we could haul him up and once, we almost lost him. When we did top him out of the well, he looked like he'd been dragged by horses.

Harve found a tarp and we laid him on it and carried him to the house. He was in bad shape, bad enough shape that I knew he'd die no matter what we did—a dying man gets a certain look in his eyes and Jake Feathers had that look.

We did the best we could for him, wrapped him in blankets, and fed him whiskey, most of which spilled from his lips.

"Tom," he kept saying over and over. "Tom, Tom."

I asked him where Tom was and his eyes grew startled and shifted from me to Teddy Blue to Harve and back to me.

"Is Etta with Tom?" I asked.

He blinked several times and I asked again.

He nodded his head.

"Gone," he said. "All gone."

"Where?"

Harve spilled some more whiskey in him, then took a pull himself.

"Where are they?" I said again. "Where are Tom and Etta?"

He looked toward the door, then up to the beamed ceiling.

"Gonzales . . ."

I wasn't sure I heard him right, but he repeated it. The name didn't make any sense, but nothing did.

"Who did this to you, old timer?" Teddy Blue said.

"Hi . . . him . . ." he muttered.

"Who?"

"Man . . . knife . . ."

"Gypsy Davy?" I said.

Jake Feathers looked at me, looked at Harve, at Harve's empty sleeve, then rolled his eyes, took a breath, and died.

"Who's this Tom?" Teddy Blue said.

"His boy," I said.

"You know him well?"

"Well enough."

"Can he fight, McCannon? Can he stand up to a man like Gypsy Davy?"

"I have my doubts."

"Then we better get going."

"Where?" Harve said.

"Any ideas, McCannon?" Teddy Blue said.

Before I had a chance to think about it, the ground

thrummed with hooves. We went to the front door and there topping a ridge was maybe a dozen riders.

Teddy Blue stared at the bunch and said, "That would be Colorado Charlie Utter and his assassins."

"How can you tell?"

"Their hats," Teddy Blue said. "See the way they wear them pinned back?"

CHAPTER 11

Colorado Charlie Utter was a short, thick-set man who wore a cream-colored sombrero with the front brim pinned back to the crown. He also wore a heavy buckskin jacket that had beadwork, fringes, and doeskin gauntlets. He wore a brace of pearl-handled revolvers and I could see the brass-fitted stock of a Remington long-range Creedmore rifle like the one I owned tucked into the boot of his saddle. He was a grim-looking son of a bitch who looked loaded for bear. The men with him were typical waddies: broad-brimmed hats pinned back like his, chaps and spurs, and equally well armed. I counted ten of them.

"We're looking for a man named Feathers," Utter said. "One of you, him?"

"He's in there," I said, "but he's not up to conversation just now."

Utter leaned forward, resting his hands on the pommel of his saddle.

"Why ain't he?"

"He's as dead as Moses," Harve said. "Some feller tossed him down a well after he dragged him."

Utter looked beyond the three of us as though he were trying to see through the log walls of the main house, trying to see if Jake Feathers was really inside, dead as we'd said he was. Then he said something to the man next to him, a tall, lanky yahoo wearing batwing chaps and three pounds of pistol on his hip. He told the man to go see how dead Feathers really was. The man sniffed the air and swiped at his sandy mustache before climbing down from his horse and going inside. He came right back out again.

"Sumbitch's dead, Charlie, these fellers weren't lying. And his ears is cut off."

Utter took off his gloves and slapped them together, then said, "Well ain't that a piece of bad news." Then he looked at me and said, "We're looking for a lady, don't suppose you've seen a woman about?"

"Saw no woman," I said before Harve or Teddy Blue could say anything. "Why are you looking for her?"

He looked at me with his dark buggy eyes, the lids half-closed, as though he were already tired of our conversation.

"That'd be none of your business, mister."

"You're the man who buried Hickok," I said.

He blinked.

"You heard of me, huh?"

"I know who you are," I said.

"Then if you know anything, you know I'm a serious man. If you know about this woman I'm looking for—her name'd be Etta Devearux—then you'd best tell me about it. I find out otherwise, me and my men here might just come looking for you boys."

"You don't want to come looking for me," Teddy Blue said in his flat voice that was as cold as iron.

"Oh, you don't believe so, eh?" Utter replied.

"You don't want to come looking for me, mister," Teddy Blue repeated. "You want to track down women to hang them, you go ahead. Maybe that's your speed, but you don't ever want to come looking for me."

Some of the riders visibly shifted their weight, but not Colorado Charlie Utter—he was a man with too much bulk to shift easily. He tapped his gloves in one hand and measured Teddy Blue, measured his speech and the level empty gaze.

"You know why I'm after her then," Utter said at last. "I find out you boys know the whereabouts of this woman I'm after, I won't forget that."

"We don't know anything about this woman," I said, making sure to cut off Teddy Blue's challenge to the man. Getting into a shoot-out wasn't going to serve anyone's purpose, especially not our own, considering we were outgunned three to one.

Utter tugged on his gloves, took up his reins, and turned his horse back in the direction they'd come and rode out. The other riders followed, slapping the end of their reins over the flanks of their mounts, throwing up clods of dirt as they peeled up the ridge.

"Maybe I should have killed that man here and now," Teddy Blue said. "Might have saved us all some future troubles."

"Maybe so," I said. "But a wise man has to pick and choose his place and time and this was neither the place nor the time."

He shifted his gaze from the distant riders.

"We'll meet those men again, McCannon. And when we do, we'll have to kill or be killed."

"I've already counted on it, Mr. Blue, but maybe next time, we'll have the odds a little more in our favor."

"What now?" Harve said. "We going to ride or are we just going to stand out here and watch it rain and talk about gun-shooting?"

"I'm with you, Mr. Sweetwater," Teddy Blue said. "We're just burning daylight standing around here."

"Well, we might find us a way to narrow down just exactly where Etta and Tom Feathers are headed," I said.

They both looked at me and said, "How?"

We rode back into Ogalala and stopped in front of the city marshal's office. Bittercreek Newcomb was sitting inside, his feet in a pan of hot water. He looked up when we walked in; wide-eyed and ruddy-faced, he was already working up a sweat at just the sight of us.

"What the hell you yahoos doing back here?" he shouted.

"Keep your feet in that pan," Harve said. "Or I'll pull this hogleg and shoot you in both of them wrinkled dogs."

Newcomb grimaced at the threat.

I told him about finding Etta's aunt and Jake Feathers and his men. He got a sour look on his face.

"Cut off their ears?"

Harve started to go into detail about Gypsy Davy

and his penchant for human ears, but I stopped him before he could get windy.

"The man who killed them," I said, "is someone we need to find before he finds Etta and Tom Feathers. The old man's dying word when we asked him the direction they were headed was 'Gonzales.' You want to tell us what that means?"

Bittercreek looked at the three of us like we were rotting buffalo hides some fool had dropped off in his office as a practical joke.

"Well even if I did, you think I'd give two shits about you boys finding him, or anybody else, for that matter?" His gaze was fixed stonily on Teddy Blue.

"You know how hard my daughter cried when I told her you killed her husband?" Newcomb said. "You know what my baby's tears felt like running over my hands as I tried to wipe them from her eyes? You've any idea how much she loved that man?"

"This ain't about that," I said. "Maybe next time she will have better judgment in men and won't marry a killing rapist."

Newcomb's gaze shifted to me with as much vehemence as it had held for Teddy Blue.

"I aim to kill you boys, just thought you ought to know."

"Go ahead and shoot him in the feet, Harve," I said.

"Hell, yes!" Harve said and pulled his Buntline Special. "I finish with you, you'll have to crawl for your supper and sit to take a piss."

"Hold on now!" Newcomb cried.

"Tell me what you know about this Gonzales," I said.

He grumbled for a moment, then saw that Harve would have no trouble crippling him by shooting him in the feet. Convinced, he told us that he'd seen Feathers and Etta passing through town three days before on the south road with luggage tied to the back of Tom Feathers's hack.

"Jake owned a cattle spread in Gonzales, Texas," Bittercreek said. "That's all I know about it."

"That road they took, where's it lead?" Harve asked, still aiming his long-iron at the feet of Bittercreek Newcomb.

"Take you all the way to the goddamn Gulf of Mexico, I reckon, if you stayed on it long enough."

"Kansas, then across the Oklahoma panhandle and on into Texas," Teddy Blue said. "We better get after them."

"They ain't alone," Newcomb said. "Feathers has got a nigger hand of his with them—one who can shoot in the dark."

Harve blinked.

"Nigger that shoots in the dark?"

"That'n can," Bittercreek said. "The old man hired him special, had him brought up here from the Nations 'cause a his reputation. Fact is, I'm the one who told Jake about that nigger—how he can see in the dark good enough to shoot a man at a hundred yards. You give him daylight, he'll kill you from a mile out with his buffler gun."

"That doesn't mean spit to me," Teddy Blue said, already turning to leave.

"Maybe that nigger will shoot you in the dark and save me the trouble," Newcomb said. That's when Teddy Blue came round in one forceful motion and struck the lawman hard across the cheekbone, knocking him out of the chair and his feet out of the water pan.

"You want to shoot me, get to it, you fat tub of guts, or keep your mouth shut!"

That was all there was to it. Bittercreek Newcomb didn't say another word as we turned and walked out of his office.

"We have to look at it this way," I said as we walked our rented horses back to the livery. "If Feathers has got an extra man with him who can shoot, it can't hurt if Gypsy Davy or Charlie Utter catches up with them before we do."

Harve chimed in by saying, "I knew a trick shot in Fresno who shot glass balls off his wife's head while wearing a blindfold."

"That's damn risky business on her part," Teddy Blue said.

Harve laughed and said, "No, he wasn't wearing the blindfold—she was."

It broke the mood somewhat, Harve and his stories.

We needed to buy horses and asked the owner of the livery if he had any for sale. He clapped his hands and said, "I do." We bought three of his best, which were of average horseflesh, but they'd have to do.

"You think these mounts will hold up under a hard ride?" Teddy Blue said as we saddled up. The horses cost us twenty dollars each; the saddles, forty.

"Only one way to find out," I said.

We rode until dark and made a dry camp by a branch of the Platte.

A meal of beans and river water coffee, a quick

shuck, and a pull off of Harve's whiskey flask to ward off the chill and we found ourselves in our bedrolls, staring up at a half-moon behind shifting silvery clouds. I don't know why, but I had a bad feeling that we wouldn't find Etta before Gypsy Davy found her—or Colorado Charlie Utter and his assassins.

As I lay there watching the big emptiness overhead, I kept thinking about the surname Utter had given Etta: Devearux. The more I learned about her, the more I understood how little I knew.

CHAPTER 12

We rode three days south into Kansas. One thing about Kansas, there's not much to take up your attention. Endless seas of prairie grass and hardly any trees. You wanted to hang a man in Kansas, you'd be hard pressed.

"This is a godless place," Teddy Blue said after lonely hours and days of riding and seeing little more than an occasional soddy. "What would possess a man to bring his family way out here?"

"Free land," I said.

"It's not hard to see why it's free," he said. "Who'd want it?"

Harve rode along whistling happily until he ran out of bug juice.

"Need to stop and buy some supplies," he said, holding forth the empty flask trying to shake out the last drops.

We rode on.

Eventually we came to a burg called "Sweet

Jesus"—it was painted on a board a hundred yards from the nearest set of raw lumber buildings; I counted four in all.

"It ain't hard to see how it got its name," Harve said as we rode past the sign. "The first feller probably stopped here and said, 'Sweet Jesus, I can't go no farther! And Sweet Jesus, there just ain't no reason to.' "

Among the buildings there was a whiskey den, a mercantile, a restaurant, and a blacksmith—everything a prairie town needed to survive, it would seem. Harve wanted to go straight to the whiskey den, but I suggested we might do well to have a meal at the restaurant, that all the hardtack and beans we'd eaten on the trail were getting plenty tiresome.

"Well, I'll meet you boys at the hog house," Harve said. "I've got to warsh my throat."

Teddy Blue and I rode over to the restaurant while Harve tied up in front of a place called Big Mary's.

We went inside and grabbed chairs at a table near the window. I have a need to sit by windows where the light is good and I can observe the street—it's an old habit from my days as a lawman, and also from my days while on the dodge.

We sat there a long time without anyone taking notice even though we were the only patrons. Then finally a man came out of a back room, wiping his hands on a greasy apron. He had a head full of thick hair and was as big around as he was tall and when he saw us, he came right over.

"Scusa," he said. "I'm in the back and don't hear you gentlemen come in."

He had the same accent as Billy Cody's wife—Italian.

"Two plates of grub," Teddy Blue said. "Make it steak, if you got it and no beans!"

"Sì, sì, signore. I fix them right up for you."

"Wonder how it is a man comes all the way across the wide ocean to end up out here on this godless frontier?" Teddy Blue said. "Think of all the places a man could end up. This place doesn't even seem like it would be on the list."

"Maybe he was trying to get to California or Oregon and just couldn't go no farther, like Harve said."

Teddy Blue reached in his pocket, took out his watch, and wound it. He checked the time, then put it away again.

"You catch the name Colorado Charlie used when he spoke of Etta?" he said.

"Yeah, Devearux," I said. "Was that her maiden name before she married you?"

"No, it was Simpson, leastways that's what she told me at the time."

"Then she's using an alias," I said.

"Sounds like."

"You as concerned about her as I am?"

He looked at me for a long hard moment.

"You forgetting who it was came to you for help in the first place?" he said.

"No, I haven't forgotten."

We ate our steaks in silence. Gnawed the meat off the bones like we were pilgrims just landed, which in a sense I guess we were, only instead of an ocean behind us, we were in a sea of grass.

I was rolling myself a shuck when I saw something I didn't believe. It was a naked man riding a flea-bitten mule down the center of the town. Naked, that was, except for his hat, a pistol belt and a revolver, and his boots.

Teddy Blue saw him, too.

"I thought I'd seen everything," he said. "I was wrong."

I called the waiter over and asked him who the man was.

His eyes got big and he said, "Oh, that's Signore Allison," he said.

"Clay Allison?"

"Sì, that's him. Sometimes he comes to town like that."

I looked at Teddy Blue.

"The last I heard Clay Allison was in New Mexico, married with a wife and several children."

"Last I heard he was in jail in El Paso," Teddy Blue said. "Somebody ought to go tell him to put some clothes on before he's spotted by a decent woman."

"Be my guest," I said.

He looked at me in that hard flat stare of his.

"Maybe I just will."

"Let it go, Blue. Why risk getting killed because the man's a fool?"

"Doesn't this place have any law?" Teddy Blue asked the waiter.

He nodded sadly.

"Sì. We got Signore Redbird, but he's asleep a lot or drunk and asleep. Sometimes he's a fishing in the river, too."

"Where's his office?" I asked.

"Over there." He pointed toward Big Mary's, the saloon Harve had gone into to drink his lunch.

We found Ned Redbird stretched out on the pool

table asleep. Harve was chatting with a woman in a red dress in a far corner near the piano and paid little attention to either Clay Allison, who stood along the bar with his bare buttocks sticking out like loaves of unbaked bread, or me and Teddy Blue when we came in.

Teddy Blue shook Ned Redbird awake and he sat up scratching his eyes and said, "Who are you and why are you disturbing my sleep?"

Teddy Blue pointed toward the naked gunfighter.

"Is it your custom to allow lewdness in public?"

Ned Redbird looked at Clay Allison then back at Teddy Blue. "Why hell, that's Clay Allison. What'm I supposed to do? That man's killed more people than the pox; you think I'm going to tell him he has to dress up to come into my town?"

"You're the law, aren't you?" Teddy Blue said.

"Am the law, but that don't mean I got to die being it. 'Sides, what's the harm? He ain't shooting or stabbing nobody. Wake me up if he starts shooting or stabbing somebody," Ned Redbird said, and stretched back out on the pool table.

"Why? Does that mean you'll go arrest him if he starts killing folks?" Teddy Blue said.

Ned Redbird opened one eye and peered disdainfully at the Ranger.

"No, it just means that if he starts stabbing and shooting people, I want to get on down the road before he stabs or shoots me."

Teddy Blue uttered an oath, then looked at me and said, "That is just plain indecent."

"Let it go," I warned him again. "You see anybody complaining except you?"

The woman Harve was talking to laughed suddenly and I saw Clay Allison look in their direction.

"Naomi, you damn cheating bitch!" he bellowed.

"That's it," Teddy Blue said, and crossed the room to where Allison stood against the bar.

"Mister, you are a damnation to look at. Why don't you go put some clothes on like a decent man?"

Clay Allison drew his head back sharply as though he'd ducked a punch. He blinked, unaccustomed, I suppose, to having anyone say anything to him about his appearance or manner. I eased my way into position to shoot him if he went for his pistols. And if he did go for his guns, some of us were going to die and I wanted to make sure it wasn't all of us.

Seeing for the first time Clay Allison's state of affairs, Harve cawed from the table, "What's that you say, you bare-assed son of a bitch!"

Allison's gaze shifted from Teddy Blue to Harve; my movement in taking up a position on him also caught his attention. Suddenly, he looked like a bad dog surrounded by three other bad dogs. *Which one to fight?* That's what was going through his mind.

"Let it go, Clay," I said from the shadows. "You pull your iron, one of us is going to kill you."

His gaze came to full rest on me, least what he could see of me, standing where I was, where the light was bad and off to his left.

Harve had moved away from the table where the woman seemed to shrink herself as small as she could. There wasn't a backdoor and no place to run except past Clay Allison, so she stayed where she was.

"That," he bellowed, "is my goddamn woman sitting with that one-armed son of a bitch and I don't allow no man to sit with my woman, especially one-armed sonsabitches!"

"He didn't know," I said. "He does now."

Harve was itching to pull his hogleg and let fly, but I knew Allison would probably kill him before either Teddy Blue or I could shoot the man down.

"Ease off, Harve," I said.

Teddy Blue and the gunfighter were no more than three feet apart. I kept waiting for one of them to make a move, hoping the whole time that Clay Allison would see he was in a delicate situation.

"Three against one, Clay," I said. "Even a blind man can see those are poor odds. Why die like this, naked in a saloon? Think how your wife and kids would feel hearing the news."

He gave it one more moment, then tugged his hat down hard enough to bend his ears and stomped out. Teddy Blue and I walked to the door and watched as he mounted the flea-bitten mule, cussing to himself as he did so, then rode back out of town in the same direction as he'd come.

"He's likely to get good an' chafed," Harve said, joining us, his arm around the waist of the woman. "That man don't have no sense."

"I can't wait to get back to Texas," Teddy Blue said, shaking his head. "Men in Texas don't ride around in their altogether and they don't insult women. Kansas is a raw and untamed place, godless as any I've yet seen."

"Maybe it's all this nothingness they got out here," Harve said. "Maybe so much nothingness makes folks crazed."

Naomi, the woman, said, "That's twice in three

days that I've seen a crazy man. First there was that man wearing a string of ears around his neck, then today my lover comes riding in naked as a jaybird. I believe he must be on dope or something!"

It got our attention, the part about the man with the ear necklace.

CHAPTER 13

Naomi said a tall, handsome stranger had come through a few days earlier and had stopped in Big Mary's and drank a bottle of whiskey and offered her twenty dollars to give him a bath and scrub his back and wash his hair.

"Twenty dollars to give him a bath?" Teddy Blue asked incredulously.

"Yes," Naomi said. "At first I thought he was fooling. Most cowboys want to buy my services, but the last thing they want is a bath. Fact is, most of them would rather shoot off their big toes than take a bath. Whiskey and fun, that's what they come here for, not baths. But this man wanted a bath and so I gave him one. For twenty dollars, wouldn't you?"

"I surely would not," Harve said. "I wouldn't give a man a bath for a thousand dollars!"

"Well, that's you, honey, that ain't me. Out here, money is as scarce as trees. Somebody offers you twenty dollars for anything, you take it. He offered and

I took it. Hell, he could have had the whole package for five—bath and all!"

Ned Redbird stirred from his position on the pool table and sat up again.

"A man can't get no decent sleep anymore," he groused. "Might as well go cut me a willow pole and go fishing."

"Where you going to find a willow pole when there's not a tree to be seen in any direction for a hundred miles?" Teddy Blue asked, his mood still sour over the encounter with Clay Allison. "I didn't even see a creek for any fish to be in."

"Well, there is a pond about a mile from here 'at's got fish in it and I got a willow pole I brought with me from Ohio. I just don't know where I left it at. But if I can find it, I'm going fishing."

"Go right ahead, mister," Teddy Blue said. "Maybe you are better at catching fish than you are at catching criminals and keeping the laws of decency. This woman says there was a man through here a couple of days ago—tall man wearing a necklace of ears. You see this fellow, see which way he went when he left?"

Ned Redbird scratched himself all over and muttered he was feeling gamy.

"Well, did you?" Teddy Blue repeated.

"Yeah, I saw somebody riding a big white horse. I didn't see if he was wearing ears around his neck or not. I never seen a horse that big a'fore. Must have been eighteen hands tall if he was an inch. All white, except he had a black tail and mane. And that feller's saddle was covered in silver. Had more silver stuck to it than what they had down at the bank before it got robbed and burned to the ground."

"Which direction did he go, that's all I care about," Teddy Blue said. "I don't care how tall his horse was or how much silver he had on his saddle or even how much money there was in that bank."

"Well, I had fifteen dollars in that bank when it got robbed and burned down," Ned Redbird said bitterly. "It was my life's savings. Those dirty, ornery Canadian River boys came through and robbed it and burned it and I'm once more broker than a hard-shell Baptist."

"Canadian River boys?" Teddy Blue said. "I've never heard of them."

"Well, you're lucky you ain't. They're the meanest bunch of yahoos I've ever seen in my life. They shot everybody in the bank, then robbed it, then burnt it down!"

"Where were you when all this was going on?" Teddy Blue said. "You're supposed to be the law."

Ned Redbird scratched at a spot inside his shirt, then withdrew his fingers and checked them.

"I was fishing! And it's a good thing I was or I might have lost more than just my life's savings. Those Canadian River boys murder any lawmen they see just for the fun of it, Them boys is all breeds—Mexicans and half-Induns and coloreds—and they hate lawmen, white lawmen especially!"

"You're a disgrace to that badge," Teddy Blue said.

"Here, you want it?" Ned Redbird said, unpinning it from his cowhide vest and holding it forth. "Be my guest, mister."

"All I want from you is to tell me which way that man on the tall horse went when he left here!"

Ned Redbird pointed with his nose.

"That way, south," he said. "And good riddance to him and good riddance to the Canadian River boys as well. I hope not to see hide nor hair of any of them. Fact is, if I can save me another fifteen dollars, I'm going back to Ohio. There is nothing out here on this frontier but grass, people who live in mud houses, and wild gangs of thieves and murderers."

"Maybe it's best you do," Harve said. "How did you get to become the lawman in this burg in the first place, scared of your own shadow as you are?"

Ned Redbird looked duly contrite for a moment. Then Naomi said, "He took it off of Two-Finger Gus!"

"Who's Two-Finger Gus, hon?" Harve said.

"He was my common-law husband and owner of this whole durn town and everything in it till he passed on. He was also the mayor, postmaster—though we don't have a post office yet—justice of the peace, and town marshal. Course, a town like this doesn't need much law—there's only eight folks lives here, was eleven but three got shot and killed during the bank robbery. That's how Gus met his end, fighting those Canadian River boys. They shot him full of holes and left him out on the street dead as any dog." At this, Naomi spilled a tear from her eye and Harve was quick to wipe it dry with a fancy red kerchief.

"Now, now, hon, take it easy. I'm sure those Canadian River boys will try and rob the wrong bank and end up swinging from ropes before too long. Not to worry."

"Well how long do you intend on standing around comforting this woman?" Teddy Blue said. "I'd like to get moving. What else can you tell us about this feller that had the ear necklace?"

She sniffled and laid her gaze on the Ranger like she was a cow looking at new grass.

"Well, he had good skin," she said. "I seen that when I was giving him his bath."

"I don't care about the good skin he had," Teddy Blue said. "I want to know did he tell you anything, where he was going, was he chasing somebody, anything like that?"

Naomi blinked several times, then said, "I remember asking him what was a fine, handsome man like himself doing way out here at the edge of nowhere and he said he was after a woman, a lady friend of his, and he thought for sure she'd come through here not long ago. Yes, I believe those were pretty near his exact words."

"Let me ask you something," I said. "Didn't you think it was a little strange giving a bath to a man wearing a necklace made of human ears?"

She looked at me then like I'd just asked her if she knew how to fly to the moon.

"Well, he wasn't wearing them at the time," she said. "He only wore them when he came into town and when he left again."

"Fine, fine," Teddy Blue said. "Enough of this jaw-breaking. Let's get moving."

I looked at Harve.

"You staying here with Naomi?" I said.

"No, sir, I'm not one to quit a job before it's finished." He turned to her and said, "You'll just have to wait on me, hon, and hope I get this way again and if I do, I'll pay you to give *me* a bath and I won't be wearing no string of ears around my neck, either. How'll that be?"

"I can't make no promises," she said. "The wind could come through and blow me away, or who knows? Those Canadian River boys could come back and steal me and take me off to their hideout and make me their slave and who knows what all. You want me, you better take me with you now."

"Well, what about your boyfriend, the naked feller?" Harve said. "Won't he be brokenhearted if I was to take you away with me?"

"Him!" she snorted. "He's nothing but a dope fiend and a married man to boot. What future would I have with someone like that? I'd be better off marrying a cow."

Teddy Blue and I were already riding the south road when Harve caught up to us. He had a wide grin on his face.

"Boys, that's some woman, ain't she? Last woman I knew like that who had pretty white hair and a sweet smile such as Miss Naomi's was Squirrel Tooth Alice, who is now married to a Calvinist and lives a stark and pious existence. You'd never know it to look at her now that she'd bedded about every yahoo that ever rode up the Chisholm Trail."

"I'm not interested in your experiences with womanhood, Mr. Sweetwater," Teddy Blue said. "It's not a decent thing for a man to discuss his doings in public, even if it is with whores."

"Suits me to a tee. I just thought it might help pass the miles, I was to tell you about my experiences with Squirrel Tooth Alice, but if you'd rather just ride along and be bored to death, that's fine by me."

"I'd rather be bored plum out of my hat than to listen to a man discuss his private doings with a woman," Teddy Blue said.

We rode for another few hours like that, hearing nothing more than the creak of saddle leather and the plod of our animals' hooves and the swish of prairie grass when the wind washed over it.

"You thinking about Gypsy Davy?" I said to Teddy Blue, who looked deep in thought, his brow furrowed, his gaze fixed straight ahead, where there was little more than grass and horizon and you could see fifty miles in any direction.

"I know where Gypsy Davy is," Teddy Blue said. "Ahead of us somewhere."

"Then what?" I said.

"What I don't know is where Colorado Charlie Utter and his bunch are." He turned his attention to me for a brief moment. "You know they're out there somewhere. Thing is, where?"

It was something to think about.

"You know what I'm concerned about?" Harve said. Before either Blue or myself could answer, he said, "Why that Gypsy Davy didn't cut the ears off Naomi after she gave him his bath?"

"Maybe he's got no more room on his string," Teddy Blue said irritably. "Maybe his string is too full and he just couldn't fit another pair of ears on it."

"Hadn't thought of that," Harve said. "But you could be right."

Two crows flew out of nowhere and crossed overhead, casting their winged shadows over the grass.

" 'At's a bad sign," Harve said, looking up, "seeing two crows together like that."

"Who says?" Teddy Blue said. "I've seen lots and lots of crows and I've never known it to be a bad sign. Fact is, there is even an entire tribe of Indians named Crows. Fierce warriors known for their strong medicine. A handsome people, too."

"I don't know about none of that," Harve said. "All I know is every time I have seen two crows flying close togther like that without cawing and on a cloudless day such as this, trouble has soon followed."

"I'll keep that in mind," Teddy Blue said, and spurred his horse on ahead, as though he didn't want to hear any more about crows and bad signs and Harve's encounters with women. To tell the truth, my own ears were getting a little sore from so much talk. All the palaver about crows and whores and bad men didn't take my mind off the fact that ahead of us somewhere was a woman I thought I was in love with, one who was running from something terrible, and with a man I much disliked. It was a bitter pill for me to swallow, knowing that she had sought out Tom Feathers for help. But then, I was beginning to realize there was a lot about her that I didn't understand. I didn't want to believe that I'd let myself be fooled, and I didn't want to believe that everything I thought I knew about Etta Landrow was a lie. Because if it was a lie, then everything she and I had shared was also a lie. I needed to find out the truth and the only way I was going to do that was to find her before Gypsy Davy or Colorado Charlie Utter did.

We rode until the dusk chased us into a dry camp beside a stream and settled in for the night.

Off in the distance you could hear the rumble of thunder. The plains were like that. One minute the weather was peaceful and the next it was at war with you. There were no trees, no sort of shelter if a storm did strike us. Maybe Harve had been correct in saying that the two crows were a portent of bad things to come. I'd seen men drowned in rivers, trapped by sudden wildfires swept by high winds, and hammered until bleeding by hailstones the size of apples. But the worst thing I ever saw was an outrider struck by lightning; it killed him and his pony in a heartbeat and fused his spurs together.

The rumble of thunder came closer like it was marching right in our direction.

I watched streaks of lightning snake through the sky off to the west and thought of the outrider who had been dozing in his saddle one minute and struck dead the next instant. The lightning had also set his hair and shirt afire. I tried hard to keep my thoughts off both Etta and the approaching storm. Then I felt the ground rumble and knew we were in for it.

CHAPTER 14

"There's a cyclone coming, boys! Run for cover!" Harve was already out of his soogan, shouting at us above the wind, its roar like a fast moving train.

"Damnation!" Teddy Blue swore. "This is the most godless and inhospitable country I've yet to be in!" At that instant the wind snatched his bowler and carried it off into the darkness and driving rain.

"There's no place to run!" I shouted. "No place to hide, except we immerse ourselves in that creek!"

"That's good enough for me," Harve cawed, and dove in, belly first.

The water was cold, but we hugged it like it was our momma while the lightning, wind, and rain rushed over us, the wind growing so loud we could barely hear each other.

"The horses!" Teddy Blue shouted.

"Nothing we can do," I yelled in return.

"My ears feel like they're exploding!" Harve cried.

Bolts of lightning struck the ground all around us,

then the rain turned to hail the size of prairie chicken eggs and pounded us while the creek water churned and frothed over us.

"Good Lord! Look at that, would ya!" Harve cried during a strong series of lightning flashes that lit up the prairie in a strange ghostly light. Through squinted eyes I saw a gray funnel cloud not a hundred yards distant, our horses running ahead of it, but it was plain to see in that moment, they weren't going to out-run the funnel of wind. Then the darkness closed in again and the roar made it impossible to hear one an-other as we clung to the muddy sides of the creek un-der the assault of hailstones and a pounding rain and waited.

In minutes it was over, except for the rain. We climbed out of the creek, soaked to the skin, and stood there trying to see into the dark.

"You reckon it took the horses?" Harve said.

We listened for a time without hearing anything more than the claps of thunder as the storm receded into the darkness.

"Nothing we can do until morning," Teddy Blue said. "It's wet and we can't even find a tree to build a fire. Damnable place, this Kansas is."

"I wonder if that cyclone went through Sweet Jesus and blew all the buildings away?" Harve said. "I won-der if it blew Naomi away? She said a big wind might come through and blow her away, or that the Canadian River boys might come and steal her. Maybe she's one of those people who can tell the future."

"That wind took my hat," Teddy Blue said. "That

was a pretty good hat; I bought it just before I left Amarillo. I used to wear a Stetson, but I sort of liked the way that bowler looked on me when I put it on. Now it's gone, taken by that cyclone along with our horses and every blasted thing we had."

We stood alone and defenseless, drenched like kittens someone had tossed in the creek. Teddy Blue's wrath was plain in his croaky voice.

"Come daylight, I'm going to go look and see if I can find my hat and whatever else that wind swept away. I don't like going about bareheaded."

"Could be we'll find Naomi, too," Harve said. "Along with your hat and our horses. She might have gotten blown clear to China, and maybe so did your hat."

"Mr. Sweetwater," Teddy Blue said, "I think it's time you passed around that whiskey flask you keep in your pocket. I'm terribly wet and cold and it's going to be a long night without a fire to dry our clothes. I'm by nature a temperate man on most occasions, but I reckon the good Lord will forgive me for drinking some of that devil water."

Harve gladly pulled his whiskey flask from his pocket and passed it around and we were for once mighty grateful for twenty-dollar whiskey. It was small comfort, but comfort nonetheless.

After a long, restless night, day broke with a line of silver clouds off to the east and we took survey of our situation.

"Good Lord," Teddy Blue said. "That wind blew away our entire camp. Why, we don't even have a saddle between us, nor a gun or pistol. Even our footwear has been blow away!"

It was true, the cyclone had plucked us clean as chickens at a Mormon picnic. Even the grass was cut like a gigantic scythe had bored along, inches above the ground, and we could follow the cyclone's path like a crooked green road.

We began walking, following the path laid out before us. We had little choice if we were to find some of our gear or our horses. We were in sad shape, worse than beggars, wearing nothing but the wet clothes we had on when the cyclone hit; we were bareheaded and barefooted and without weapons or horses. We would have been easy prey for road agents or renegades. Fortunately, it was an empty land devoid of much life. In three hours of walking, we didn't see as much as a single antelope or coyote.

"I told you those crows we saw yesterday were bad luck," Harve said finally as we shared the last of his whiskey. "I know now why they were flying so low and fast—they were trying to outfly that storm."

"I'd at least like to find my hat," Teddy Blue said. "My head's beginning to broil under this hot sun." With the passing of the storm, the sky had turned to a pure blue without a single cloud and the sun had turned fierce. Another mile on we found the horses. They were dead, piled one atop the other in a small arroyo, their bodies twisted, their legs stiff and sticking straight out.

"Well, least we found them," Harve said. "If we had a knife among us, we could cut us some horseflesh and eat it like the Apaches do when their horses is kilt or they've run them to the ground."

"Well, we've no knife, nor wood to build a fire to

cook with," Teddy Blue said. "Unless you want to try and eat those animals right off the hoof."

"I ain't walked that far or gone that long without a meal that I'd eat a dead horse raw," said Harve. We moved on.

Another mile and we found a single boot, but it wasn't one of ours.

"Who do you reckon this boot belongs to?" Harve said, trying it on, only to learn that it was too small and wouldn't fit.

"Maybe if we're lucky it belongs to Gypsy Davy. Maybe the storm caught and killed him like it did our horses," Teddy Blue said.

"You taken inventory of our luck lately?" I said.

"Yeah, you're right," he said. "We wouldn't be that lucky, would we?"

"Well, whoever it was had mighty small feet," Harve said. "I've always prided myself on the size of my feet, but this feller's got me beat." He tossed the boot aside.

"We're in a tight here," Teddy Blue said. "We could walk a thousand more miles and not see a living soul. I guess the government didn't give away enough of this free land, or else we would have come across one human being by now."

"We could always walk back to Sweet Jesus," Harve said. "It can't be more than fifty or sixty miles."

"If that cyclone hit through there," I said, "it would be a wasted walk. Best we keep moving south, forget about finding any more of our camp."

"Poor Naomi," Harve said. "She was a sweet woman, even if she was a whore."

"Well, we can only guess whether the cyclone blew

that town off the map or not," Teddy Blue said. "Your lady friend aside, it would be no great loss to the world if that big wind blew Sweet Jesus clean to Texas, which is where I wish I was right now. In fact, if that cyclone blew away all of Kansas, it wouldn't be any great loss in my book."

"Too bad we ain't cows," Harve said after several more hours of walking. "We could eat some of this grass."

"And if we had wings, we could fly," Teddy Blue said sourly. "Like those crows."

"I wish I was a crow," Harve said. "I'd fly and find us a place to get some grub and buy some horses."

"I guess we can complain all the way to the Gulf of Mexico," I said, "but that won't make the trip any shorter."

We fell into silence after that and continued to walk due south, considering that if we walked long enough and far enough, we'd end up in Texas.

Late that afternoon as the sun was beginning to angle low and cast our shadows into long dark shapes over the beaten grass, we saw a soddy, its lone stovepipe curling up black smoke. There were two sorry-looking horses staked nearby—a bay and a swayback stud.

"We've been saved," Harve said. "I never thought I'd be saved by folks who lived in a dirt house."

"We're not saved yet," Teddy Blue declared. "Those folks might not be friendly, and if they are, they might not be friendly to three half-dressed and shoeless men. Look at us; we look like bummers."

"But we ain't bummers," Harve said. "I'm a rich man, thanks to my late wife."

"You don't look rich," Teddy Blue said. "You look like a bummer of the worst sort."

"Well, I ain't no bummer."

We approached the soddy to within fifty yards and I hallooed the house. No sense taking chances of walking all day just to get shot by a nervous sodbuster.

"What you boys want?" came a man's voice from behind the long barrel of a musket poking through an open window.

"We were caught in a bad storm last night," I called. "It swept away our horses and gear, left us afoot as you can see."

"How do I know you ain't those Canadian River boys that's been raiding all over Kansas?"

"Mister, take a good look at us," Teddy Blue said. "We don't even have a single horse among us or a pistol, neither. How you figure we'd be raiders?"

"You look like trash to me," the man said.

"We ain't trash either," Harve said. "I'm a rich man from Denver."

"Shit," the man cursed. "You a rich man, then I'm Ulysses S. Grant and I got ole Abe Lincoln in here and we're discussing the Congress."

"Look," I said. "We just need some grub, maybe buy a horse or two if you have some you'd like to sell."

"Nearest town's forty miles one way, sixty the other. You came from the north, you went through Sweet Jesus—that's the one's sixty miles. The other's south of here—Hump Dance—outside of Dodge City; it's the Sodom and Gomorrah of Kansas. Full of cutthroats and painted whores and whiskey dens. I'm betting you can buy all the grub and horses you want once you get there, or steal them. Better move along before you miss the party!"

"The only thing that cyclone didn't blow away was my pants with my lucky gold piece in them. I'll give you that twenty-dollar goldpiece for a pistol and some bullets and one of those sorry-looking horses," Harve said. "We could at least protect ourselves from road agents and the like if we had us a pistol."

The man snorted.

"Road agents? What would road agents want with you bummers?"

"Now look here. . ." Teddy Blue started to say. I cut him off before he could rankle the man further.

"Mister, we'd be grateful to you for something to eat. This man's a Texas Ranger and we're after a pretty bad actor. And maybe if you'll help us, we'll catch him before he comes along and kills you and whoever else lives here with you." I was hoping to play to his sympathies and if not his sympathies, then his fears.

There was a slight pause while the man thought about what I'd said.

"He'll cut your ears off if you ain't careful," Harve said. "He likes to cut the ears off folks and wear them on a string around his neck."

"Anybody comes around here trying to cut off my ears, I'll give him a gutful of lead," the man said. "Now git along 'fore my finger gets itchy and I start shooting you boys to ribbons."

I saw the scowl on Teddy Blue's face and said, "Come on, let's keep moving."

We walked until dark, then stretched out on the open prairie with nothing but stars for a blanket and the ground for a pillow; but at least we weren't having to sleep in a creek or in wet clothes.

"We walked a damn long ways today," Harve said.

"Farthest I've ever walked at one time," Teddy Blue said. "And I don't aim to walk this far tomorrow. I might just go back and confiscate that man's horses."

"Then you'd leave him in the same condition we're in," I said.

"Yes, sir, I know. It's all that kept me from doing it in the first place."

"How far did that man say it was to Hump Dance?" Harve said.

"Forty miles," I said. "Less what we walked since then."

"Forty miles." Teddy Blue said it like a curse.

CHAPTER 15

Noon two days later we saw something.

"What is it?" Harve said.

Someone was moving across the prairie on foot pushing something.

"Without my hat to shade my eyes," Teddy Blue said, "I can't hardly make out who or what it is."

I hallooed and the figure stopped and seemed to look in our direction, then after a moment or two, sat down.

"Let's go," I said.

When we reached her, the woman looked like she'd walked as far as she was going to go. She was old and thin and wore a dirty gingham dress and a Mother Hubbard bonnet from which peered a pair of the most forlorn eyes I've ever seen. She had a plain and simple face that was long and narrow, and reflected, no doubt, every weary, mournful year she'd spent on the prairies. The thing she'd been pushing was a wheelbarrow with a dead man in it.

The man was as thin as she, dressed in faded denim coveralls and a cotton shirt that was frayed at the collar and cuffs. His brogans were dusty and his skin was grayish. His bony limbs hung over the edges of the wheelbarrow.

"Madam," Teddy Blue said, "why in God's name are you pushing a dead man around in a wheelbarrow out here in the middle of nowhere?"

Her eyes flicked white in the shade of her bonnet as she took in the Ranger. She seemed almost too weary to answer, but then said, "Taking him to town."

"What on earth for?"

"Taking him to his harlot," she said.

"Harlot?" Harve said.

"He loved her, not me. Let her bury him; I won't."

The three of us looked at each other.

Teddy Blue was shaking his head. "Strange country, McCannon. Must affect people's minds."

"How far is this town, ma'am?" I said.

She turned her head and stared into the distance, toward a horizon that offered little but grass and sky. The wind ruffled her bonnet.

" 'Nother mile, maybe two. It's hard to say when you're pushing a heavy load like Judiah here. He may appear slight, but he's all deadweight. You ever try and push deadweight more than a mile or two?"

"No, ma'am, not in recent memory," I said.

"Well, 'tain't no easy chore, I can assure you that. Goddamn and son of a bitch, I don't believe we should have ever left Indiana and come to this country. This is a goddamn useless place that just eats up a body's soul. And now that harlot has eaten up Judiah and she can goddamn well have what's left of him."

It was rare to hear a woman cuss, but she did a right smart job of it.

"What he die of," Harve said, "your mister?"

"Syphilis is what the doctor said he had," she said. "I reckon it was that; it wasted away his brains. The last few days he talked all sorts of crazy talk, tried to jump off the roof to kill himself, only the roof wasn't high enough to even break a leg and all he done was jam his knees and complain about that. Tried to drown himself in the well, but only managed to get stuck and I had to winch him out. Night before last, found him standing on a pail trying to screw the milch cow, calling it Jezebel and slapping its flanks. Had to strike him with a shovel to get him to stop. Milch cows is hard to come by this far out—almost as hard to come by as husbands."

There were four bloody dots on his shirt front.

"Looks like buckshot holes," she said. "But they ain't. I didn't shoot him. What finally happened was, he rammed himself into a pitchfork and that finished him. Judiah never had that much sense to begin with; the screwing disease poisoned what little mind he had. Pitiful way for a man to come to his end, but that's what sin will do to you—bring you to a pitiful end."

"You don't look like you are going to be able to wheel him to town," Teddy Blue said. "Better just leave him right here and go back home, ma'am."

She sat there staring at the horizon.

"This is the bitterest place I've ever been," she said, then began to weep.

"Where is your place, ma'am?" I said.

She pointed over her shoulder and we saw the soft

rut that the barrow's wheel had cut leading off toward the east.

"Let us help you take your husband back there and bury him proper," I said.

"I wanted her to have him," she said. "His Jezebel."

"Well, the dead deserve our respect," Harve said. "Even if they strayed in life. Which one among us has not strayed along the path of life?"

The woman looked up at Harve, her dirty cheeks now stained from her tears.

"Are you a preacher?" she said.

"No, ma'am. Long ways from it. Maybe your husband done wrong by you, but this ain't no way to get even with him, hauling his carcass to a whore. Best let the good Lord sort out such matters. You've done about all you can for him."

"You're right," she said. "But I just couldn't scrape out a hole and drop him in it. You know what they say about a woman scorned. Me, I am right proper feeling scorned. Now Judiah's dead as last winter's skunk cabbage and I'm left alone out here in this goddamn nowhere. All alone with naught but the wind to keep me company." She looked at the dead man and gave him a bitter stare. "You did me wrong, Judiah, and I shall never forgive you for it. May your soul burn in the lake of fire!"

We walked the mile or so back to the woman's homestead—a soddy in the middle of nowhere. A milch cow was staked nearby with not even a chicken or a horse to keep it company.

"If you'll bury him, I'll fix you men something to

eat, if you don't mind eating corn dodgers and slab
pork, that is."

"No, ma'am, we don't mind eating anything,"
Harve said. "You got a spade?"

It took us half an hour between Teddy Blue and
myself to dig the grave while Harve looked on, oversee-
ing the burial.

"Better go deep with him so the coyotes and
wolves don't come along and dig him up. That poor
woman probably couldn't take seeing this make an appearance again. I'm sure she's glad shet of him. Imagine how she'd be affected, was she to come out some
morning and find him lying there, dug up by wolves,
gnawed on and such."

"You want to dig this grave, you're welcome to it,"
Teddy Blue said, a bit irritated at all the advice. "I've
buried lots of men and I've never yet had to have anyone tell me how to do it."

"I'd have a hard time digging a hole with having
only this one arm. If I had two, I'd pitch in and help
you boys. Someday I intend to go find my other arm, or
what's left of it. I reckon the coyotes and wolves et
everything but my arm bone, but still, it would be good
to have it so when they bury me, I'll have all my parts.
I'm a firm believer in departing this world with all that
the good Lord gave you when you came into it."

"You think having all your parts in the hereafter is
going to make a difference?" Teddy Blue said.

"Well, it can't hurt," Harve said. "Suppose I have
to end up wrestling the devil to fight my way into the
pearly gates?"

We finished planting the man then washed up in a
barrel of rainwater before going inside and eating the

corn dodgers and slab pork she'd prepared for us. We sat at a small handmade table in the dim light and ate ravenously while the woman sat and watched us in stony silence. Finally we finished what had been set before us, then shoved back from the table feeling as though we'd just dined at the finest establishment in seven states.

"There's some cider," she said, pointing to a jug. "You boys might as well have at it, Judiah sure ain't going to be missing it and I'm a teetotaler and would never allow hard liquor to pass my lips. Whiskey steals a body's brains," she added. "The raw frontier has stolen about everything from me there is to steal and I'll be hanged before I let my brains get stole, too."

Harve looked at us then, with a shrug, reached for the jug and pulled the cork with his teeth.

"Well, let my brains get stole," he said, and took a long pull and smacked his lips.

"You gents look poorly," the woman said after we'd finished passing around the jug. "What happened to you and how come you're out here without so much as a horse among you?"

I explained to her about the storm.

"Oh, yes," she said. "I heard it howling two nights ago after I hit Judiah with that shovel to get him offa the cow. I thought for sure the wind was a sign from the Almighty and would blow all this dirt down on us and kill us. Maybe I'd be better off if it had. Least I wouldn't have to live with the shame of a straying man."

"I guess there'd be nobody to know that but you," Teddy Blue said. "You're the first person we've seen for nearly two days."

"It's high lonesome, that's a fact," she said.

"We were trying to get to that town, Hump Dance," Teddy Blue said. "Is that where you were headed with your husband?"

"Yes," she said. "The most sinful place in God's creation. Full of syphilitic whores and evil spirits. I hope that storm went through there and blew it to kingdom come. It is a blight of humanity and maybe if it got blowed away, some decent folks would come through and build a new town where a woman could walk the streets without being molested by tramps and liquored up men, and a husband could go without getting drawn into the lair of harlots."

"Well, we best get started," Teddy Blue said. "We've a lot of ground to cover."

"Judiah's clothes are in that trunk yonder; you gents are free to help yourself to any that will fit you. What need do I have of a dead man's clothes?" she said.

We thanked her for the offer but none of us really had need of a dead man's clothes, either. We headed for Hump Dance.

Harve kept an eye on the sky saying he was watching out for more crows.

"I reckon we'll be lucky if we don't see no more crows this trip," he said.

"I see any more crows," Teddy Blue said. "I'm going to chunk a rock at them."

"You'd have to have a pretty good arm to chunk a rock at a crow and hit it," Harve said.

"If you don't stop talking about crows, I might take a rock and chunk you with it," Teddy Blue said.

"My disposition is sour and all this talking about crows isn't improving it any."

Harve was about to reply, for there was little he liked better than arguing a point, when we heard the drum of hooves and turned to see riders bearing down on us.

"Hope they ain't road agents," Harve said. "We don't have even a stick to fight with."

"They're not road agents," I said. "That's Colorado Charlie Utter and his bunch."

CHAPTER 16

They sawed at their reins until they pulled their ponies up just short of where we stood. Colorado Charlie Utter looked disdainfully at our condition and said, "You boys look like you been rode hard and put away wet. What happened, some road agents come by and rob you?"

Teddy Blue glared at the man.

"Never seen me a bunch of barefooted stragglers out on these plains that lived to tell about it," Utter said. "Why you boys would be easy prey for any yahoo with bad intentions!" This said, he looked at his crew and hooted like we had tickled his funny bone.

"You best ride on out of here, mister, and leave us alone," Teddy Blue said.

Colorado Charlie blinked like an owl.

"Why, we could rope you boys and drag you around behind us like you was tree stumps," he said. "How'd that be?"

"Move along, Utter, before you talk your way into

a fight," I said. I was feeling some of Teddy Blue's wrath at being fooled with by a bunch of assassins.

His sidekick, the one with the batwing chaps and Walker Colt on his hip, leaned off to one side and spat and said, "Hell, Charlie, let's just shoot the sonsabitches and be done with it. They'd be as easy to kill as prairie chickens."

He was right, of course. They were armed to the teeth and all we had was our pride and not much of that.

"Hold off, Miller," Utter ordered with the raise of a hand. "No use wasting good bullets." Then he leaned forward, spat, and looked at me and said, "Why, it'd just be a good waste of bullets. I reckon these yahoos will plumb walk themselves to death." With that, he spurred his horse and rode away, the others close on his heels, except for "Batwings."

"I ought to shoot you boys just for practice," Batwings said.

"Yeah, maybe you should," I said. "Hell, you'd be doing us a favor, I reckon. We don't find water and food soon, we'll die a hard death. A bullet would be a blessing."

He seemed to like that, the fact we'd die a hard death. It caused him to smile like a mule eating briers and I thought, If he doesn't shoot us, I'll find him and make him wish he had.

"You gents have a good walk, hear." Then he rode off.

Harve whistled and said, "Thought the son of a bitch was going to plug us with that big iron."

"I'll remember him," Teddy Blue said.

"Yeah, me, too," I said.

We made Hump Dance in three hours. When I say "made," I mean we limped in. Our feet were bleeding, but our bellies were full of corn dodgers and fatback the widow had fed us, so we probably weren't nearly as bad off as we appeared. I did see this: women grabbing up their children and ducking inside whatever door was nearest when they saw us.

"They act like we're heathen savages," Harve said.

"We probably look worse," I said.

"I still got that twenty-dollar gold piece in my pocket," Harve said. "Let's stop in that whiskey den and have us a beer and then I'll see if this burg has a telegraph and wire Denver for funds so we can buy some horses and re-outfit ourselves."

A spot along the bar cleared when we approached. It was either the sight or smell of us, or maybe both. We drank our beer in silence, then Harve ordered a second round and we drank that.

"You boys look like you could use a whore," the bar dog said. "You ain't got no boots and no hats but that don't mean you ain't got no need." He had his eye on Harve's double eagle lying atop the bar.

"We need a lot of things, mister," Teddy Blue said. "Whores ain't one of them." Teddy Blue's voice was rough and tired and mean from the long walk. He said earlier that if he didn't get himself a hat and a horse soon, he might kill the next man who gave him any guff.

Harve wiped the foam from his lips and asked the bar dog if they had a telegraph in town. "Sure, sure," the man said, then told him how to get there.

"We might as well wait here for you," I said. "At a

table near the back where we won't be a living spectacle for every yahoo in Kansas."

We took our beers and found a table where the light was dim. We sat there about five minutes before Teddy Blue said, "I've never been in such poor shape in my life, not even fighting Comanches in Texas."

"Well, a Comanche is one thing and a cyclone is another," I said. "We just had the misfortune to be in the wrong place at the wrong time."

"You ask me, this whole state is the wrong place."

"I won't disagree with you. What I've seen of it so far hasn't exactly made me want to go find a wife and move here."

"The rate we're going," he said, lifting the glass of beer to his mouth, "we won't ever catch up with Etta and that man she's run off with. Either Charlie Utter will, or that murderous fool, Gypsy Davy. I'm afraid it's too late for us, McCannon. I've got a down and dirty feeling about this mission."

"Well, maybe if we don't catch up with them, neither will Colorado Charlie or Gypsy Davy."

"Those are long odds, McCannon. Leastways far as we know, they've got horses. We don't even have a single rusty pistol among us. I am thoroughly disgusted!"

"You can give up," I said, "you feel that way. Go back to Texas and forget Etta."

He stared at me. Even in the shadows, I could see the light in his eyes.

"Technically, she is still my wife; what kind of man would I be to quit and go back to Texas and forget about her? Worse comes to worst, I'll give her a decent burial."

"I understand," I said.

"I try not to think about it," he said. "But my mind keeps turning it over, what they'll do to her if they find her first."

I let my own thoughts push aside my weariness. If we were going to stop Utter and his bunch, we'd just as soon do it sooner rather than later. I knew that, and I think Teddy Blue knew it as well.

"We'll have to kill him," I said.

"Who?"

"Utter, most of his men, next time we run into them."

"I know."

"You up for that?"

"I never killed a man who hadn't yet committed a transgression," he said, "or hadn't cornered me in a fight."

"You killed Comanches," I said.

"That was different."

"Maybe not as much as you think."

"Don't tell me what I think, McCannon."

"I'm just saying if we take on Utter and his bunch after the fact, it will be a little too late, don't you think?"

He bobbed his head.

"Yeah, way too late."

"Then we stop them the next time we run into them."

"I'll do whatever it takes," he said. "You?"

"I didn't walk halfway across Kansas just to get fainthearted now."

"Well, if your friend doesn't get the money wired here, we might have to chunk rocks at them."

"Like David slew Goliath," I said.

"Our aim will need to be true," he said.

"Let me ask you something," I said. "You ever wish now that you hadn't chased Comanches and run them to ground?"

There was a moment of thoughtful silence between us before he answered.

"Yes, many times. They were a noble people, but sometimes they committed wrongful acts—that's why I did it. But I miss not having them as adversaries; they were a worthy breed—not at all like Colorado Charlie Utter and those pistoleers that ride with him, or that ear-wearing maniac, Gypsy Davy. Such men don't compare with the Comanches."

"It feel a little odd to you?"

"What's that?" he said.

"That we both love the same woman."

"Not so odd. Etta's an easy woman to love."

"I guess the strange part is," I said, "neither one of us seems to know her as well as we thought we did."

He finished his beer.

"Do we ever really know another person?" he said.

"No, I guess not."

We sat and nursed our beer for half an hour more before Harve returned, looking like the cat that had swallowed the canary.

"We're fixed up boys—got us a line of credit at the bank," he said, waving a telegram. "Had my bank in Denver send a confirmation of my resources. We're back in tall cotton, boys. We can walk over to the mercantile, get us some duds, pistols, boots, and a new hat for you, Mr. Blue. Then we'll take a walk down the street where I'm told there's an Injun who has horses for sale."

"Well, things are looking up again," Teddy Blue said. "Maybe we will find Etta yet, before the others do."

We bought the clothes we needed; Teddy Blue selected a broad-brimmed hat the color of a dove; and when Harve asked didn't he want another bowler— there were several on display—Teddy Blue said, "No, sir, I think that fancy bowler was nothing but bad luck to me. And besides, I probably looked foolish in it. It was a vanity on my part. This one will do just fine." And he set it squarely down on his head.

"Well, at least now you look like a Ranger and not some fancy dan," Harve said approvingly.

We each bought weapons. I chose a .45 Schofield because I liked the heft of it. Teddy Blue favored a Russian model .44 Smith & Wesson and Harve picked out a double-action .45 Colt with bird's-eye grips. We also bought Winchester repeating rifles and plenty of shells, boots, saddles, and blankets.

"Throw in a few cans of those peaches, too," Harve told the clerk. "I got a sweet tooth for peaches."

We walked out of the mercantile different men, dressed and armed and looking dangerous.

"I don't feel naked now," Teddy Blue said, shifting the .44's weight in the scabbard of his pistol belt. He wore it crossed over on his left hip, butt forward.

"We'll go down there and see that Kiowa the man told me had the horses," Harve said. "Then we'll find us a bathhouse, scrub off this prairie, and get the nits washed out of our hair. Afterward, we'll eat like hogs and get a fresh start in the morning."

None of us disagreed with the plan.

That night as we sat in the saloon, having filled our bellies with steaks, fried onions, potatoes, and corn bread, I couldn't help but feel guilty that we had been delayed in our pursuit of Etta. Outside the wind was whistling and rattling the windows and we were sitting around, cozy and content. Who knew what depredation Etta might be suffering at that very moment? I feared that with every passing hour, our chances of finding her before the others did grew slimmer and slimmer. I saw the distant stare in Teddy Blue's gaze and knew he was thinking the same thing. Men in love, I thought. We were willing to do anything to save the woman we both loved. It occurred to me that if things turned out badly, this might be the last trail for all of us. I drank my liquor and listened to the wind and rolled myself a shuck. The wind sounded like a woman moaning—like Etta crying to us from the grave—and a chill ran down my spine. For the first time since we'd begun our journey to find her, I was afraid that maybe we were already too late, that maybe Teddy Blue's earlier premonition was right.

CHAPTER 17

We continued south for several more days without change of scenery. The prairie seemed as endless as an ocean, the grasses stirred by constant winds. Large white clouds drifted overhead and every so often, we would see herds of grazing antelope in the distance but could never get within rifle range to bring one down. The meager supplies we'd purchased in Hump Dance were again running low, and so were our spirits, since we hadn't yet come across any sign of Etta and Tom Feathers. Hell, I was starting to doubt if we were even on the right trail. They could have gone off in any direction at any time. But if the information we'd gotten was correct, they were heading for Gonzales, Texas, which put us on the right road.

Night found us camped along a tributary twenty miles north of Dodge City, according to Harve, who claimed he was now familiar with the country.

"This here is Pawnee Creek," he said as we unsaddled our horses.

"Looks more like a river than a creek to me," Teddy Blue said. "Why, a man could drown in this river you call a creek."

"A man did drown in it," Harve said. "His name was Jim Bones, and he drowned right in this very creek whilst trying to ride a paint horse across it. Paint horses ain't very good swimmers. I'd never ride a paint horse across no creek, or no river, either."

"I've never known paint horses to be worse swimmers than any other horse," Teddy Blue said. "Whatever gave you such an idea?"

"Having to write a letter to poor Jim's folks back in Missouri is what gave me that idea," Harve said. "Why, if he had been riding any other color horse than a paint, he might be alive today. And so might the horse. As it was, we never found either of them."

Teddy Blue waggled his head as he shook out his blanket and placed it on the ground. He and Harve Sweetwater seemed made for each other; they bickered like two old maids on just about every subject that struck their fancy. But I had a feeling that they genuinely liked each other and would have missed the company and the chance to argue if one hadn't come along.

"What do you say, Quint?" Harve asked, not content to let the matter drop. "Ain't a paint horse just about the worst swimming horse there is?"

"I guess a paint horse can swim just as good as any other color horse," I said. "And Jim Bones might have drowned no matter what he was riding. River crossings are always iffy and come tomorrow, we'll have to find ourselves a place to cross this one."

"I know one thing," Teddy Blue said, wrapped up in his blanket now. "A mule will never put itself in harm's way. If Jim Bones had been riding a mule, he might not have drowned at all because no mule will cross deep water."

"Well, I have heard that mules are smarter than horses," Harve said. "But it is unseemly for a man to go about on a mule. Anybody want to share this last can of peaches?"

"Not me," Teddy Blue said. "I'm not partial to peaches."

"*Hmmp,*" Harve muttered. "I never met anybody who wasn't partial to peaches."

"Well, you have now."

"I guess you two will argue until the stars fall out of the sky," I said. "Maybe we ought to get some shut-eye."

Harve looked up at the sky as though he expected to see the stars falling, then chuckled and ate his peaches, making slurping sounds before tossing the can aside and rolling up in his blanket. We could hear the river slipping its banks and it seemed like just one more obstacle to finding Etta.

The next day, we found a place to cross and came out the other side in fine shape and by mid-morning, we rode into Dodge City.

"Let's go check in with the law and see if we can learn anything about strangers passing through in the last few days," I suggested.

"I'll catch up with you," Harve said, "I've got to get me a refill on this flask and buy some more peaches."

I asked a kid with a spotted dog where the city

marshal's office was and he pointed and said, "Yonder is Mister Earp's office."

The name struck an old chord with me. Wyatt Earp's common-law wife, Mattie Blaylock, had nursed me back to health after a colored prostitute had shot me, trying to prevent me from taking her man to jail. It was one of those acts of kindness on Mattie's part that I won't ever forget and I remembered her telling me how Wyatt had run out on her and left her alone on the frontier. That was something else I hadn't forgotten and I'd always promised myself that if I ever ran into him, I'd let him know what I thought about his behavior.

"What's eating you?" Teddy Blue said.

"Nothing," I said.

"That kid mentioned Earp's name and you start looking like you want to bust somebody in the mouth. You and him have a past, do you?"

"Not really," I said.

We tied off in front of the office; I was determined to hold the grudge until we learned whether or not Earp knew anything about Etta or Tom Feathers's having passed through, or about seeing any of the others— Charlie Utter or Gypsy Davy.

He was a much bigger man than I imagined him to be. He was sitting behind a desk writing something on a piece of paper when we walked in. Another man sat in the corner reading an issue of the *Police Gazette*. Both men wore black frock coats and city marshals' badges and both looked up.

"Help you gents?" the one behind the desk said.

"You Earp?" Teddy Blue said.

"Yes, sir," he said, and I could see the instant precaution in his gaze. "Who's asking?"

"I'm a Texas Ranger and this man's accompanying me. We're looking for a woman who might have passed through here a few days ago traveling by hack. She'd be with two men, one of them a colored."

Earp had a sandy mustache that drooped below his chin and slate-gray eyes. The other man reading the *Gazette* could have been his twin.

"No, sir, I haven't seen anyone of that description, but you might ask my brother, Wyatt."

"I thought you said you were Wyatt?" Teddy Blue said.

"No, sir, you asked me if I was Earp and I am an Earp, but I'm Morgan Earp. That'n in the corner is Virgil. Wyatt is running a faro game over at the Alahambra."

"Which way is that?" I asked.

He looked at me, then said, "Out the door, turn right on Front Street, take it to First and take a left. You can't miss it—Kelly's Opera House is upstairs, Hungerford's meat market is right across the street, and George Dieter's Centennial Barbershop is two doors down same side, case you're thinking of getting a haircut whilst in the city."

It was a little more information than we needed, but we took it and left and I could feel Morgan Earp's gaze on us as we did.

"Looks like the Earps are the entire police force," Teddy Blue said.

"They usually are, from what I know about them," I said.

We found the third brother dealing faro.

"Better let me ask him," Teddy Blue said. "I wouldn't want you to go busting him in the mouth before I get an answer."

"I'd like a word with you, marshal," Teddy Blue said, interrupting the game. Several players grew scowls and one started to protest the interruption, but Teddy Blue cut him off with a hard stare. Earp, on the other hand, shuffled the deck between the fingers of one hand; the other hand, I suspected, was holding a self-cocker somewhere below the table.

"I'm off duty," Earp said. "Come see me in my office tomorrow you want to talk."

"I'm a Texas Ranger looking for someone," Teddy Blue said. "I'd appreciate your cooperation as a fellow lawman."

I saw Earp grow a half-smile on his lips.

"This is Kansas, son, Texas is two states down."

"I know where Texas is," Teddy Blue said. "I'll ask you again for your cooperation, then I won't ask a third time."

Earp's gray-eyed stare was cold and calculating. I could see he was taking the measure of Teddy Blue, just as Blue had already taken the measure of him. I knew by reputation that Earp wasn't a shooter. He was known for striking men across the head with the barrel of his Peacemaker, what they called buffaloing a man. I think he knew after a moment of contemplation that he wasn't going to buffalo Teddy Blue without paying a heavy price for the trying.

"All right," Earp said. "Charley, take over." A man with a patch over his left eye and garters on his sleeves took Earp's place and the three of us walked over to the bar where Earp ordered whiskey and branch water.

"So, what's so all-important you need me to leave my business?" Earp said after tossing back half the glass of liquor.

"We're looking for a woman and two men who might have passed through here two, three days ago. One of the men is a colored; they would be driving a hack, maybe the colored on a horse outriding, a bodyguard. You seen anybody fit that description?"

"Yeah, I saw them, they came in a few nights ago, stayed at the Dodge House, except for the Negro, who stood watch out front. Left first light the next morning."

"Which direction?" I asked. Earp looked at me.

"We met?" he said.

"Not directly," I said.

"What's that supposed to mean, not directly?"

I started to tell him what I thought about his having left Mattie Blaylock high and dry, when I saw her out of the corner of my eye coming through the doors.

"It means I've heard of you," I said in response to his question. "That's all."

"What's your name?" he said. I told him. I could see him running it through his mind. "The name sounds familiar, but I can't place where I've heard it."

"Wyatt," Mattie said as she approached. She glanced at me and smiled. "Quint, how have you been?" Earp gave her a hard look.

"Wyatt, this is Quint McCannon, a second cousin of mine from back in Illinois."

Earp's jaw muscle twitched.

"I heard you'd gotten married, Mattie," I said.

"Yes, Wyatt and I have been married for quite some time."

Teddy Blue was restless with all this small talk.

"We've got work to do, McCannon." He turned his attention back to Earp. "Which way did they go when they left here?"

"South road," Earp said without taking his gaze from me.

"You see anybody else come through here, a lone man wearing a string of ears around his neck?"

"Ears?" Earp said.

"I guess you haven't or it wouldn't surprise you. How about a bunch of riders got their hats pinned up, you see them?"

"Saw some riders, yesterday—United States deputy marshals."

"Hats pinned up?" Teddy Blue repeated.

"Yeah, hats pinned up. What about them?"

"They're not lawmen," I said.

"They had the papers and badges to prove it," Earp replied. "I checked."

I exchanged looks with Teddy Blue.

"Judge Beam made them official by deputizing them," he said. "To make it look like less than a squad of assassins."

"What the hell is this all about?" Earp asked.

"Nothing," Teddy Blue said. "Leastways nothing that should concern you."

Earp was getting red around the gills.

"I hope you are taking good care of my cousin, marshal," I said. "I wouldn't want to think that she's not well cared for here on this rough frontier."

His gaze narrowed, uncertain what I knew or didn't know about him and her.

"Blood runs thick in our families," I added. "Always did, always will. One thing, we take care of our own."

Mattie gave a lighthearted laugh and touched my wrist.

"Did I ever mention, dear Wyatt, how serious some of my cousins can be about family?"

"You gents ought to get moving if you're after that woman and her friends," he said. "They got a good three, four days jump on you."

"You're right," Teddy Blue said, and turned to leave. Then he paused and said, "You coming, McCannon?"

I gave it one more second to see if Earp wanted to take it further, but nothing happened and Mattie kissed my cheek and said, "Tell the folks hello for me when you get back home, Quint. Tell them everything is fine and that I miss them." The look in her eyes appealed to me to let the matter drop and so I did.

"You take care of yourself, Mattie, you know how we all worry about you."

"I will," she said.

Teddy Blue was already tightening the cinch on his saddle when I caught up with him.

"Well, did you get all your good-byes said?" he asked. "And where is Grumpy?"

Harve was just coming out of the Long Branch, carrying several bottles of liquor.

"We leaving?" he said.

"What's it look like?" Teddy Blue said.

"Looks like we're leaving."

As we rode past the Alahambra, I saw Mattie and Wyatt and his two brothers standing on the walk and thought to myself that someday he was going to give her untold heartbreak.

"You boys learn anything?" Harve said.

"Yeah," Teddy Blue said.

"I learned something, too," Harve said.

"What's that?"

"That a man can't hold his hand against a glass jar that has a rattlesnake in it when the snake strikes."

"What on earth are you talking about?"

"In that saloon they had a rattlesnake thick as your arm in a glass jar and the bartender was taking bets you couldn't hold your hand against it and not jerk it away when the snake struck the glass. I bet him a dollar I could. I lost."

"Next time you want to throw a dollar away," Teddy Blue said, "throw it my way."

"I could have won five," Harve said. "Seemed like good odds at the time."

"Men who fool around with rattlesnakes are foolish, indeed," Teddy Blue said. "I knew a preacher down in Tascosa who believed you could let a rattlesnake bite you and not kill you if you had enough faith in the Lord. To prove it, he let one bite him one day in a church full of women and children and died on the spot."

"That is foolish!" Harve said.

"Do not tempt the Lord, the Bible says."

"I guess maybe that preacher didn't read that part."

"Well, now he won't ever get the chance," Teddy Blue said.

"Maybe if we spent less time talking about paint

horses and rattlesnakes and preachers," I said, "we might concentrate better on the task ahead of us."

"He's a mite touchy," Harve said to Teddy Blue.

"He found out his cousin is married to Wyatt Earp."

"Hmmm . . . I saw Earp bust a cowboy's skull in Abilene once with his pistol. Horsewhipped him."

"I doubt he'd horsewhip a woman," Teddy Blue said.

"I'd almost as soon be horsewhipped or snake-bitten than to listen to the two of you jabber all the way to Texas," I said, and put the spurs to my mount. Harve was right, I was a mite touchy.

CHAPTER 18

We found the bodies an hour after breakfast. They were lying in a circle around a cold fire of buffalo chips—eight, maybe ten men sprawled out.

"Christ and Jesus!" Harve said.

"Massacre," Teddy Blue said, "is what it looks like."

"You notice?" I said.

"Yeah," the Ranger said. "I noticed first thing."

"Their ears are cut off," Harve said.

I dismounted and took a closer look.

"That's not what killed them," I said. "These men were shot."

"How could one man shoot this many men without himself getting killed?" Teddy Blue asked. Gypsy Davy wasn't among the lot.

Turkey vultures wheeled in the sky above us.

"A smart piece of shooting, if one man did it," Harve said.

"Looks like perdition," Teddy Blue said. "Like Armageddon, like these men were smote by the hand of God."

"Or the devil," I said.

One of them had a tintype clutched in his hand; it showed the picture of a woman with dark ringlets of hair, her eyes staring into the camera.

"They won't meet in this world again," Teddy Blue said, taking the tintype and looking at it before placing it back in the dead man's hand.

Then we heard a moan.

Harve jumped two feet and stared at the bodies.

"Which one said that?"

A hand twitched and we rolled the feller over. Harve took his canteen and spilled water over the man's lips, his head was bloody, one of his ears had been sliced off, his face was black from gunpowder.

He rolled his eyes when the water touched his lips and he moaned again. There was a knot in the middle of his forehead the size of a turkey egg.

"This boy's been coldcocked, it looks like," Harve said. "Look at the size of that knot on his head."

"Coldcocked and cut," Teddy Blue said, "but I don't see a bullet hole in him."

"Then he's lucky."

"What's your name, son?" I asked. He looked young—eighteen, maybe not even that old.

He blinked several times, licked his lips, and stared at us.

"They call me the Cincinnati Kid," he said. "But my true name is Joe McCarty."

"The Cincinnati Kid, huh?"

He nodded.

"What happened here?" I said.

"Turrible bad fight, mister."

"We can see that, boy," Teddy Blue said. "How'd it come about?"

"Was camped," he said. "That's all. Then these fellers rode down on us like blue hell and started shooting us to ribbons. We didn't stand a chance."

"Why did they shoot you to ribbons?" Harve said.

The boy waggled his head.

"I guess they thought we were the Canadian River boys done all that bank robbing and killing. We figgered they was the law come to do us in."

"Canadian River boys?"

"Yes," the Kid said. He looked around, saw the dead, and added, "God, they're all kilt but me."

Harve snorted, looked around at the gaggle of dead men, and said, "You boys sure as hell don't look like no serious outlaws. Why, take a gander—there ain't one among the bunch looks like he's old enough to shave."

The boy looked at me, blinked again, sat up, let out a groan, and felt the knot on his head.

"Yes, sir, I'm admitting it, that's who we were: the Canadian River boys, worst bunch of yahoos in three states. Robbed and killed everybody we could; shot 'em, stabbed 'em, dragged 'em, even run over some with our horses. We were mean, mean, mean. Wasn't nobody or nothing that we ever feared until yesterday." Then he rolled his eyes and groaned.

"You don't look like a yahoo that could even kill time," Harve said. "Why you can't be more'n a dang child!"

"Well, sir, I was part of these here dead boys, alright. I may have even been the worst of the bunch, truth be told. I've done things I'm nearly shamed to admit."

"I ain't buying it," Harve said. "You don't look like you could whip a schoolgirl, much less rob and murder folks."

The boy looked contrite.

"I don't know," Teddy Blue said. "It's been my experience that killers and thieving trash come in all ages and stripes. Maybe we ought to take this boy to the nearest town and see him hanged for his crimes."

The boy nodded.

"Yes, sir, you'd be right in doing it. I deserve to hang for what I've done."

"Hell, maybe we ought to just shoot him and leave him here for those turkey vultures," I said.

He looked up, saw the swarm of dark-winged birds circling overhead.

"First they pluck out your eyes," Harve said. "And you don't even have to be dead yet. Birds like that, find eyes to be the tastiest of morsels. Then the wolves come and tear open your guts and eat them."

Teddy Blue said, "Seems to me, that's a better fate for a killing, thieving, no-account rascal such as yourself."

"They'll probably chew off your other ear, too," Harve added.

The boy reached up and felt the ragged fringe where his ear had been, winced, and pulled away bloody fingers.

"I thought it was a dream I was having," he said, his eyes wide with startlement. "I thought I was only dreaming that a feller was cutting off my ear. Oh, Lord, I'm violated!"

"That's nothing compared to what's going to happen to you," Teddy Blue said. "Let's go." We turned to mount our horses when the Kid shouted.

"Don't leave me for the buzzards to pluck out my eyes and the wolves to eat my guts!"

"You said it yourself, boy," Teddy Blue said, putting a foot to the stirrup. "You are the worst kind of breed there is. Best you die hard—maybe you'll get your reward in heaven but not here on this earth."

"I was lying!" the boy said. "I ain't no killer. Why, I ain't hardly fired my pistol at nothing but jackrabbits, and even then I didn't hit nothing."

Teddy Blue strolled over to the boy and looked down at him.

"Honest, mister. I just joined up with these fellers yesterday, ran across their camp here and asked could I stay for some coffee and hardtack. I just happened to be in the wrong place at the wrong time, 'at's all."

"Why'd you make up that story then?"

The boy dipped his head, moaned, looked up again.

"Me and my brother Henry come two thousand miles with our ma," he said. "She died and Henry went to New Mexico to seek his fortune. Me, I stayed right here in Kansas seeking my own. Henry's made a big name for himself as an outlaw and I wanted to be wild and wooly just like him. So when these boys told me who they were and what all they'd done and asked me to throw in with them, I couldn't hardly say no. That'n there—the one with the greasy pants—he's their leader. Called himself Sunny Jim. He's the one said I could either throw in with them or taste lead, meaning he'd shoot me down like a yellow-dog if I didn't. That'n next to him is Muddy Water Bill. Those others I hardly remember their names."

"These riders that sent you boys to perdition," Harve said, "what'd they look like?"

"Hats pinned back," the Kid said. "That's about all I remember; that, and they could shoot awful good. Killed us all in about ten minutes, except for me."

"How come they left you?" Teddy Blue said.

"I guess they thought I was kilt like all the others. How it happened was, Muddy Water Bill swung about to shoot one of them and knocked me senseless with the barrel of his Winchester. I reckon I was standing too close behind him. Next thing I know I'm dreaming of some yahoo leaning over me with a knife."

"One of the pinned hats?" I said.

"Uh-uh," the Kid said. "This feller wasn't wearing a hat. Fact is, he had long dark hair. And another thing: He was wearing a . . ."—his eyes grew wide—"a string of ears around his neck."

"No pinned hat?" Harve repeated.

"No hat."

"Gypsy Davy," I said.

"And the others were Colorado Charlie Utter and his bunch."

"Why you reckon they shot us?" the Kid asked.

"Practice," Teddy Blue said.

"Practice?"

"There was no way they could have known you were outlaws. My guess is, they just got restless to shoot someone and you boys were it. You are a lucky man, Kid," I said.

"Well, why'd that feller come along and cut off my ear, you reckon?" The Kid had buckteeth and his eyes were slightly crossed. He again touched the side of his head gingerly. "What'd make a body do something like that?"

"Souvenir," Harve said. "He's got a thing for ears. Be glad he didn't cut off both your ears or you wouldn't have no way to hold your hat. As it is, it will fall to one side more'n the other, but that's not so bad. Lots of men with two ears wear their sombreros like that."

"Well, I'm mighty mad I was violated in such a manner," the Kid said. "I intend to find that man and get my ear back and teach him a lesson in the doing!"

"You best hie on back to Cincinnati or wherever it was you said you were from," Teddy Blue said. "The frontier is no place for a tenderfoot to be, as you can plainly see if you were to look into a mirror. That ear will be a long time growing back, but if those fellows had shot you full of lead like your compadres, you'd be a lot sooner dead."

"No, sir," the Kid said, standing up then wobbling like a newborn colt. "I intend to track that rascal down and get my ear back."

"Well, good luck to you, boy," Teddy Blue said, and mounted his horse.

"We can't just leave him here," I said.

The Ranger gave me a flat stare.

"We're closing ground on them," he said. "You want to slow us down by hauling this yahoo along?"

"Well, then, at least have the decency to shoot him," I said. "It'd be a more generous act than leaving him out here alone on foot, him leaking a blood trail the wolves can follow."

Teddy Blue looked thoroughly disgusted at my suggestion.

"Okay," he growled, kicking a foot free from his stirrup. "We'll ride him double to the next town."

"Dodge is back yonder," young Joe said as we started out on the south road again.

"We ain't going to Dodge," Teddy Blue said.

"Why ain't we? It's the closest town."

"Because we've already been there. Now stop yapping."

In spite of my concern for the boy's welfare, Teddy Blue was right, even if he was as hard as nails about it. Having to ride the boy double would slow us down considerably. Each hour, each day that passed without us catching up to Etta and Tom Feathers only decreased our chance of finding them alive. Colorado Charlie Utter and his bunch, along with Gypsy Davy, were leaving a bloody wake across the landscape. It seemed all we were doing was following after them and cleaning up the mess.

CHAPTER 19

There wasn't spit for the next two days and riding an extra man, even one as light and slender as the Kid, made the going slower than it should have been. The landscape was more of the same, except the country became a little more hilly, the soil turned reddish, and the rivers and creeks more muddy. We were even seeing more trees, scrub oaks and blackjacks.

"I know this land," Harve said. "Crossed it many times droving. What they call no-man's-land, Oklahoma territory. Bad place to be unless you are an outlaw. Hideout of killers, thieves, rapists, and every sort of bad actor you can imagine." He turned and looked at Joe, who was riding behind me.

"Why, you ought to be right at home here, Kid. You being the cold-eyed, one-eared only surviving member of the Canadian River boys." Harve took great delight in japing the Kid about aliases and falsified reputations.

"Why would any thieves or killers want to come

here?" the Kid said, looking about. "We ain't seen nary a mercantile or even a drummer to rob or kill."

"They come here because the law is afraid to. Those federal marshals sent out of Judge Parker's court over in Arkansas won't come this far. No fool in his right mind who wears a badge would come to such a hellish place."

Teddy Blue's eyes snapped.

"I'm wearing a badge and I came here," he said sourly.

"Well, I must admit," Harve said. "You're a rather odd duck to begin with."

"What do you mean by that statement, Mr. Sweetwater?"

"Just meant that there ain't many men who'd go clear to hell to find an ex-wife. In fact, most men would head in the *opposite* direction when it comes to ex-wives."

"Well, I ain't most men," Teddy Blue said.

"That's sure enough plain as paint."

Harve, who was riding slightly in the lead, drew up short.

"What is it?" I said.

"Look," he said. "Ain't that the biggest rattlesnake you ever saw in your life?"

A diamondback rattler was stretched out on a rock in the warm sun near the road; its body was the thickness of a man's arm, its length well over six feet.

Before I knew it, the Kid leaped off the back of my horse and quickly grabbed up the big snake by the tail and cracked it like a whip, snapping off the head.

"Dinner!" the Kid said, holding it up proudly.

"Dinner?" Teddy Blue said. "What sort of fool would eat a snake?"

"You ever et one, Mr. Blue?"

"No, and I ain't never going to eat one, either."

"Tastes like chicken, you fry 'em right."

"I'd just as soon eat a real chicken if I wanted something to taste like chicken."

"How 'bout you, Mr. Sweetwater? Mr. McCannon?"

"No thanks, Kid," we said in unison.

He shrugged and said, "Suit yourself."

The horses needed a blow and there was a small, meandering, muddy stream nearby, so we made noon camp and smoked cigarettes, except for Teddy Blue, who said he preferred cigars but had forgotten to purchase any in Hump Dance. Harve produced one of the bottles of twenty-dollar whiskey from his saddlebags and offered it around while we sat and watched the Kid skin and cook his snake over a mesquite fire.

"You know it was the devil in the form of a serpent who tempted Adam and Eve in the garden," Teddy Blue said. "It's why God didn't give legs to a snake."

"Imagine if He had," Harve said. "What terrible creatures they'd be. Why suppose a big ole rattler like that'n had legs and could run as fast as a horse? Wouldn't this be a mighty dangerous world?"

They both seemed to think about that for a while. My own thoughts were on Etta. Thinking about her and the things that had transpired since I'd last seen her, I could only wonder how different our fate would have been if I had asked her to marry me when I had the chance. Just those few words could have changed everything for us.

It's easy for a man to imagine all sorts of things, given the time and inclination. Lately, I'd been doing a lot of thinking about life, what lie ahead for me, given the fact I was a year older than Bill Hickok, who, like most of my contemporaries, had already been sent to the grave. A man my age and with my past, surviving on the frontier, gave me cause to think. But if I did have many more years ahead of me, I'd like them to be in the company of a woman like Etta.

I watched the Kid squatting before the fire, content, I suppose, to be alive, the prospect of a full belly and all the world yet ahead of him had probably healed some of the pain already. It seemed like only yesterday that I was as young and foolish as Joe McCarty; a jug-eared cowboy hardly green broke, chasing the ass-end of longhorns and eating their dust up the Chisholm, Bandera, Goodnight Loving, and a lot of other trails. In a way, it seemed like it never happened, like a dusty dream. But it had happened and I'd grown long in the tooth and I knew that my gun hand was slower than it once was, and that I couldn't stay in the saddle forever. Sooner or later, I would have to find a place to light and take root or end up dead, maybe on some sawdust floor like Hickok. The taste of lost opportunity turned bitter in my mouth.

The Kid pulled smoldering chunks of the rattler off his roasting stick and ate them, seeming delighted with his repast while the rest of us squatted on our heels and watched.

"You fellers don't know what you're missing," he said.

Finally it got the best of Harve and he said he'd try it.

"Damn, the Kid's right," Harve said, tentatively chewing on a piece of the snake. "Does taste like chicken—sorta. Let me have another piece of that serpent, Kid."

I thought, What the hell? My belly was starting to scrape my backbone and I was hungry enough to eat cactus. It wasn't so bad—fried snake—once you got over the thought of it. But Teddy Blue would have none of it.

"Some things are just too vile for a man to put in his mouth," he said. "You'll not catch me eating a creature that crawls on its belly—that includes horny toads and Gila monsters."

"Horny toads and Gila monsters got legs," Harve said.

"Little bitty ones," Teddy Blue said. "Not enough to count. They are just serpents with little bitty legs."

We rode the rest of the day and as dusk started to overtake us, we saw some lights off in the distance.

"Could be a town," Harve said.

"Don't care what it is as long as we can buy a meal, something other than serpent to eat," Teddy Blue said.

Actually, it wasn't a town but a collection of shacks built around a large garden.

"We'd best be cautious in our approach," Teddy Blue said. "What Mr. Sweetwater says is true about this territory—it's a refuge for the bad actors, decent folks will be jumpy about the approach of strangers."

But we'd already been noticed. Several men stepped out of the shadows, each had a shotgun cradled in his hands. These were the dark faces of Negroes.

"What you men want?" one of them said. He was an older gent with a cotton-gray fringe of hair.

"Meal, if we can get it," I said. "That and a place to water our horses."

"Be hard pressed to get a meal round here," the man said.

"Why's that?" Teddy Blue said.

"Look at you," the man said, then glanced at the others who stood spread out.

"What about us?" Teddy Blue said.

"You white," the man said.

"I'm also a lawman," Teddy Blue said. "Texas Ranger."

"This here ain't Texas, mister, and all the law that exists is these." He waggled the barrels of his shotgun.

"If I had a dollar for everyone who's told me this wasn't Texas, I'd be a rich man," Teddy Blue replied. "I *know* it ain't Texas; fact is, I'm dang glad it *ain't* Texas, for if it was, I'd be ashamed to be a Texan."

"Insults ain't gonna buy you much except trouble, mister," the man said.

"Not trying to insult anybody, trying to buy a meal."

Harve spurred his horse a little ahead and said, "The color gold matter to you gents, whether it's a white man's gold or not?"

The men looked at each other.

"Gold money?"

"Double eagle. Give you one for a meal for my friends and me and some grain and water for our mounts, how will that be?"

"That'd be just fine, but I'd like to see the money a'fore I feed you."

Harve flipped the man a coin and he caught it and examined it before slipping it into his pocket and lowering the scattergun. The others were slow to lower theirs until the old man said, "Welcome to Nowhere."

"That what they call this place?" I said. "Nowhere?"

"That's what it is," the man said. "So that's what we call it."

He told us where we could wash up and water our horses and had one of the younger men pour out some grain in nose bags for our mounts. Inside the shack, the old man sat at the head of the table. Up and down both sides sitting on benches were children. I counted twelve.

"These are my young'ns," he said, and named them each and every one. "And that's my wife, Hattie, doing the cookin'." A large black woman stood at the stove with her back to us and only every now and then glanced over her shoulder at us. The room was filled with the smell of fatback and beans and corn bread. It was a good smell.

"What happen'd your arm, mister?" a youngster about halfway down the right hand row of children said. He was maybe five or six years old, wide-eyed and curious.

The old man spoke up, told the boy to mind his manners, but Harve grinned and said it was okay, he'd gotten asked the same question lots of times.

It was plain, however, that the loss of an arm was not fit conversation around the supper table so Harve didn't go into the grisly tale.

After supper, the old man, who said his name was Israel, asked us to join him out of doors, which we did.

The sky was just turning a dark shade of plum against a dark-silver background and some of the other men were standing around a large fire of blackjack stumps, the flames trapped in their eyes.

Israel introduced all around and told us this was all one family, cousins and brothers of his, nephews, men who'd brought their wives and children to this far end of the settlements to be shed of the "troubles that still existed for a colored man closer in." He told us that he and some of the older men had fought the Cheyenne, Sioux, and Apaches as buffalo soldiers in the Ninth and Tenth Calvary Regiments; how after they'd all been blooded and after the fighting was over, they went home to the same hard conditions they'd left.

"Don't seem to matter none what you did or didn't do for this country," he said, looking sharply into the flames, the stem of a corncob pipe clenched between his teeth. "You a black man, you still just a slave in most white men's eyes. 'At's why we came out this far, figgered no white men here to contend with. Ain't, either, except the occasional dodger. You see now why we carry shotguns and take notice of strangers."

"Pays to be alert," I said. "No matter whether you're white or black or red in this country."

"Got that right, mister."

We talked at length about the war, about crops and rain and outlaws while Harve produced a fresh bottle from his saddlebags and passed it around. Then the conversation turned to what our business was this far from anything and Teddy Blue told them. The mention of Etta and Tom Feathers brought a pall over the talk.

"You seen these folks?" I said. "It's important we find them before some others do."

"Ain't seen nobody," Israel said. "Nobody's been through here in a month."

Logic said that was hard to believe, considering that we'd been traveling the same road since Dodge, which lay just a hundred yards to the north of the settlement.

"You sure?" Teddy Blue said. "I don't see how you could have missed seeing them."

"Ain't seen nobody like you described or like you ain't described, either. I guess we best be turning in, getting late, lot of planting to do tomorrow."

It was a signal to the others to slip off into the shadows and head toward their homes. Israel said we could camp the night but would appreciate it if we were gone by daylight.

"Nothin' 'gainst you," he said. "Jus' that, well . . ."

"We'll be gone," Teddy Blue said.

After the men left Teddy Blue said, "They saw them."

"I agree," Harve said. "Clammed right up when you asked them."

"I'm sure they've got their reason," I said. "Out here, middle of nowhere, man's best to keep to himself."

"They seemed like honest enough men," Harve said.

"Honest to a point," Teddy Blue said.

"The outrider," I said. "Bittercreek Newcomb said he was a black man."

"Then that's it," Teddy Blue said. "They wouldn't say anything against him because he's one of their own."

"Makes sense," Harve said. "Feathers's man could have told them they were being chased by a pack of white devils—don't we look it, truth be told?"

"Hell if we don't."

"Maybe the lack of an answer is our answer," I said.

The boy, Joe, strolled back into the fire's light.

"Where you been, Kid?" Harve said.

"Relieving myself."

"Of what?"

Joe grinned sheepishly.

"Say you didn't?"

"Didn't what?"

"Wander off into the bushes with one of those young gals."

"I might have taken a stroll down by the creek out yonder," he said. "And maybe one of them young gals happened to come down there for a pail of water. And maybe we even exchanged a few pleasantries."

"Jesus, Kid, you want to get us shotgunned by some outraged daddy?"

"Didn't do anything, me and her, just exchanged some pleasantries."

Teddy Blue warmed his hands in front of the dying flames and stared into them. A knot worked along his jawline. I thought he would light into the Kid for his indiscretion, but instead he said nothing.

"From now on," I said, "stay close to camp, understood?"

The Kid looked at me, lowered his gaze to the flames.

"Yes, sir."

"Was she sweet?" Harve said. " 'Cause if you are

going to die over a gal, she ought to at least be pretty and sweet."

The Kid blushed, the fire sputtered and crackled, and a thousand stars were flung across the sky.

Among us, only the Kid seemed to be enjoying the moment.

CHAPTER 20

I thought Billy Cody and others like him had wiped out all the great herds of buffalo on the plains. You ever been to places like Ft. Griffin and Dodge and seen the mammoth pile of buffalo skulls and bones, smelled the stink of hides waiting to be shipped east, you'd know what I mean about the eradication of the beasts. Once was a time you could see herds so vast that you could practically walk from Texas to the Canadian border atop their backs without ever setting foot on the ground; top a rise and see before you a carpet of dusty brown hides, humps and horns that went from horizon to horizon. So many, a crew of hide hunters could set up shop half a mile downwind and melt the barrels of their Sharps rifles, trying to kill them and still not make a dent. So many, the land became littered with their rotting carcasses after the slaughter and if the wind was right, you could smell death twenty miles away. So many, the wolves got so fat and lazy trying to eat up all that meat, you could walk up and club them. As one old Cheyenne who'd remembered put it, "The white man has emptied the prairies of the buffalo."

So when I first felt, then heard, the rumble and jumped from my blankets in time to see a large herd of the shaggy beasts coming directly out of the gray dawn at full charge, bearing straight down on us and the settlement, I thought I was dreaming.

Teddy Blue and Harve Sweetwater leaped from their blankets, too, their Winchesters at the ready. The people of Nowhere came tumbling out of their shacks, the men carrying their shotguns. The charging herd seemed an implausible sight to behold, and for a full few moments we were all mesmerized by it.

"Holy shit!" Harve squawked.

"They're coming straight for us," Teddy Blue said. For the first time, he looked uncertain. I saw the people of the settlement—the old men, the women, and children—and saw destruction and death if the herd continued their course and overran us.

"Get inside!" I shouted. "Get in and stay there!"

Israel looked at me, his eyes keen, a hard-eyed stare as though our presence, the presence of white men, had brought this misfortune with them.

"Take your families inside!"

"I ain't never seen nothing like it!" the Kid cawed. "Why, there must be a hundred of them!"

"More like several thousand!" I said. "Mount your ponies and we'll try and turn them before they reach the settlement."

"Huh!"

"Hell, yes!" Harve shouted. "Like in the old days before Cody killed them all! Hell, yes!" and he was the first to run for the horses.

"Get inside with the others, Kid, and stay there!"

He looked at me for a split second, then ran for all he was worth.

"We don't stand a chance in Hades of turning that herd," Teddy Blue said as we ran for our mounts.

"No, but we have to do something or else they'll run right over us!"

We stepped into leather and wheeled the horses about and slapped their flanks with the barrels of our Winchesters. They were balky about charging full-head at a thundering herd of buff, and who could blame them?

"Try and shoot the leaders!" I shouted. "Come at them from the flank and knock as many down as you can!"

It was risky business. Hell, it was always risky business when you shot buffalo from a galloping horse. One misstep and you were under their hooves. One quick turn and they had their horns up in your pony's belly. They were five hundred yards from the settlement and we closed the gap quickly, then swung wide and came alongside the leaders and commenced firing into them.

Harve had taken the reins between his teeth and was firing and jacking shells by levering the Winchester with his one hand after every shot. It was a hell of a piece of shooting and horsemanship and anyone who saw it knew he'd hunted buff before and knew his business. The roar of the thundering hooves drowned out the crack of our rifles as we dropped several of the leaders by firing almost point-blank into them. You had to shoot them just behind the front shoulder—shooting them in the skull was useless, the bullets would simply bounce off.

I was concentrating hard on one exceptionally large bull who'd taken the lead when suddenly the horse stumbled, then caught itself just as I pulled the trigger. My shot struck the bull in his haunch and in the quickness of a breath, he turned suddenly, his horns goring into the ribs of my mount, just barely missing my leg.

The horse went wild with fear and pain; blood spouted in a pulsating stream as the big bull ripped and butted its horns. I felt the horse rear, felt us going over backward, the thundering herd of buff swarming around us, sweat stinging my eyes, my mouth full of dust. Falling, falling.

No time to think, I braced myself for the pain of trampling hooves as I was slammed into the ground, my pony swept from under me by the goring bull. My head struck something hard and my world went mercifully black.

Death seemed pleasant enough: a sweet peaceful void.

I awakened to flames of pain in my ribs, back, and right knee. I tried to move and it hurt like hell!

Harve and a black woman were leaning over me, the woman had a wet cloth she was pressing to my face.

"Back from the dead, Quint—how was it?"

"Preferable to what I'm feeling being alive," I said, every word like a dagger in my chest. I knew I was going to cough, tried not to, and when I did, blood flecked the pan I'd grabbed from the nightstand.

Harve offered a look at the contents, then tried to smile it off.

He was dusty and sweaty and so was Teddy Blue.

"We turned them," Blue said. "I don't know how we did, but we turned them."

I tried to sit up but it felt like a rockslide on my chest.

"Busted ribs, podner," Harve said.

"Put a bullet in me," I rasped.

"You're lucky all you got was busted ribs," Teddy Blue said. "I once met a man who was struck by lightning on two different occasions and lived to tell about it, but he wasn't half as lucky as you. I never heard of any man losing his saddle in a herd of charging buff who lived to tell about it."

"Fell into an arroyo," Harve said. "That's what saved you."

Lucky, I thought. I'd been shot and didn't feel half as bad.

"Thing is, McCannon. You'll be some little time before you can even sit on a horse—we can't wait around that long."

I wanted to argue, to crawl out of the bed and prove him wrong, but just breathing was pure torture. I cursed my damn poor luck.

"We'll go on ahead, try and catch up to Etta and Tom Feathers," Harve said. "We'll head on to Gonzales and see if we can locate this ranchero Feathers, see if he and Etta are there."

Teddy Blue shifted his weight and said, "We're leaving the Kid, too."

I nodded, too damn angry and in too much pain to argue.

"I'll leave you this," Harve said, placing a bottle of whisky on the bed. Then he handed the woman a pair of twenty-dollar gold pieces and said it was for my care and feeding.

"Don't let him get too fat and lazy, miss."

We shook hands and I heard them ride off.

"You wants anything, mister?" the woman said.

"Yeah, some . . . ribs that ain't . . . busted."

She looked at me and shook her head before leaving the room.

The old man, Israel, came into the room and stood at the foot of the bed.

"Want to thank you gents for what you did," he said.

I didn't want to say what I was thinking, about how I'd maybe traded Etta's life for theirs for getting myself stove-up.

"Least we got our homes left, our garden saved, and plenty of meat to eat," he said. "Guess misfortune brings fortune at times, don't it?"

"I don't see how," I said.

He smiled knowingly, like he had secrets locked up inside his head only he was privy to.

"You'll see," he said. "There's a silver lining in every cloud, you'll see."

"You don't mind, I'd like to drink about half this whisky my compadre left me."

He nodded his head.

"Lottie will take good care of you long as you here," he said, indicating the woman who'd just left the room. "She's a dandy cook as well. You up to some sweet buff hump for supper?"

I'd had about all the buff I could stand for one day.

"The whiskey will do me just fine." It was like I had to squeeze every word out.

"I'll look in on you after a time," he said. "You need anything, you tell Lottie."

I felt alone and useless. Etta was somewhere on the run and I couldn't do a thing about it. The world for me at that moment was a very damnable place to be. And as far as silver linings in the clouds—well, all I could see or think about, were rainstorms.

I didn't know how things could get much worse. But being a fairly sensible man who'd seen my share of misery, I knew that they could, and they probably would.

I heard the happy laughter of the folks from the settlements as they sallied forth to the killing fields where we'd shot a number of the great beasts—maybe truly the last roving herd of buffalo anywhere on the plains. Taking with them their skinning knives and baskets for the meat, they were about to harvest the shaggy brown manna. Israel and his people's silver lining, not mine. Mine was there in the form of a bottle of expensive whiskey. Seemed a far cry from deliverance.

Another knock at the door and the Kid ducked his head in.

"You doing okay, Mr. McCannon?"

"What's it look like?"

"I guess I must be some sort a bad-luck charm," he said. "First I join up with the Canadian River boys and they get themselves shot all to pieces, then I join up with you fellers and the only dang buffalo herd left on these plains nearly runs us over. You ever heard of anybody with such bad luck?"

"Just me, Kid."

He blinked, half-smiled. "Well, I guess I'll leave

you be, go out and help 'em skin some of those buffs. You need anything, you just holler."

I nodded.

He closed the door and I started looking for that silver lining Israel spoke of in the bottom of the whiskey bottle.

CHAPTER 21

Later that day, Israel and some of the men came into the room.

"We got us enough meat to last the season," he said.

"You came here to tell me that?"

He offered me a benign look.

"We need to wrap those ribs, that knee of your'n, too. Looks twisted."

"Not in my lifetime."

He shook his head.

"Could be one or two a them ribs is busted clean in two. We don't wrap 'em, they could stab you in the heart, lungs maybe."

"There's not enough whiskey left in this bottle to kill the pain."

He eyed the bottle, nearly gone now. He looked at one of the men, a big, broad-chested man with thick brown arms.

"You help lift him, Ezekiel, whilst I cut off his shirt and Lottie wraps his ribs."

"Leave me be," I said.

" 'Fraid I can't."

Strong hands lifted me as gently as they knew how, but it still hurt like hell and I wanted to bite my tongue off against the pain. Jesus, it was like being suddenly plunged into ice cold water.

Seemed like it took forever before the woman had my ribs wrapped sufficiently to suit Israel. And when they finished, he told her to go to work on my right knee, watched as she split the pants leg up the middle.

"Fat as a mater," Israel said. "Best not jump around too much."

"I'll keep that in mind," I said through clenched teeth, the sweat stinging my eyes.

"I'll have Lottie come later and give you a bath, get some of that dust and blood off'n you."

"No, thanks . . . I'll do my own bathing."

Israel looked at me as though he had all the sympathy in the world for me.

"Best let her do it," he said. "It won't hurt half as much."

I closed my eyes, tired from the pain and with no more energy to argue. I was lying on a feather bed and between it and the whiskey all I felt like doing was closing my eyes and that's what I did. I remembered turning once in my sleep and having the pain shoot up through me like bolts of lightning, waking me up, the room black as pitch.

I slept fitfully, on and off, waking when someone would come in the room, waking when someone pressed a cool rag to my face or put water to my lips.

Waking when I felt my clothes being removed and my skin being bathed. The whiskey had done its job in part, but not completely.

Finally I came out of the fog and the pain came full bore and I cussed it as hard as I did my luck. Lottie came into the room with a plate of mush and buffalo meat.

"You up to eating?"

I shook my head.

"Israel says best you eat."

"Can't, won't."

She set the plate down on a stand next to the bed, shrugged, turned, and started to leave.

"Where are my clothes, miss?"

"Gettin warshed," she said.

"I had some tobacco, papers, and matches in my shirt pocket."

"Right there," she said, pointing to a small shelf just above my head, then reached and handed them to me. "You want me to fashion you a cigarette?"

"I can do it."

"You sure are an independent and grumpy man."

"Thank you," I said, and waited until she left the room before fumbling with my makings. I couldn't even roll a damn smoke.

I felt something stiff above my left eyebrow, reached a finger, and felt a ridge of dried blood. I must have been a sight.

It took three precious days for the pain to ease up enough so I could sit on the side of the bed, use the privy without Lottie sliding a chamber pot under me. Israel came in several times a day to check on me.

"Ribs look good, but that knee looks out of kilt," he said. "Looks like I might have to set it back in place."

"Let's get it done," I said.

"You won't be able to stand it."

"Hell, tell me something I don't know."

He took a pouch from his pocket, poured some of its contents—a whitish powder—into a tin cup of water he took from the nightstand, then swirled it around and told me to drink it.

"What is it?"

"Something to put you out of the misery I'm going to cause you," he said.

I looked at him.

"Mambuto," he said. "It's more powerful than any whiskey or any drug."

"Never heard of it."

"It's from Africa, where my people come from, handed down. Comes from a certain plant found there. Nothing like it here on the frontier."

"You ever had the pleasure?" I said, eyeing the contents; the powder had tinged the water a yellow.

"Not me personal, but I've seen it taken."

"For what?"

"Cousin I was with in the Apache campaign got hisself shot in the nuts."

"It helped?"

"He died, but at least he died without knowing it."

"That's a comfort to know. How do you know it wasn't the Mambuto that killed him and not the getting shot in the nuts?"

Israel shrugged his shoulders. "Couldn't say for certain. Least he didn't die miserable."

"I think I'll pass on the Mambuto," I said.

He looked at me, shook his head.

"Okay." Then he called in the men and told them to hold me down. I near flew out of bed when his hands took hold of my knee and began moving it about. I drank the Mumbato and waited. I didn't have to wait long. A soft hum began inside my head and my blood felt thick in my veins. Everything seemed to slow down at the same time my entire body felt like it was floating off the bed. I tried to say something but couldn't be sure that the words even came out or what they sounded like. The faces of the men above me became distorted and when Israel leaned in close to look at my eyes, I saw a blue light surrounding him. The first moments created a fear in me, then I felt a deep calm, as peaceful as anything I'd ever experienced. If I was dying, I thought, I welcomed it, surrendered completely to it. I felt a mixture of sadness and joy, of surrender and triumph even as my mouth grew dry as grit and I had trouble swallowing. I floated to the ceiling and looked down upon the men surrounding my bed. Amazingly I saw myself lying there on the bed and continued to watch as Israel went about manipulating my knee, aligning it, then binding it.

I heard him say to the others, "For a white man, he's tough as they come."

Then I watched as they left the room before my world went black.

I awakened to the sound of a harmonica and someone thumping on a guitar. Singing. The shuffling of feet and the clapping of hands. It was dark in the room, and through the only window I could see the night sky flung with stars. There was a flickering yellow light licking at the blackness. Instinctively I moved my right leg and was surprised that I felt no pain in my knee, just a bit of stiffness. The rest of me still hurt like I'd fallen off a cliff. My throat was parched and I reached for the tin cup and the pitcher of water that had been on the nightstand. I fumbled for it, only to knock it to the floor. The music stopped briefly, then started up again. Israel came in holding a lamp, shined it in my eyes, and said, "You ain't dead."

"I could use a drink," I rasped.

He shined the light on the tin cup then called some of the men and had them carry me outside and place me in a chair. Then he told Lottie to bring me some water and something to eat.

"Last time he wouldn't eat a thing," she said.

"Don't be quarrelsome, woman, bring this man some victuals."

Israel handed me a jug and said, "Drink some a this."

"More Mambuto?"

He grinned.

"Cider—hard cider."

"What's the occasion?" I said, taking up the jug and watching as couples danced to the music around a huge bonfire.

"It's Saturday night," he said. "End of the workweek. Tomorrow's Lord's Day. But tonight, we celebrate."

"Celebrate what?"

"Lots of things," he said. "Our freedom, for one.

Fact we ain't all killed or slaves or on the run from the law. Fact we got ourselves a place we can call home.

"Fact," he said, "we got plenty a meat and a mouth harp and an old guitar and somebody who can play them. You think of any more reasons to celebrate?"

"A good horse and healed ribs," I said, taking a hard pull from the jug.

Lottie brought me a plate covered in buff meat and red beans cooked in fat and this time I was up to eating, and that's what I did and licked my fingers when I'd finished.

"Here, I brought you this, too," she said, handing me my makings.

"Grateful," I said. "And I didn't mean to be grumpy with you before."

She was as plump as a laying hen and had a round dark face and wore a red kerchief around her head. And when she smiled, she looked like the happiest person in the world.

I leaned back and rolled myself a shuck and offered the makings to Israel. He declined, said he never took up the habit. I asked why and he said because of being a poor man. To let himself take pleasure in something he couldn't always afford, he reasoned, was just another road to more misery and he'd had enough misery in his life that he didn't want to give himself more by developing bad habits he could ill-afford.

"How about the cider?" I said, holding forth the jug. "Isn't that a bad habit?"

"Cider's something a man can always make if he knows where to find apples or berries. A man needs seed for tobacco and the right weather. Seed costs money and the weather you can't ever count on. I hear back East, they make cigarettes you don't have to roll that come in a package you can buy for a nickel."

"It would take away half the pleasure of smoking," I said, "not being able to roll your own."

"That Kid," he said, watching Joe trying to dance to the music even though he didn't have a partner. "He's a lively boy. What happened to his ear?"

"It's a long story," I said. "You mind passing that jug again?"

They seemed happy, the lot of them. There wasn't anything around for miles, no sign of civilization, no towns to gamble or drink or whore in. No churches to pray in, no outsiders to mingle with or bargain with. It was just them, left to their own devices, dependent on one another for their survival and for their joy. They were not so different from their ancestors, the first people God had led into the wilderness in search of the promised land. Maybe *this* was the promised land and they'd found it. It certainly seemed that way as I sat and smoked and listened to the music and watched them dance. The happiness creased into their dark faces as they laughed and sang.

I felt something I hadn't felt in a long time: envy.

CHAPTER 22

I busied myself by watching the men and women plant and cultivate their large garden and talking to young Joe. He related to me the story of his past with his brother, Henry, who was making a name for himself down in New Mexico.

"Some call him Kid, some Billy the Kid," Joe said. "I guess he's shot some people down there. You said you were a lawman once in Texas, you ever hear of him?"

"No, must do all his killing local," I said. "There's lots of bad men between Texas and the borders."

"Our real name was McCarty. Mother moved from Cincinnati to Silver City and married a man there named Antrim. Thin-faced son of a bitch, ugly as a boot. My mother was a handsome woman—beautiful Irish, with strawberry red hair and eyes with the green of Ireland in them. She married Antrim 'cause she was sick with the lung fever and desperate and wanted somebody who could take care of me and Henry—his true name—once she'd passed on. Trouble was, soon as she took her last breath, Antrim got shed of us quicker'n a dog tries to shed himself of fleas. Henry ended up stealing a Chinaman's clothes for a feller named Sombrero Jack. This Sombrero Jack offered him fifty cents to do it, and Henry landed in jail for it. I helped bust him out—dug him out with one of Mother's old kitchen spoons. Why, that jail wasn't nothing but some mud slung up on some mesquite poles. That's the day our life of crime began. He fled to Arizona where he shot his first man, a blacksmith who was molesting him. I took out for Dodge City, where I heard there was plenty of opportunity. Ended up swamping out saloons, emptying the spit of men like Wyatt Earp and Bat Masterson. Wild Bill Hickok, too. I suppose you heard of them?"

I generally didn't go in for a lot of yap, but since I didn't have a hell of a lot else to do while waiting for my ribs to heal but sit there and listen, I gave the Kid his head.

"Tell you something, Mister McCannon, spit is spit, don't matter whose mouth it comes out of."

"I'll keep that in mind."

"I met a gal there in Dodge," he said. "It was the one good thing that came out of going there. Her name was Maggie and it didn't matter a lick to me that she was a whore."

"She break your heart?"

"When she drank poison and killed herself, she did. I wanted to marry her, asked her to but she said I couldn't offer her much being nothing but a saloon swamper. She was right. I told her I wasn't always go-ing to be swamping out other men's spit and she looked at me and said, 'Why, you're just a kid and I'm nearly twenty-three. Time you get around to a regular profession, I'll be old and ugly and worn out.' That was the saddest moment of both our lives, I suspect. I think she loved me, but not enough to keep her from drinking mercury. You ever seen the look on someone's face that has drank mercury?"

I shook my head.

"That's when I decided to make something of myself. I wanted to go and become an outlaw because I didn't have no education or skills for nothing else. And I sure didn't want to end up drinking mercury."

"So you met the Canadian River boys and decided to join up with them."

"Truth be told, yes." He squinted into the glare of the slanting sun.

"Well, I didn't know who they were when I came into their camp. And once they told me and what all they'd done, I was a little afraid of getting mixed up with such bad yahoos. I mean, I wanted to be a regular hombre, a mean blood and all that, but I didn't take to killing innocent folks. Robbing banks seemed okay, for it's the rich man who owns the banks and I reckoned it wouldn't hurt them so much to 'share a little of the wealth,' as Henry used to say when we'd talk about becoming outlaws."

"So you've never done any actual crime-committing?" I said.

"No, sir, never did get the chance. I was a member of that gang exactly three hours when we got shot all to pieces by those fellers with the pinned hats."

"That tell you anything about being an outlaw?" I said.

"Tells me I'd better get a damn sight better at it or find another occupation to take up."

"Now you want to ride the vengeance trail, find the man who cut off your ear, and do him in," I said.

"Well, what would you do, Mister McCannon, was it your ear he'd cut off?"

"An eye for an eye, the Bible says."

"Exactly, only this time it's an ear for an ear."

"You're going to cut off his ear?"

"Cut off both of them, I get the chance."

"This man," I said, "he's a bad hombre. I'd cut my losses, so to speak, and find myself a steady job like clerking; find an honest woman to settle down with; raise some children, a garden. Take a look around you, Kid, what do you see?"

"Folks hoeing and planting," he said.

"Exactly. That's the way we were meant to live: in harmony with one another, not killing and robbing and cutting off each other's ears."

"You sound like a preacher," he said.

"I'm about as far from a preacher as this here place is from the moon, Kid."

"I miss Maggie," he said. "If she hadn't killed herself, I would be with her today, still have my ear and maybe an honorable profession."

"Most likely she would have broken your heart one way or the other, Kid. Some women are like that. She sounds like she was doomed from the get go."

"Maybe so."

"It smells like rain," I said.

"They could use it for their crops," Joe said.

"That gal you met down by the creek the other night. You still meeting her?"

"Some," he said.

"I'd be careful with that. These are good people here, but I don't think they'd take well to you courting one of their daughters."

"I know, cause I'm white. She's already said that. Still, we sort of are taken with each other."

"Then I'd go ask her folks was it okay with them you meet her."

"I know I should."

"I ain't your daddy, Kid. You'll have to work it out however you work it out. Thing is, these folks are kind enough to let us hole up here until I can step into leather and ride out. I'd not want to abuse their kindness."

"I understand," he said.

The rain came that night, hard and slanting and I could hear it ping off the tin roof and spill off the eaves. For some reason, it created a deep loneliness in me. The story Joe had told me about the prostitute who drank mercury crept into my thoughts. The wind picked up and turned into a low, mournful moan, like Etta's voice calling for me to come find her before it became too late. Christ, I couldn't let myself think about her being dead.

CHAPTER 23

Another ten days passed before I could stand on the bum knee and take a breath deep enough that I felt like I could ride a full day without falling out of the saddle. In that time, I'd grown damn antsy from sitting in the shade and staring at my toes and Gila monsters. The Kid had busied himself by pitching in with the hoeing and planting and tossing secretive looks at a light-skinned gal, who I learned was the daughter of one of Israel's cousins. Her name was Iris. I'd oiled my pistol and practiced the art of rolling shucks and tried hard not to think of my compadres, of Etta Landrow and Gypsy Davy, of Colorado Charlie Utter and his assassins. Ten days was long enough, I figured; it was time to get back on the trail.

I was about to call the Kid over, tell him I was leaving, when I saw a rooster tail of dust in the distance. I whistled and the bent backs straightened from their hoeing. When Israel's gaze fell on mine, I nodded toward the dust. He wiped his hands on the rump of his jeans then pulled a blue bandanna from his pocket and wiped the sweat from his brow as he watched the dust get bigger.

He told the men to go get their shotguns and told the women to take the youngsters into the house, then walked to where I sat and said, "Could be anybody, could be nobody. Best to be prepared for whoever it is." Then he disappeared into one of the shacks and came back out again with his shotgun, as did the other men.

"What should I do?" the Kid said. "I ain't got a pistol nor even a knife if it comes to a fight."

"Might not come to that," I said.

"Mister Israel and the others sure enough act like it might."

"They've a right to be cautious, Kid. Maybe it's better you wait inside."

"With the women and children?" The indignation in his voice was sharp, high-pitched.

"I've got my Winchester inside, you can go get that, you want."

"Yes, sir."

I stayed seated, but fixed it so my pistol was handy on my left hip. Joe came out of the house and stood next to me, the long-barreled Winchester nearly as tall as he was, clutched in his hands.

Israel took up a position a few feet away.

"Looks like it might be half-dozen riders," he said.

"Maybe them fellers that shot us Canadian River boys to bits," Joe said.

"Well, they come down around here shooting, they'll get all they want," the old man said, his eyes white with determination under the brim of his straw hat.

It didn't take long before we could make out several riders, their ponies lathered, the foam flecking off their chests and forelegs, their tongues lolling against the iron bits.

"Oh, no," Israel muttered when the riders were still a hundred yards out. "Rufus." He said the name like it was a cuss word he hadn't meant to say.

Ten feet from the shacks the riders jerked hard on their reins and the dust swirled up around them then settled slowly, leaving a fine coat of golden dust on their hats and clothes.

The one in front had oily dark skin and eyes as black as obsidian that came to rest on me and the Kid.

"Rufus," Israel said. "What you doing this far west of the territories?"

It took a long slow moment for the dark eyes to swing from me and Joe to Israel.

"Uncle," he said. "Me and my boys need something to eat, a place to rest our horses."

Israel stood motionless for a second.

"You taking in white people?" Rufus said, jerking his head in our direction. "Slaves, I hope."

"Don't be rude, boy."

"Well, can we or can't we rest our ponies and get some grub from you, Uncle?"

"Yes, you welcome to squat and rest up. I'll have some of the women fix you something to eat. Anybody following you?"

The dark face turned my direction again, the stare as hard as flint. I counted seven of them. Indian, Negro, a mixture of both. All of them bad news and on the dodge, judging by the way they were dressed and the sidearms they carried. Not a one in the bunch looked much older than Joe. The one called Rufus might have been nineteen, if that.

"Them's some hard-looking hombres," Joe said in a low voice when the riders walked their ponies to the water tank, then dismounted and took up places around the long table kept in the yard for purposes of community meals.

"Keep a low profile about yourself," I said. "Don't give them cause to start up trouble with you. The way I see it is, after they get through filling their bellies and watering their mounts, they'd probably like nothing better than to dust a white child such as yourself."

"What about you?" he said. "I'd say you're as white as me."

"They'd probably want to save me for dessert."

He gave a nervous laugh.

Israel came over after a time of sitting with the bunch.

"That's my brother's boy, Rufus Buck," he said. "His mother was a Cherokee. He's got a bad spirit. I'm his goddaddy, else I'd tell him to keep riding."

"No need to explain," I said. "Kin is kin."

"Better I do," Israel said. "Thing is, he hates white people, any white people, and lawmen most especially."

"He wouldn't be the first to feel that way. You can tell him we're not the law."

"I told him not to start no trouble with you boys, but he's got a boil on his butt about seeing you here."

"It's your place," I said. "You want us to leave,

we'll leave. You've already done more than your share."

Israel looked at me.

"You'ns turned them buff, kept them from over-running our settlement. I owe you for that."

"Let's just call it even then. Me and the Kid will ride out, save everybody the trouble."

"Thing is, you do that, I won't be able to protect you if Rufus and his bunch decide to take up with you."

"What do you suggest then?" I said.

"I don't know, just trying to clue you boys in that they could start some trouble with you."

"I don't mean to insult your family," I said. "But I won't be laid a hand upon by any man."

"Understood," he said. "I'll do my best to see he don't kick up no sand round here."

"Appreciated."

"We in for a fight, you reckon?" Joe said after Israel returned to the table.

"Could be. You think you can hit anything with that Winchester?"

"I'm a good shot," he said. "Me and Henry used to pop rabbits with Antrim's needle gun, though he wasn't aware of it or he'd have skinned us."

"Popping rabbits ain't nearly the same thing as popping a man," I said.

"I'll do what needs doing, I reckon."

"Anything starts up, let me make the first move. Don't go shooting anybody over words. We walk away from this thing if they give us half the chance. Under-stood?"

He nodded. I wasn't convinced. Fear makes a man

jumpy. Lots of fear makes a man lots jumpy. I knew men in the war who became so overwrought with fear and the battle raging around them, they'd forgotten to load their muskets. Least the Kid was holding a repeater and wouldn't have to reload. I just hoped if shooting broke out, he wouldn't shoot me by accident.

I told the Kid to go inside and pack up our gear.

"Now?"

"Yeah, unless you're planning on sticking around and marrying that gal you're so sweet on."

He arched an eyebrow then ducked back inside the house. I turned my attention back to the callow youths sitting at the table, hunched over, feeding their faces, and talking among themselves. Every so often, Rufus Buck would look over his shoulder at me. I made sure he saw I was watching him, too.

In a few minutes, Joe returned.

"All packed and ready to go when you are."

"Hold tight, Kid. Let's see how it plays."

The Kid looked nervous, shifting his weight, stealing glances at the table, seeing them cast hard looks in our direction.

"What do you think?" he said.

"I don't know."

"I ain't scared," he said, meaning that he was.

"Go ask Israel if I could speak to him a minute," I said.

Joe did as asked and I saw the hard look Rufus Buck gave him as he stood at the table talking to Israel—like an owl eyeing a field mouse.

"What can I do for you, Mistuh McCannon?" Israel said, carrying the shotgun in the crook of his arm, his eyes weary because of the tight spot he found himself in.

"I'd like to buy a horse off somebody, a good one that will ride two men to the next town."

He gauged my words.

"Might be Mose would sell you that big bay a his. He's talked about selling it 'cause he can't get it broke to a plow."

"Tell him I'll pay twenty dollars and throw in a good pistol to boot."

Israel weighed it then said, " 'At bay ain't worth twenty and a good gun."

"Today it is."

He went off, toward where the other men had gathered watching Rufus Buck and his gang eating up a good share of their buff meat and beans. These men were obviously not much more comfortable with the presence of Rufus Buck than was Israel. I saw him speak to the one of the men, a stump of a man with a straw sombrero. They palavered for a moment, then the man walked in my direction.

"Israel said you'd give me twenty dollars for my bay horse and throw in a pistol to boot. 'At it?" he said, looking at the self-cocker on my left hip.

"Twenty and this pistol, that's the deal," I said, unholstering it and handing it to him.

"Done," he said.

"Time we parted company," I said to Israel.

"You sure?"

"I've burned too much time as it is," I said. "I've got something to do and I can't see it done lying round here. Kid, go get and put my saddle on that big bay in the corral."

"I can't promise your safety once you're out of the settlement," Israel said.

"I can't promise I won't kill your godchild, either. Let's just hope they've got better things to do today."

"I'd feel mighty bad you was to kill him," he said. "Those others is just trash. Rufus might be trash, too, from the stories I've heard about the depredations those boys have caused in Indian territory. But he's still my kin, still got my blood in his veins."

"Let's hope he's got some of your good sense, too."

"I sure enough hope it don't come to trouble, Mistuh McCannon."

"I do too, Israel." I offered my hand and he shook it.

Joe returned with the horse saddled and said, "I'm ready, you?"

I said in a low voice, "You see one of those yahoos make a move, don't be slow in letting me know."

I grabbed horn and when I swung myself up, the ribs still bit into me, reminding me I wasn't whole-hog just yet. Once in the saddle, I left a stirrup for Joe to swing up behind me and put the bay into a fast walk until we hit the the south road.

"I'm going to miss meeting Iris down by the creek," the Kid said.

"You'll get over it."

"Glad we didn't have to fight them fellers, Mr. McCannon."

"You might have to fight them yet, Kid. Best be on guard, keep a check over your shoulder now and then."

"Oh," he said.

We rode till the sky turned crimson and was banded by a long line of silver clouds.

"You think we're in Texas yet?" the Kid said as we set up camp.

"Texas, Oklahoma Territory, what's the difference? We'll get there when we get there."

"Just that I ain't found nothing good about Oklahoma," he said, " 'Cept Iris, and her I didn't have a Chinaman's chance with."

"There'll be plenty of others to strike your fancy. I'll take first watch; you grab some sleep. I'll wake you in four hours."

" 'Cause of Rufus Buck?"

"He's one reason; there could be others."

He stared into the encroaching darkness.

They came just past midnight.

CHAPTER 24

Shadows in the moonlight, seven riders strung out in single file scouting for our camp. I clamped a hand over the Kid's mouth and shook him awake.

"Don't say anything, don't cough, fart, or make a sound," I whispered.

There was a hunter's moon and I figured even half an Indian could find us in that much light.

I already had the Winchester at the ready. With just one weapon, I'd have to wait until they came close enough and by that time, it might be too late. Seven hard cases against a busted up yahoo and an unarmed kid wouldn't be too much of a fight—unless they weren't as hard as they thought, or as ready.

I could hear the Kid breathing rapidly through his nose.

"Any I drop," I said, "you run and take his weapon and shoot anyone but me."

I could almost hear the sweat dropping off his brow.

I heard the snuffle of their ponies, the clink of iron bits, the creak of leather—sounds that grew louder as they closed the distance between us. I put a firm hand on the Kid's shoulder, indicating for him not to move. They were a good fifty paces from us—still not close enough to suit me.

"Fucken white men," I heard Rufus say. "We find them, we cut off their nuts." Some of the others grunted, a few laughed.

We waited as they walked their ponies through the sage, the shod hooves snapping mesquite twigs. And waited.

One of them said, "I think maybe they'd be over there by that wash, where there's a little water. I think maybe I see something over there."

They turned their ponies just fifteen paces away from where the Kid and I lay.

"Hey, I see their horse," one said.

"Shut your mouth!" Rufus said. "You want them knowing we're coming?"

"Too late," I said, and fired into them. Even with the moonlight, it was hard to tell which was which. I'd have preferred to take out Rufus with my first shot. Maybe the rest would quail. I couldn't tell which of them I shot first, which was second, but two flopped off their ponies and hit the ground hard.

"Go get their weapons, Kid!"

Flashes of gunfire spewed from the muzzles of their guns, but the shots went wild as they were caught up in the excitement of a sudden firefight. The Kid duckwalked to the nearest body and snatched the pistol from his belt but was having trouble firing it.

"Shoot the goddamn thing!" I shouted as I fired

two more rounds, one striking a rider but not unseating him and the other missing its mark.

"I'm trying!" he yelled. Suddenly it was as though they'd figured it out, where the killing was coming from, and the ground around me exploded with their shots. I rolled behind a fallen blackjack tree and the lead from their pistols chewed up bark and whanged away at it. The Kid was fumbling with the bandit's pistol when one of the riders closed ground on him, the horse striking him before he could bring up the pistol and get a shot off. I snapped off a quick shot, then the next round jammed in the breech.

I broke open my Barlow knife and pried the shell loose and quickly jacked another round into the chamber. But not quickly enough.

The rider had the hooves of his pony thrashing the Kid and when I came up and drew a bead on him, I saw the man take aim and fire three quick shots into the Kid—three white flashes that lit up the Kid's frozen features. It was just enough for me to see, too, the oily face of Rufus Buck. I took aim and pulled the trigger and watched him pitch from his horse and fall next to the Kid.

A flurry of rounds rained all around me; a splinter of wood stung my cheek and instantly I could taste blood. I rolled away, the lead from their guns chewing up ground. But the dance of their ponies threw off their aim enough for me to scramble to the Kid and the man who'd killed him. My rifle jammed again. I grabbed the pistol from Rufus Buck's still-warm fingers and rapid-fired into the remaining four riders. One pitched from the saddle and the others turned tail. The whole fight had lasted less than five minutes but it exhausted me and for a moment, it seemed like I could barely move. I swiped more blood from my face and lips with the back of my sleeve. My mouth was parched and my ribs ached like a broken jaw, but those things didn't seem to matter just then.

There in the paleness of moon, I saw Joe lying faceup, his mouth open, his eyes partly so, a bloody wound to the throat, two more to his chest. Rufus Buck lay next to him, facedown, unmoving, the two joined in death. I felt sorry for the Kid. He'd wanted to be an outlaw; now he was never going to be anything. Maybe the Almighty knew the Kid wasn't cut out for a criminal's life: the loneliness of a prison cell or a hangman's rope. I thought of a line I'd read in the Bible once: *Death comes like a thief in the night.*

I tucked Rufus Buck's pistol, a Colt Peacemaker, in my belt, grabbed his Deane Adams and Smith & Wesson, and then bladed out the jammed round from the breech of the Winchester, then used it to help me up to hobble to where I'd staked out the bay. By the time I'd gotten the saddle on him, I was too damn tired to take another step. Still, I pulled myself into leather. The remainder of Rufus Buck's gang had scattered off toward the west. I doubt they'd return for an encore. If they knew how defeated I felt right then, they might be tempted, but running into an ambush will take some of the stiff out of your pizzle and I think those boys had about all the fight they wanted for one night. I know damn well I did.

I would have liked to have buried the Kid, but I had no shovel and no time and what was done was done.

And after all that, the rain came.

CHAPTER 25

The rain hammered the land with a vengeance and hammered me along with it. Rained so hard the water seemed to boil up from the ground—a cold slanting rain that lasted until dawn before it let up. And with the dawn I could see the roiling gray clouds scudding low over the broken red earth. I thought of the Kid lying back there among the dead; the coyotes and the wolves that would surely find their corpses if they hadn't already; the circling vultures. There was nothing I could do for him, there was nothing anyone could do for him. I rode on, through the dull light to a destination unknown. My life, it seemed, had come full circle. Thirty years previous, I'd ridden away from a farm in Indiana—from a widowed mother and three brothers—off to make my fortune, to find my glory, only to go bust in the goldfields and end up fighting in a war in such far-flung places as Cold Harbor and Gettysburg, where I saw lots of boys with the same frozen mask of death on their faces as that of young Joe McCarty. And just like the Kid, I could do nothing for those others, either, except leave them to the ages and the ravages of the land. At least with the boys on those battlefields, men would come later, scooping up their bones and skulls into wheelbarrows for burial in mass graves. No such honor would befall a restless young man who'd gone off wanting to be like his brother, an outlaw. Here's to you, Joe McCarty, I thought in my silent passage. To you and all the others like you.

I must have dozed in the saddle, for when I awakened, my horse was standing still and a raven-haired woman stood in a yard before a small whitewashed house with several children clinging to her skirts. She held a Sharps saddle gun in her hands, the kind of rifle used by the United States Cavalry.

"You there," she said, "better keep moving before my husband gets back."

My eyes felt like they had grit in them and every bone in my torso ached. I probably didn't look too good, either, my clothes still wet, the brim of my hat battered down by the rain, my pony slathered with red mud.

"I'm afraid you're just going to have to shoot me," I said.

"Why's that?"

"Because I don't believe either this pony or me can go another step without rest."

The children—three girls and a boy—all looked up at her, their eyes big with wonderment.

"Ma, you gonna shoot that feller?" the boy said.

"I just might," she said.

They seemed to shrink back.

"You'd be doing me a favor," I said.

"What's wrong with you?"

"Nothing a change of dry clothes, some Arbuckle, and hot grub wouldn't cure."

"You a thieving man?" she said.

"If I am, you can see I'm poor at it."

"Killer, maybe?"

"Nobody who didn't deserve it."

"How come you to land in this far-flung place?"

"I didn't, my horse did. I just came along for the ride."

She looked uncertain what to do with me. What indeed do you do with a man who's shown up in your front yard looking like a bad version of death? That was the question behind her eyes. A rooster crowed and one of the kids jumped.

"We ain't got nothing if you came here to rob us," she said. "Just these kids and that rooster; two, three laying hens."

"I didn't come here to rob you or otherwise bring you harm," I said. "You mind I step down?"

She motioned with the barrel of the Sharps and I eased myself out of leather and leaned against my pony to keep from falling.

"You hurt?"

"No, not really," I said. "Just a little stove-up. Place I can water my horse?"

Again, she used the barrel of her rifle to indicate a water tank off to the side of the house. I led my mount there and let him drink his fill.

"I reckon you could stand something yourself,"

she said. "You wait out here, I'll go fetch you something."

"Suits me down to my heels," I said.

I took a seat on a stump that looked like someone had tried unsuccessfully to pull from the ground, then tried burning it out, and finally gave up on doing anything with it. It made a tolerable chair. I reached for my makings and found the papers and tobacco wet. Didn't bother to reach for a drink 'cause I know I wasn't toting. Wet on the outside, dry on the in—a bad fix for a man to be in.

The children seemed fascinated by my presence; they stood around in a semicircle gawking at me and I said, "I'm not a circus elephant," and that made them laugh.

"You look like a mud puppy," the boy said, and that made them laugh, too.

I looked at my clothing and said, "You are right, I must have fell asleep and fallen off my horse." More laughter.

The woman returned carrying a plate of biscuits and fatback and a cup of coffee.

"It ain't much," she said apologetically.

"It'll do," I said. "Thank you."

The lot of them stood and watched me eat but I didn't mind. The biscuits were tasteless and the fatback greasy, but I licked my fingers when I'd finished and washed it down with the Arbuckle and I felt as if I might live until noon.

"Much appreciated," I said.

"Your leg need mending?" she asked. "Saw you limping like a three-legged dog."

"Bum knee," I said. "Had an accident."

"What sorta accident?" the boy said. He was maybe ten years old, a mop of corn silk hair fresh cut in the shape of a bowl. Gaping teeth.

"Fell off my horse," I said.

"You fall off'n your horse a lot," he said, making his sisters giggle.

"Good thing I came along," I said, "or you young'ns wouldn't have anything to laugh about." The girls giggled some more.

"You kids go on and finish your chores," the woman said, "and leave this feller be."

They scampered off and I wondered what chores they could have, given the spare conditions of their existence. The roof on the house looked leaky and the front door was missing a hinge and a good, hard wind seemed like it might blow the whole shebang into the next county. Still, it wasn't my place to question; I was grateful to have a bellyful of grub and a little coffee to ease the chill in my blood.

"You want," she said, "I could wash and dry your duds."

"Thank you, but I've already put you and your family out enough."

"No trouble," she said. "I'm fixing to do a wash now, anyway."

"How'd it look your man come home and find you washing my duds?" I said.

She brushed a sprig of her hair away from her eyes where the wind had worked it loose from the tortoise-shell combs.

"Truth is," she said, "I don't believe you have to worry none about my man coming home."

I thought about it a moment, looked up at the foreboding sky. It didn't look like the sun would come out anytime soon. The thought of riding another fifty miles in wet clothes made my skin crawl.

"If you're sure it's no trouble," I said.

"None. You can take 'em off inside. Wrap yourself in that old blue quilt I got hanging on the wall."

Time passed slowly, the children came and went, laughing, acting as children will do. No schooling to occupy them, they spent a lot of time chasing each other round and round the house until they tired of that, then took out after the rooster causing it to squawk and flap its short red wings and run a jagged course. The woman called them to leave off on the rooster lest they frighten it to death, which only made them laugh all the harder until her voice grew stern. Then they slunk off like cats to an old shed, where I supposed there was something equally interesting to occupy their minds.

She'd built a fire under a wash kettle and scrubbed the clothes with a bar of yellow soap, then rinsed and wrung them out by hand and hung them on a single line of wire that ran from a nail in the side of the house out to a dying blackjack tree.

"They'll be forever drying without any sun," I said when at last she'd finished and sat on the top step of the porch next to me.

"Not with this wind," she said. "If it don't rain, those duds will be dry in less than an hour. One thing we got in this territory is lots of wind. Makes for drying clothes good, but not much else."

"Your man," I said. "He run off, get killed, something like that?"

"Don't know," she said. "He went out hunting one day and never came back. I went looking for him for a month; had an old mule I rode out as far as I dared looking for Albert. Never found him, never found a trace of him. Like as not, he got carried off by a bear, or he just grew tired of all the responsibility of a wife and young'ns and trying to scratch out a living from this hardscrabble."

She brushed her forehead free from more sprigs of hair with the back of her wrist.

"Seems like a poor place to bring a family," I said.

"Not if you're wanted by the law, it ain't."

"On the dodge, your man?"

"Albert used to rob banks in Missouri," she said. "Till it got to be unprofitable."

"How does robbing banks become unprofitable?" I asked.

"The Jameses, Jesse and Frank and their cousins, the Youngers," she said. "They were a lot better at robbing banks than Albert ever was and that got the Pinkertons and most of the law in Missouri down on bank robbers. Pretty soon, it got so you couldn't walk in a bank that didn't have at least one or two armed guards. Albert was a lot of things, but he wasn't a gun artist. The other thing was the new safes the banks installed. Albert said you couldn't blow one 'cause of the amount of dynamite a man would have to use—that the explosion would blow up the whole bank and all the people and money in it. Albert wasn't no murderer like those James boys. He had a good heart in him. Couldn't kill a sand flea. Those new banks and armed guards just put him right out of business."

She folded her arms against the chill wind and stared off toward the horizon.

"It's just as well," she said. "Sooner or later Albert was bound to be murdered." She turned her head just enough to look at me over her shoulder. Her eyes were the same color as the sky—smoky gray.

"You ever know an outlaw who came to any good end?" she said.

"Most die young," I said. "Least the ones I've known."

"Albert just never liked the thought of regular work. He had a good heart but was shy when it came to hard work. Still, I miss him something terrible, and so do my kids."

"Maybe if a bear didn't get him," I said. "He will change his mind once he's been gone long enough and come back."

She sighed and stared at the horizon as though if she watched it long enough, Albert might appear.

"I wonder how long is long enough," she said. "He's been gone a year already."

"Why stay on if that's the case? Don't you have some family back in Missouri?"

"Sister," she said. "That's about it."

"That's something, anyway. A place to start."

"No," she said. "I best wait and see if Albert *does* come back. I light out, he might not know where to look for us."

"How long you reckon you can hold out?" I said.

She shrugged her shoulders.

"Maybe another six months, leastways up till winter."

"Then what?"

"Then . . . well, I imagine I'll have to take my kids to an orphanage and find myself some work in the nearest town."

The wind blew steadily out of the northeast.

"You down to just biscuits and fatback?" I said.

She nodded and said, "And not much of that."

"There any sort of town near here that'd have a mercantile?"

"Jack Ass Flats," she said. "About twenty miles that way," pointing with her chin.

She'd been right about the wind, in an hour my clothes had dried cold and stiff. I still felt like hell, but at least I had clean clothes and a half-full belly. I thanked the woman for her kindness as I stepped into leather.

"My manners are poor," I said. "I never caught your name. Mine's McCannon."

"Charity," she said. "And those wild'ns are Minerva; Jessie; Laura; and Albert, Jr."

They grinned up at me like possums and I tipped my hat to them.

"Hope your man comes back soon," I said. "He's out there and got any good sense, he will."

She offered me a weak smile as though she knew there wasn't a chance she would ever see him again but still held to the slimmest of hopes.

I rode away, thinking that the reason the frontier was so vast was because of all the misery and heartbreak it had to hold.

———

Jack Ass Flats was west and would take me out of my way, but it was a trip that needed taking and that is where I went.

CHAPTER 26

The first thing I noticed about Jack Ass Flats was the man hanging from the telegraph pole. The corpse twisted in the wind to the creak of the rope that held him. The streets were empty and I felt a little like I had ridden straight into a bad dream. I saw a string of ponies tied up out front of a saloon; it seemed like the place to stop.

The bar was lined with yahoos of all sizes and shapes. They were in a celebrating mood. A few threw looks my way when I stepped up to the oak and ordered a whiskey. The bar dog said, "two bits" and I placed it on the oak next to the glass, then stood for a moment before knocking it back and let its burn fan out in my blood.

"You Cecil?" the man next to me said.

"Cecil?"

"Why, yes," he said. "Cecil Trotter, the executionist from Tahlequah."

"Sorry, I said. "I'm neither from Tahlequah or an executionist."

"Too bad," he said. "Was hoping you were."

"Why's that?"

He grinned wide enough to show that his incisors were gold-capped.

"Just so's we'd have the pleasure of telling him Sombrero Jack's already been executed. Imagine you saw him when you rode in—feller what's hanging from the telegraph pole."

"Hard to miss," I said. "What was his crime?"

"Pony thief, adulterer, and murderer. Killed his lover's husband; the husband caught them in bed together."

"Sounds like a bad situation," I said.

He nodded knowingly. "Was for him."

The man gave me the once-over. Maybe I looked like a pony thief or a murderous adulterer.

"So this Cecil from Tahlequah is going to be a bit disappointed," I said. "Riding all this way for nothing."

"It got boring waiting," the man said. "Town like this, you take your fun when you can get it."

I thought of Teddy Blue and how he would think it was unseemly to leave a dead man hanging from a telegraph pole where the corpse could be seen by women and children.

"There a reason you just left that fellow hanging?" I asked.

"Well, hell, we was to cut him down right away," the man said, turning to make sure he had the attention of his compadres, who by this time were all ears, "it'd just get boring again."

"Yeah," said the man next to him, a short yahoo

wearing a Navy Colt with ivory grips. "The Flats ain't exactly St. Louis, case you ain't noticed. Ain't much to do here but watch paint dry and listen to the wind blow."

"So hanging a man is a real big deal," I said.

"Like the Fourth of July."

"Which way to the mercantile?"

"Down the street to your right, stranger."

I was tempted to order another whiskey, but I wasn't up to the company of men who would leave another man hanging from a telegraph pole for the sport of it.

I found the mercantile and told the man what I wanted: beans, flour, sugar, coffee, cured beef in tins, some horehound candy. Then I asked that he deliver it to the woman and gave him directions.

"I know you've got a telegraph in this town," I said. "I saw a man hanging from one of the poles. Which direction is it?"

"Cross the street, down two doors."

The telegraph office was closed, a sign on the door said "Out to Lunch, Back in Thirty Minutes." I figured the telegrapher was among the yahoos celebrating in the saloon. I started to cross the street to seek him out when I had to step back on the walk to keep from getting run over by a spring wagon pulled wildly by a pair of high-stepping Percherons. Holding the reins and trying to keep her seat was a female dressed in a buckskin shirt and leather breeches. I wasn't sure whether she had control of the team or not until she brought them to a hard stop just beneath the pole where the dead man hung.

I watched her for a moment, saw her stare up at the body, then lower her head until her shoulders shook once. Then she climbed into the back of the wagon and took a knife from her belt and began sawing away at the rope.

"Better let me help you," I said.

She looked down, saw me, said, "Who are you?"

"Just a stranger passing through," I said. "Better let me help you."

The dead man's size made her agreeable. I climbed in the back of the wagon and hefted the corpse while she cut the rope, then laid him out in the back of the wagon.

"This your man?" I said.

She had short cropped red hair that was as glossy as a rooster's feathers and sea-green eyes and a splatter of freckles across her nose.

"He's my father," she said. "Name was Flea Mc-Tavish."

"I'm sorry for your loss."

"Why should you be, unless you are the one who hanged him up there and left him like that?"

"No, I had nothing to do with it."

"Then don't apologize for what you had no hand in. You want to feel sorry for someone, feel sorry for them who did this."

She jumped from the wagon, reached back in under the seat, and took out a shotgun with sawed-off barrels and a whittled down stock—to fit her own diminutive size, I suppose—and headed across the street to the saloon.

I took hold of her elbow.

"You planning on getting some justice?" I said.

She looked at me hard.

"Just that there's probably twenty or thirty yahoos inside and everyone of them is drinking and armed."

"I don't see where that's your concern," she said.

"You don't think they'd shoot a woman, liquored up and growing bored again?"

She pulled free from my grip and started across the street.

I don't know why I felt it was any of my affair what the people in this town did—seemed like they were all hell-bent on killing one another—but I fell in step alongside her, and followed her through the double doors of the saloon.

All the celebrating that had been going on stopped at the sight of the two of us, most of the attention on the woman and the shotgun she was carrying.

"Who did it?" she said. "Step away from the bar."

For a whole minute the yahoos stood frozen, beer mugs and shot glasses held in their hands, disbelieving looks on their faces.

"Who's the ones who hanged him?" she demanded.

The yahoo who had been so talkative to me earlier said, "Diana, that thing loaded?"

"You do it, Woodrow?"

He shook his head. I saw some of the others ease away from the man, snake out along the bar out of harm's way.

"How about you, Frank? You hang him?"

Frank, the one with the Navy Colts, lost his grin.

"Every man in this room knows what your daddy did," the man said. "Hanging was too good for him."

"Step away from the bar, unless you want your friends to die with you," she demanded.

"Ain't nobody dying today, Diana," a voice from behind said. "Put that greener down before you shoot somebody."

I turned enough to see a familiar face, only this time he was wearing a nickel badge and holding a pistol.

"Stay out of it, Bill," the woman said without taking her attention from Frank.

"Can't," the lawman said. "It's my town."

"Was your town, then where were you when they hanged Flea?"

"Collecting taxes," he said. "A man can't be everywhere at once."

"You should have been here," she said.

"I'll see that things get righted," he said. "But you cut loose with that scattergun, you'll just end up making it worse."

"You there, mister, step away," the lawman said to me. He failed to recognize me, it had been a long time since we'd last run into each other. Then Bill Tilghman said to the men at the bar, "Put your iron on the oak and step away."

They did, quickly enough.

"Now," Tilghman said. "You shoot any of those men, Diana, unarmed like they are, it'll be the same thing as what they did to your daddy. Let me handle this, woman."

She took a deep breath, let it out, then turned to face him.

"Goddamn you, Billy Tilghman, for letting them do it!"

"It was my responsibility," he said, "and my mistake of thinking it would be done legal. Cecil was on his way over from Tahlequah; I thought he'd be here by now."

Her eyes filled with a bitter pain.

"I'm holding you and this whole town responsible for what happened here."

"You might hold your daddy a bit responsible, too," Tilghman said. "Trouble with one wrongful act is, it often leads to others. Wasn't for his crimes, none of us would be standing here now."

She looked at him for a long hard second, then strode out of the saloon, brushing past him and through the double doors.

Some of the men along the door snorted until Tilghman told them to "shut their cake-holes." He eyed me for a moment.

"We met?"

"Once," I said. "Long time back on the Chisholm Trail. You were ramrodding beeves and I was looking for work."

He stepped closer where the light was a bit better, then with what for him probably came as close to a smile as you would see on Bill Tilghman, said, "McCannon. You sure found your way to hell and gone."

"Looks like you did, too," I said.

"I've some work to do here," he said. "Maybe after I'm finished we can meet up at the café and have some coffee and catch up on old times."

"I'd like that, Bill, but to tell the truth, I've got to keep moving."

"You on the dodge?"

"Not to worry," I said. "You'll find no papers on me."

"I heard sometime back you was wearing a badge down in Del Rio. What happened with that?"

"Long story," I said. "I killed a bandit and had to quit."

"Why's that? They don't like lawmen killing bandits down along that border?"

"Not when the bandit is a cousin to most of the population," I said.

"I see."

I started to leave, then took a moment to say, "Glad you didn't shoot that woman, Bill."

"I'm glad I didn't shoot her, either," he said. "She's my fiancée."

"Well, then that would have made a rough start of it for the marriage," I said.

"You're telling me."

I could hear him telling some of the yahoos at the bar they were being placed under arrest as I walked out to the street again. The woman snapped the reins over the rumps of the Percherons, turning them around in the street, then when she arrived at where I was standing, brought them to a halt.

"If you are seeking a long and prosperous life, this ain't the place," she said, then snapped the reins again and drove away.

I made for the telegraph office and this time found the telegrapher in.

"How much to send a wire to Gonzales?" I said.

CHAPTER 27

In Amarillo, I sold the bay, saddle, and a few of the pistols I'd taken from the dead after the fight with Rufus Buck's gang. I needed money and I needed a quick way to Gonzales so I bought a ticket for the stage to take me from Amarillo to San Antonio; from there I could easily make my way to Gonzales with hopes of hooking up with Teddy Blue and Harve Sweetwater. I'd sent a wire from Jack Ass Flats to be delivered to whatever local law enforcement was to be had in Gonzales that explained the situation and asking him if those two yahoos were in the vicinity, to let them know I was coming.

There was a man named Beaver Smith who ran a private stage line out of Amarillo, what he called a mud wagon, and there were two other passengers besides myself: a gaunt-looking drummer with a large mole on the tip of his nose, and a woman.

The woman wore a green, tie-back dress with black trim and a Western hat with a large ostrich feather pinned to the crown. She had a long face with dark curious eyes, an unattractive woman whose silence was disturbing. The other thing that was disturbing about her was the single scabbard with the mother-of-pearl-handled pistol on her hip. It was highly unusual for a woman to wear a sidearm. Most kept a derringer or knuckle duster in their reticules, but few openly wore pistols. This one did and she fancied a small riding crop laced around her left wrist. She had a certain way of running her gaze over you that made you feel like prize livestock she was considering buying.

The drummer seated next to her seemed quite interested in this homely woman and for the first several hours of our ride out of Amarillo, he could not seem to take his eyes from her. She appeared not to notice but when the mud wagon pulled into the first way station and we'd gotten out to stretch our legs, I heard her say to the drummer, "Something about me that's got you so all fired dumbstruck?"

The drummer flushed red and he adjusted his trousers by hiking them up over his narrow hips. They were baggy on him as were the rest of his clothes—baggy and dusty.

"No, ma'am, just that I couldn't help but notice that fancy piece you're wearing. Unusual for a lady to go about fixed with a pistol. You ever shoot anybody with that iron?"

"Only those who took liberties with me," she said, giving him a hard stare.

He grinned weakly.

"You care for a dipper of water?" he said, nodding toward a well that stood in the sun twenty feet from the corral. "I'd be happy to fetch some for you."

"That would be pleasant of you," she said, to which the drummer then hurried off, grateful, I suppose, to be out of her glare. I noticed when she spoke she had large, horsy teeth that did nothing to improve her looks.

She then looked my way. I was rolling a shuck and anticipating how long it would take to make a change of the team and get back on the road again. This Beaver Smith, the man who owned the line, said we'd make San Antonio in two, maybe three, days, depending on the weather.

"What's weather have to do with it?" I said.

"I mean whether or not they is any road agents, busted wheels, or other disasters that might befall us along the pike," he said, then grinned foolishly like a man who'd just played a great joke purely for his own amusement.

"What about you, Bub?" the woman said.

I licked the edge of the paper and finished the roll before twisting off the ends and striking a lucifer off my heel.

"What about me, what?" I said.

"You interested in why I carry this pistol proud on my hip?"

"Not really," I said.

"Why ain't you? Most men are, they see a woman with a hogleg strapped on to her skirts."

"Just not," I said. "Free country, you can wear what you want, it's none of my business."

"Now I like that in a feller," she said.

"Like what?"

"His willingness to live and let live. That's the way my Sam is, too."

I really didn't want to engage her in conversation and was relieved when the drummer returned with a dipper of water, which he handed her. She placed it to her lips but did not drink genteelly. She drank more like a man would, spilling a good portion of it, then wiping her chin with the cuff of her sleeve, never once taking her gaze from me. Finished, she handed the dipper back to the drummer and asked if he might go inside the little way station and see if they had any hard candy.

"I'm partial to candy," she said. "The hard kind, got teeth like a squirrel's, you know what I mean." She gave the drummer a lascivious wink, which caused his knees to buckle.

"Yes, ma'am," the drummer said, and quick-stepped it to the way station.

"Amazing what a man will do just for the sniff of a woman," she said.

"Amazing," I replied, then strolled over to the corral to look at the horseflesh.

The next thing I knew she was right there beside me.

"Going to see my husband, Sam," she said. "Got him in jail in San Antonio."

I didn't say anything.

"Planning on hanging him."

"That's too bad."

She breathed through her long nose; it was an audible sound. When I didn't say anything, she added, "Sam was always a man with bad luck on his side."

"In my experience, it's usually more than just bad luck that gets a man hanged," I said.

She snorted, and I could smell the faint odor of

sweat and rose water as she stepped in a little closer to me.

"You're right," she said. "It's me that's the one with the bad luck. Every man I've ever had a thing to do with has come to a terrible end—Sam's just one. I had a lover went to prison for twenty-five years; serving time this very moment in Illinois. Blue Duck, you ever heard of him?"

"No." I was content to simply smoke my cigarette and watch the hands exchange teams, turn out the old ones and round up four fresh mounts to put in the traces. One particular animal they were having trouble with—a stout gelding with a blazed face.

"I spent a little time myself in the calaboose down in Dallas once," she continued, as though I'd encouraged it somehow. "They claimed I was fencing stolen horses. Can you imagine that?"

I could, but I didn't say anything. She had an irritating manner of speaking, her voice too loud, sharp to the ear.

"Well, if you ain't never heard of Blue Duck, you ever heard of Cole Younger?"

I nodded that I had.

"He was my first husband. It didn't work out, even though we had us a child. Cole was too restless. He was cousin to Jesse and Frank James, you know."

I didn't know why she was telling me all these things; maybe she thought I had the same fetching interest in her as had the drummer. Or maybe, because I showed no outward interest, it made it a challenge for her the way it will some women. All I knew for sure was, I had no interest in this woman and her lovers or her life or her reasons for being on the mud wagon.

The drummer returned and said, "Sorry, my sweet, but they have no hard candy, not even a twist of licorice."

He was a ferret-faced little man, barely taller than the woman. Seeing as how I was taking no interest in her, she suddenly allowed herself to warm to the man, smiled, and said, "Why that's okay. What'd you say your name was there, feller?"

"George," he said. "George Pepperstick."

"How do, George Pepperstick. I'm Belle, Belle Starr," she said, and offered him a fancy gauntleted hand.

I'd heard the name now that she'd mentioned it. It was a name much bandied about the courthouse in Ft. Smith, Arkansas, where I worked for a short time out of Judge Parker's court as one of his deputies. And though I'd never encountered Belle Starr before, or any of her roost of outlaws, I'd heard plenty of stories, randy and otherwise about her. And once, while I was in the employee of the judge, I'd heard he'd sentenced her to six months in the Detroit House of Corrections for being in possession of stolen property, mainly missing nags with altered brands illegally gained from throughout the Nations.

The driver hawed us back into the mud wagon and off we went again, only this time Belle not minding as much that the drummer's eyes were all over her and his hand was resting on her knee.

"You do well drumming, George?" she asked.

"Do fairly well," he said. "Peddle knifes, special-made, guaranteed not to dull even after a thousand uses—the secret is in the honing."

"Oh, well, that's very interesting," Belle said. "But

how much you reckon you make drumming knifes, say in a year?"

It went on like that for several hours, Belle learning of the drummer's earnings and he more than happy to brag a bit, saying how in one year alone he made almost five thousand dollars, to which she feigned great surprise and said, "No!"

His face shined like a new penny.

"Sure, sure," he said. "Why, I expect to earn half as much again this year. Everyone has need of a good knife, would you like to see an example of my wares?"

She laughed bawdily and said, "You show me yours, I'll show you mine."

After two more stops to change teams, we pulled into a jerkwater town that Beaver Smith said had a hotel and a whiskey den. The other three or four other buildings were closed that hour of the evening.

"We'll rest the night, be back here at dawn," Smith said. "You want a bed, the Alamo's the only place that's got any. You want a drink, a sandwich—something like that—you'll find it at Dirty Alice's, that way." He pointed with his nose toward the saloon.

"I don't know about you," Belle said to George, the knife drummer, "but I could stand me a drink and some pickled eggs. Care to buy a lady dinner?"

"Not at all," he said, and offered her his arm, which she dramatically took.

"You want to come along and join us?" Belle said, casting a backward glance at me.

"Maybe later," I said, and headed toward the hotel.

A man with a milky eye cast it in my direction when I entered and said, "You in on the mud wagon?"

"You have any rooms to let?"

"Sure, sure. You want one to share or by your lonesome?"

"Lonesome," I said, and signed the register and gave him the two dollars he was asking for the room. I trudged upstairs and removed the pistols, the ones I hadn't sold that I'd taken from the Rufus Buck gang: a Deane Adams, a Colt Peacemaker, and a Smith & Wesson. Then I propped the Winchester in the corner before sitting on the bed to remove my boots. My ribs still hurt like hell but the rest of me was healing fine. I figured to forgo supper and grab some shuteye; it'd be another long day tomorrow and with any luck—considering if our "whether" held—we'd arrive in San Antonio the next day. And with any greater luck, Teddy Blue and Harve Sweetwater would have found Etta and have her in hand when I arrived. I had every confidence in both men.

I lay back on the bed, which sagged under my weight, and closed my eyes and soon drifted into a light sleep.

I awoke sometime later to the sounds of laughter on the other side of the wall and it didn't take but an instant to recognize the bray of Belle Starr and the voice of the drummer. The one thing I'd noticed earlier was the silver wedding band on the drummer's third finger, left hand. Somewhere he had a wife waiting for him to return; some men were fools. I rolled over and closed my eyes and tried to shut out the sounds of their revelry, which went from loud talk and laughter to whispers and the creak of bedsprings, with Belle every now and then screaming out an epithet that would make a frontier marshal blush.

Finally, I couldn't take it any longer and pulled on my boots, rearmed myself, and went down the stairs, out the door, and over to Dirty Alice's saloon. A whiskey or two, supper, and maybe once I returned to my room, things would have quieted down. The drummer didn't look like he was up to an all-nighter with the likes of Belle Starr.

A sloe-eyed faded rose tried to join me while I stood at the bar. I thanked her for her offer, bought her a watered down whiskey, then took my sandwich and drink glass to a table where I sat alone. I tried not to think at all beyond the moment and killed an hour at Alice's before returning to my room. Thankfully it was quiet next door.

I arose at five the next morning, shaved, washed my face, and combed my hair, then armed myself and headed out the door. That's when I noticed the door to the adjoining room ajar and saw the drummer sprawled on the bed, facedown and dressed in just his socks. I knew right away what had happened.

I shook him until he moaned and his eyes fluttered.

"Well, at least she didn't kill you," I said.

He muttered something and I took the pitcher of water next to his bed and poured it over him. He came up with a start, sputtering and waving his hands. I noticed the silver wedding band was missing.

"She skinned you," I said.

"Huh?" He fisted the sleep and water from his eyes.

"Belle Starr skinned you."

He blinked several times, noticed that he was naked, and quickly grabbed at the blanket to cover himself.

"What? What?"

"You damn fool, you got skinned, cleaned out, rolled for your poke—even your wedding ring."

He looked at his left hand.

"Oh, Jesus."

"How much you have on you?"

He glanced at the corner of the room, where a valise stood open, then scrambled off the bed to check it, his pale bare buttocks exposed.

"Oh, Jesus," he said again. "My wallet is gone." Then glancing about. "So are my knife samples!"

"How much in all?" I said.

He slumped there on the floor, a sprig of hair like a long piece of seaweed hung from his otherwise bald scalp. He was calculating in his mind the losses.

"Two hundred in my wallet and the knives and case worth at least a hundred more."

"That's a lot for the pleasure of an ugly woman," I said. "You better get dressed, you want to make the mud wagon."

I walked down to the city marshal's office, but the door was locked. I figured to report Belle, not that it would do a hell of a lot of good. She'd probably stolen a horse and cleared out. I sauntered back over to the way station and waited while the driver and his assistant harnessed up a fresh team of horses. I rolled a shuck and was lighting it when I saw Beaver Smith look beyond the team and say to his assistant, "Why, that drummer forgot his shoes."

I looked and saw the drummer walking toward us in his bare feet.

"She took my shoes, too," he said.

"Who took your shoes?" Beaver Smith said.

"Why, that woman with the fancy pistol you sold a ticket to in Amarillo."

The driver grinned.

"You figured Belle to show you a good time without her getting something out of it? Mister, what sort of fool are you?"

"The biggest this side of the Chisos," he said. "Maybe the biggest in the whole of Texas. The thing I don't get is why she'd steal my good shoes."

"Why, probably to take them to her husband, Sam Starr," Beaver Smith said. "Belle probably wants him to look his best when he goes to meet his maker."

They had a good laugh over that—Beaver Smith and his assistant—as the drummer and I climbed into the mud wagon.

"This is the worst trip I've ever had," he said. "What will Wilamina say when I come home with no shoes on my feet?"

I said I didn't know and sat back for the rest of a long ride.

CHAPTER 28

We pulled into San Antonio late on the third night; a busted wheel had delayed our trip by some six hours. The mud wagon stopped in front of a gentlemen's club, the Golden Spur.

I needed to stretch my legs and decided to stroll down to the Guadalupe River less than a block away. It was late and most establishments—except for the drinking parlors, gambling halls, and bagnios—were closed for business; yet it was still too early to find a room.

The air was warm and carried with it the smell of the river. The gaslights of the bridge were reflected in the green water below. The odor was pungent: damp and fishy. Across the way, ghostly under a full moon, stood the stone chapel of the Alamo—all that was left from the battle decades earlier between a handful of Texans and Santa Anna's army of over a thousand men. The chapel was the last refuge of the Texans. But neither the chapel nor its holy walls could save them from death. I'd read that after the last Texans, including Crockett, had been rounded up, they were executed—shot in the back of the head—and thrown on a pyre, the smoke of which could be seen for fifty miles. Men died for a lot of reasons, border disputes being just one.

I listened, half-thinking if I listened hard enough I might still hear the clatter of musketry and the cries of the wounded. But all I really heard was the clatter of shod hooves on cobblestones and the cries of children playing down by the river, the voices of old men telling them to hush or they would scare away the catfish that the old men were so patiently trying to catch.

One of the old men saw me standing on the bridge and called to me "Hola, amigo." I nodded and asked if he'd caught many fish this night and he said, Yes, he'd caught a few, but that in the last hour he hadn't caught a single one.

"I have brought too many of my children with me to do any real good," he said, his face oily brown in the dim yellow light from the bridge. "My little ones like to play too much and are not serious enough for fishing."

"Sí," I said, and moved on.

For some reason I felt a deep uneasiness, as though someone were watching me, causing the flesh on the back of my neck to prickle. The sense of Etta was strong in my mind, like she was nearby, maybe just around the next corner waiting for me. I knew how foolish that was, but at one point I turned and looked behind me. It was a disturbing feeling and I knew that I was letting my mind play tricks on me, like a man on the desert who sees mirages of cool water that don't exist. I'm not a superstitious man, but I believe in trusting my instinct because it has saved my hide more than once.

I continued walking the streets, trying to pay attention to my intuition, going blindly where my feet would take me. Around every corner, I expected to run into her—the feeling that she was close was that strong. After an hour or so I gave up. I drifted back toward the center of town. Nearing the hotel I'd decided to check into, a man approached me from the shadows and I prepared myself for whatever trouble he was offering.

"Pardon me, sir, would you happen to have a match?"

He was a well-dressed man, had a dark mustache, was slight of build, and wore a cape.

I reached in my pocket and handed him a lucifer, which he struck against the brass plate of the hotel's wall. It was then, when the light flared, that I saw the familiar face of Doc Holliday. He lit his cigar, then held the light for a moment before snapping it out. He inhaled and coughed, then inhaled again, as though he were trying to do battle with himself by smoking away the lung fever in him.

"You're a long way from Deadwood," I said.

He cocked his head, trying to figure out who I was, but with the heavy shadows he couldn't tell.

"Do we know each other, sir?"

"We met in Deadwood, Doc. McCannon, remember?"

"It is truly you?" he said, his voice unable to contain his surprise. "Why, I heard that you had been killed in Cheyenne—that a man had shot you in the back. I see now that the rumors of your death were greatly exaggerated, for here you are, walking around in my town."

"Oh, when did San Antonio become your town, Doc?"

"Why, every town is my town whilst I'm in it," he said, then coughed again hard and had to support himself against the wall, his hand braced against the brass plate.

"Well, I'm sorry to disappoint you about my demise," I said. "I'm not staying long, so you'll have the city all to yourself."

I started up the street and he said, "Wait."

I turned, knowing that when I did he could be holding a derringer on me ready to pull the trigger and assure that he fulfilled the rumors of my death. Instead, he held only the lit cigar, its tip burning red in the blackness.

"I'd appreciate it if I could buy you a drink, over there at the Golden Spur. I am a member of the club."

"It's late," I said.

"It's never too late for a drink, sir. Anyone would know, it would be me: I'm the self-appointed timekeeper of drinking."

I wasn't in the mood to drink, especially not with Doc. His reputation as a mean drunk who went out of his way to pick fights only made him doubly dangerous. I wondered if Doc Holliday didn't have some fanciful, morbid wish that someone would kill him outright in a gunfight and save him from the lingering death in his lungs. If that was his intention, I didn't want to be his foil.

"I'll pass," I said. "I've had a long ride and still got a ways to go."

"A man's life should not be reduced to having to drink alone," he said. "Whatever I've done to offend you, I regret." He stood there, one hand extended to support himself against the wall, his voice a near rasp from the effort it took in coughing away his sickness. But it wasn't for those reasons that I agreed to walk with him to the club for a drink. I had a sudden thought, a question that Doc might be able to answer for me because of the dark world he operated in.

"Okay, Doc, I'll sit and have a drink with you."

"Well, sir, what are we waiting for?" With that he seemed to regain his strength and we crossed the street and entered the gaily lighted club.

Most of the patrons were well-dressed men, donning frock coats, gray fedoras, and kidskin gloves. But none were dressed any finer than Doc himself, who sported a cravat with a diamond stickpin to set off his Prince Albert coat. Hanging from the pocket of his brocade vest was a gold fob. I could see the bulge of a pistol in his pocket. He carried in his left hand a silver-tipped cane. Except for the malevolent gaze, Doc Holliday looked no different from any of the other dandies standing at the oak or sitting in red cushioned chairs.

The club itself was posh with Brussels carpeting, blue velvet drapes over the tall windows, a bar that ran one length of the room, a mirrored-back bar, and waiters in jackets and white aprons. Several paintings of fat nude women hung on the walls and a cloud of gray smoke from expensive cigars hung in the air. It reminded me a lot of the Inter-Ocean Hotel in Cheyenne, where Nate Pliers was shot to death while taking a bubble bath with a married woman.

"Over there," Doc said, pointing with his cane to a

corner with two empty chairs. A waiter came and took our order. "Two tall whiskeys," Doc said. When they came, Doc held his glass to the light as though to examine the quality of the liquor, then said, "Farewell to Deadwood and old loves, eh?" His reference to a woman that we'd both had an interest in, but one that neither of us had won, didn't escape me.

Under the light, his pallor was like that of aged candle wax, his eyes sunken into dark cavities. Still, he was a handsome man, even in his condition, and several of the women who were in attendance with their escorts cast longing looks in Doc's direction. Doc didn't fail to acknowledge a single one of them, offering them a slight nod and a wan smile.

"To old times and new," he said, hoisting his glass in a salute before knocking it back and signaling the waiter to bring another round, even though I hadn't touched mine.

"Drink up, the night is yet young."

"I have to be honest with you, Doc. I didn't accept the invitation to be sociable."

He looked at me, his brow slightly furrowed, dampened with sweat, even though it wasn't that warm in the room.

"Oh?"

"I want to ask you about someone."

The waiter came with two more drinks and Doc paid him from a fold of cash he pulled from his wallet. "Keep these coming until I tell you not to," Doc said, and the waiter smiled knowingly. Doc took up one of the glasses and pressed it lightly to his cheeks, rolling it for a moment, then set it down again.

"Would that I could absorb the demon rum

through osmosis," he said. "It would save me the time of actually having to swallow it and trigger my paroxysms. Now who was it you wanted to inquire about, sir?"

"Do you know a man named Gypsy Davy? Have you ever heard of him in your travels?"

His gaze came to rest on me in a way that seemed as though he were trying to see into my soul.

"He's a complete madman, a man without a scintilla of conscience," Doc said in that whispery, liquor-ravaged voice. "He is also a highly intelligent individual, which therefore makes him even more dangerous than your average brute. Whatever would bring you to ask about such a man?"

"I'd like for you to tell me what you know about him, Doc."

He tasted some of his liquor, the eyes seemingly darker, if that were possible.

"My first encounter with Gypsy Davy was when we met in Baltimore, where I attended dental school. Young Davy was practicing to become a physician. I met him at the party of a mutual friend. He was quite charming, Davy was. In fact, he was the most charming individual I've ever met. And most deadly, too, as it turned out. He would have made a fine doctor if he'd been so inclined to save lives rather than take them. A brilliant mind." Doc pulled a silk kerchief from his pocket and wiped his lips with it, delicately, like a woman.

"But you see," he continued, "Davy was a man with taste for blood and blooding and it wasn't contained simply in the surgical theater or to the practice of medicine. He enjoyed cutting people with his scalpel whether they be patients or simply men whom he took a dislike to. It is what ultimately brought about his expulsion from medical school.

"Tell me about that," I said.

"He killed two men in a fight in some riverside bar one night, cut their throats just like that, nearly decapitated the one. Do you know how sharp a surgical steel scalpel is? There were varying stories as to how it began, who perpetrated the engagement. But because of the notoriety, Davy was given his walking papers from the school. Some say it left him embittered enough to murder his mentor, the chief of the medical staff, because of it."

"Did he?"

Doc shrugged, dabbed at his lips some more, then smoothed his pitch-black mustache.

"The man was found with his throat neatly cut and Davy nowhere to be found afterward—he'd simply dropped out of sight. They say that one of the poor man's ears had been neatly sliced off as well, some sort of mark of Gypsy's vendetta. Nothing was ever proven and the murder went unsolved." Doc finished his drink, then started to order another when I pushed one of mine across the table.

"I need to stay sober," I said.

"Good Lord, whatever for? Sobriety only clouds the mind."

He downed half his glass, the gleam in his dark eyes told me he was well on the verge of changing moods.

"I later ran into Gypsy Davy in San Francisco, where he had become the fair-haired child of Nob Hill's effete and wealthy, regaling them with tales of his exploits on the frontier. He was written up in the *Police Gazette,* you know, several times—a regular Wild Bill." Doc spoke as if he were envious of Gypsy Davy's reputation, practically snorting the words. "It was in that yellow journalistic tome that I first read that Gypsy's trademark for killing was slicing off the ears of his victims—claimed to the reporter that he had a collection of them. Thus, I assumed that he had indeed committed the murder in Baltimore."

I reached for my drink and knocked it back.

"So what is your interest in this mad-hatter, Mc-Cannon?"

"It's a private matter, Doc, that's all I care to say about it."

"I can tell you this about Davy Devearux," Doc said. "You'd be wise to shoot him on sight like a rabid dog, rather than allow him to charm you into revealing your throat to him."

The name struck a chord.

"You certain about his last name being Devearux?"

"Why yes, I believe it was. I remember, because of its alliteration—Davy Devearux."

I could feel my blood ticking in my wrist.

"Practically rolls off the tongue, doesn't it?" Doc said, his gaze gone flat now. He seemed to be staring at a porcine man sitting a number of tables away.

"Thanks for the drink, Doc, but I've got places to go."

"I would enjoy watching the encounter if you find him," Doc said. "Beware, McCannon, his blade is quick and sharp." Doc ran a finger across his throat.

But I was already on my way out. Something cold,

like iron, pressed at the back of my skull. The questions hammered away: Were Gypsy Davy and Etta married? Colorado Charlie Utter had called Etta, Etta Devearux. It might explain why she had been involved with him. But it wouldn't explain why she'd be running from him. Had she loved him enough to be part of a murder? I had to get to Gonzales, find Teddy Blue and Harve. But most of all, I had to find Etta.

CHAPTER 29

A hard ride brought me into Gonzales late in the day. The sky was a bled-white and Gonzales seemed nothing more than a sleepy little village with plenty of natives in their cotton shirts and trousers and wide sombreros. I asked one of them where the *buscadero*'s office was and he told me in Spanish that it was above the *farmacia,* which stood at the east end of the drag. I thanked him and walked the horse I'd rented in San Antonio down in that direction. I dismounted and knocked dust from my hat and ascended a set of outside stairs that led to an office above the drugstore. It was a warm day and the door stood open. A fat-bellied man with skin as brown as saddle leather sat hunched over a desk, eating tortillas filled with beans; a bottle of mescal stood near his right hand. He had a round face and pitch-black hair cut straight across his forehead and wore a leather vest with silver conchos for buttons. Grease ran down his fingers and smeared his chin and slicked his mustache. He didn't seem happy to have his supper interrupted.

"You John Law?" I asked.

"Juan Law?" he said in a heavy accent. "No, no, señor, you got me mistaken for somebody else, eh. I am Carlos. Carlos Delgado. I am the sheriff." Some beans dropped out of his greasy sandwich and he scooped them off the butcher paper they'd been wrapped in and fingered them into his mouth.

"That's what I meant," I said. "My name's McCannon and I sent a wire to you a few days ago asking about my friends—men named Teddy Blue and Harve Sweetwater."

"Oh, sí, I got your telegram. What you want me to do with it, go find them, these men you talk about?"

It was clear this man wasn't going to be much help unless I wanted to raid a restaurant.

"So you haven't seen these men?" I said.

He shook his head. "I wasn't looking for them, they wasn't looking for me, so I guess I haven't seen them."

"You know a man named Feathers, owns a cattle spread around here?"

He suddenly stopped eating.

"Why you want to know?"

"This is important, sheriff."

"So is my supper, señor. You tell me why you want to know about Señor Feathers, maybe I tell you where he lives."

"His boy," I said. "He's headed this way with a friend of mine and I want to meet up with him."

"Oh, so if you are his friend how come you don't know where he lives?"

I didn't care for the way the conversation was going, simply more time wasted.

"Skip it," I said. "I'll find the place on my own."

"Sí, sí, you do that, señor, leave me to my meal, eh."

I started to leave, paused in the door and said, "One more thing, there are some men coming, ten of them riding together, hats pinned up. They'll be asking questions, too, only they'll not fool with you—they'll shoot you in the guts for answers. I find Feathers's boy before they do, might save you and this town mucho trouble."

Some more beans dropped from his tortilla and his eyes narrowed with concern.

"Señor Feathers lives south of town—three, four miles—you'll know it by the big water tower he's got there. Who are these men who might come shoot me in the guts?"

I was already descending the stairs.

I followed the south road until I spotted the water tower the Mexican sheriff had spoken of. The sky was now a dusty rose as twilight encroached; in the weeds I could hear crickets beginning their night song.

A trace angled off from the main road toward the tower and I followed it, pulling the Winchester from its scabbard as I went. Whoever or whatever might await me at the house, I wanted to be prepared. My heartbeat quickened when I topped a slight rise and there below stood a long house in bad need of some fresh whitewash. The house was topped by a cedar shake-roof and three chimneys. Panes of window glass reflected the ocher sky and the rockers on the front porch sat empty. There was no sign of life, no livestock, no horses tied up out front.

I spurred my pony forward, the rifle balanced across the pommel of my saddle.

Except for the state of disrepair of the main house, everything appeared to be normal. I pulled up and sat the horse.

Then a voice called from behind and above me.

"McCannon!"

I turned about slowly, not knowing if the man behind the voice was armed and dangerous. Standing on top of the tower was Teddy Blue; Harve Sweetwater stepped out from within the shadows of one of the outbuildings.

"In the living flesh! I see you finally decided to haul your bacon out of that feather bed and come join us," Harve cawed.

I waited for Teddy Blue to climb down from the tower while Harve caught me up on what had happened since we parted company.

"We ain't seen hide nor hair of any of them," he said. "I don't know how we could have missed them or got ahead of them."

"Unless," Teddy Blue said, "they got waylaid somewhere along the road. Or changed their minds about coming here."

"You didn't backtrack?"

"Was waiting for you," Harve said. "Waiting for them and you. We left, you might not find us, we might not find them; figured it best to hang close a few more days, wait and see if they show, if you showed or they did."

"The Mexican sheriff didn't deliver my wire?"

Teddy Blue shook his head.

"Delgado don't leave that office or get more than a stone's throw from a dinner plate, he can help it. I've had previous dealings with him—once came here to arrest a man who turned out to be Delgado's cousin. Never found the cousin, even though I suspect to this day Delgado was hiding him. I wouldn't count on him to spit."

"What now, Mac?" Harve said. "We wait it out?"

"No. We backtrack."

"Let's get to riding then," Teddy Blue said.

Harve squinted into the setting sun.

"Getting late in the day, we won't get far."

"He's right, McCannon, maybe best to spend the night and head out first light," Teddy Blue said.

I stepped into leather.

"Stay if you want," I said.

We rode until dark.

That night we heard thunder in the distance and Harve looked across the campfire and said, "I hope it ain't another cyclone headed our way."

"You see any more crows today?" Teddy Blue said.

"Not a single one."

"Well, at least that's a piece of good news."

Then we sat in silence for a while before Teddy Blue said, "We have to face the possibility that she's dead, McCannon."

"Then let us find her and bury her," I said.

He nodded. Harve passed around a bottle. We drank.

Stars smeared the sky above us while off to the west heat lightning flashed and occasionally we could hear the rumble of thunder. From off in the distance a coyote called, then another and another. Finally more silence.

We rolled up in our soogans and tried to sleep. Then I heard the crack of a twig from outside the light of the campfire. I slid one of the pistols from under my blanket and heard the others doing the same. The distinct double-click of cocking double-action pistols—hammers being thumbed back and the single rotation of the cylinders—had the same effect as the rattle of a snake.

More silence.

"Maybe nothing," whispered Harve.

We waited, then heard a groan, and a shadowy figure stumbled into our firelight, dropped to his knees and said, "Lord mercy!"

He was a black man and bleeding from a head wound, a red stripe that scored his scalp, his clothes torn.

"Who are you?" Teddy Blue demanded, jumping from his blankets with the barrel of his revolver aimed at the man.

"Isom," the man said. "Isom Dart."

"What happened to you, Mister Dart?"

"Was ambushed, two, maybe three days ago, maybe a day before that, I . . . I sorta lost track of time."

He looked old.

"Why?" Teddy Blue said.

The man blinked several times as though trying to understand the question.

"Give him a drink of whiskey," I said to Harve. "See if we got something we can patch up his . . ."

That's when we saw the missing ear—when the black man turned his head toward the light—the blood dark red, dried to a crust around what was left of the ear.

"Jesus," Harve said, "this feller must be . . ."

"Tom Feathers's man," I said.

The mention of Feathers's name caused the black man to stare wide-eyed.

Harve retrieved a bottle of liquor and pressed it into the man's hand.

"No, suh," he said. "I'm a temperate man."

"Don't be a goddamn fool," Harve said. "Drink some of that red devil, it'll bring you to your senses."

Reluctantly Isom Dart did as ordered and didn't stop until he'd drank a third of the contents.

"Where'd this ambush take place?" I asked once he'd revived.

"In a small canyon," he said. "Somewhere back up that way."

"Come daylight, you'll show us where," Teddy Blue said.

"Yes, suh."

Teddy Blue looked at me and said, "We're close."

We rode out at dawn, Isom Dart doubling with Harve, the black man indicating the direction.

"How can you be sure, you walking in the dark like you done?" Harve questioned.

"I can see good in the dark," he said.

"Oh, yeah, I remember Bittercreek Newcomb telling how you could see well enough in the dark to shoot a man."

"He's a fool," Dart said.

"Damn ugly one, too."

We burned three quarters of the day before Isom Dart said, "Turn off here, up in there is where the canyon is."

Teddy Blue eyed the sky, saw a wheel of buzzards, some of them dropping below a ridge of rock.

No canyon could be seen from the road, but as we cut through a stand of mesquite, we came upon an arroyo that snaked back into a small boxlike canyon. There we found the abandoned hack, the horse dead in its traces, bloated and half-eaten—the big ugly birds flapped their wings and took flight at our approach.

"Looks like he killed everything," Harve said.

"Tell us what happened here?" I said.

"We was camped, pulled in here figgering to be safe. Mistuh Feathers say we soon be to his daddy's ranch, best we not tarry along the road." Dart slid off the back of Harve's mount and walked to the buggy, then cast his gaze upon the dead horse and shook his head.

"He come outta nowhere. . . ."

"Who?"

"The Gypsy man, the one Miss Etta say be after her."

"What happened then?" Teddy Blue asked.

"He killed Mistuh Tom. Slipped up on him and put a knife to him and cut his throat with it before I could get my sights on him. Then he shot me in the head, probably thought he killed me. 'At's all I know. I come to, bleeding, thinking maybe my brains be spilling out, but they ain't—'at bullet just run a track over my skull. It don't hurt so bad as this here," he said. "Then I feel my ear ain't there anymore."

The story seemed to sap all the strength from him.

"The woman?" I said.

He shook his head, he didn't know.

Teddy Blue said, "Where's Feathers's body?"

It wasn't there.

We followed a blood-trail that climbed a rocky slope of the canyon's west wall and found Tom Feathers's body lying among the cactus at the top.

"He didn't die right away," Teddy Blue said.

"Look at the way he was cut," I said, taking closer examination of the corpse.

"Just enough to let him bleed out."

"Davy wanted him to know he was dying."

"Payback for taking Etta," I said.

"Payback," Teddy Blue said. "This is some mean son of a bitch."

"What now?" Harve said.

"We read the signs, see which way they went."

"What about him?" Harve indicated the black man still kneeling by the dead horse.

"You take him back to Gonzales, wait for us there," I said.

"I came to fight."

"We can't just leave him, Harve."

"I hate splitting off from you boys."

"You might not have to," Teddy Blue said. "Look."

A cloud of dust in the distance indicated riders headed our way.

"Colorado Charlie?"

"That's my guess."

"Then let's make a stand here and now," I said.

"Goddamn right," Harve said. "I'm tired of playing behind the eight ball."

"So am I."

CHAPTER 30

"**Y**ou up to shooting?" I asked Isom Dart when we reached him in the bottom of the canyon.

He looked at me with eyes that spoke of regret.

"I'll do what needs doing. Who you want me to shoot, anyway?"

"There's riders coming," Harve said. "Gypsy Davy wasn't the only one after Miss Etta."

We set up our positions behind rocks: Teddy Blue and Harve to the right, the black man and myself to the left—partway up the canyon's neck.

"We just gonna ambush 'em?" Isom Dart said. "Just gonna shoot 'em out from under their hats?"

"We'll give them a chance to ride away," I said. "But only if they prove to be agreeable."

He didn't ask anything more, simply wetted his thumb, wiped it over the front blade–sight of the Winchester, then settled in.

"Let me ask you something that's troubling me," I said.

He didn't take his eye from the sights.

"How come you and Feathers are just now getting this far south? You should have been here at least a week or two ago."

"Miss Etta turned sick, had to find her a doctor. She was laid up for a time, thought she might die. Delayed us coming."

"What kind of sick?" I asked. "What was wrong with her?"

"Don't know. Just sick is all."

"How was she when Gypsy Davy waylaid you?"

"Still weak as a kitten," he said. "All the color washed out a her, but well enough."

For that, I was relieved. If Gypsy Davy had meant to kill Etta, we would have found her body. It was a two-edged sword, that thought. I was glad she was alive, but the knot in my gut that she was in the company of a madman was little comfort.

We could hear the clatter of shod hooves coming down the canyon. I signaled for the others to get ready, but to wait for my play.

I could hear the echoes of voices from Charlie's bunch glancing off the canyon's walls.

"Something's dead up in here, see those buzzards circling?"

"Might be we lucked out and they all perished on their own," I heard Charlie say. They were close, just around the bend.

"Be our bad luck, I was counting on having a little time with the woman before we finished her." It sounded like Batwings, Charlie's sidekick.

"Hell, we all were!" another cawed.

"You boys shut them cake-holes. Why, if there is dead up in here, you'll wake them up."

They came into view, two abreast, Charlie and Batwings in the lead. We waited until they'd all cleared the bend then I said, "End of the trail, Utter. Don't even think about it. We've got you nailed. You do anything, this is where you'll stay, where they'll find your bodies."

Surprise crawled all over his face as he jerked hard on the reins.

"McCannon?"

"You still want to shoot us like prairie chickens?" Teddy Blue called down from his position. "Go ahead."

Batwings turned his attention to the rocks on that side of the canyon.

"Yes, sir!" Harve shouted. "Hell, it'd be my pleasure blasting you yahoos!"

"Wanna know what's your stake in all this?" Charlie said.

"We're not here to talk, Charlie. Drop your iron on the ground and dismount."

Some of the horses snuffled and pawed the ground—they smelled the death.

"Then what, we do that?" Charlie said. "You planning on leaving us afoot, something like that?"

"Something like that, but only on the condition that you hoof it back to Denver and tell the judge you failed in your mission."

"No can do. Why, I ain't never failed in my mission, ain't about to now. We got ten guns to however many you got in them rocks and my suspicion is, you ain't got much but them two other yahoos was with you last time we met—that feisty Ranger and the one missing an arm." Charlie was full of himself considering the position he was in.

"We got you in our sights, that's all you need to be concerned with. You can go tell the judge yourself or he can read about it in the papers. Makes no nevermind to me, Utter."

"The hell you say!" he shouted, jerking his pistol. I shot him out of the saddle.

Too late to do any more talking. Guns jerked from their holsters, rifles and pistols cracking, bullets ricocheting off the rocks, scattering dust and riders, men pitching from their saddles.

We shot into them with a fury and some of them scattered back up the canyon, the rest lay dead or dying. Batwings was one that scattered at first shot and Teddy Blue shouted that he was going after him. I called out to let it go, but he was already stepping into leather.

"Jesus," I muttered, and went for my own horse. Nothing like a bullheaded, right-minded, never-forget-an-insult Texas lawman to not let a fight come to a quick end. Teddy Blue was spurring his horse up the canyon by the time I made leather.

"You want me to stay here or what?" Harve shouted.

"Stay here!"

I was eating Teddy Blue's dust when the *pop! pop!* of pistol shots opened up ahead of me. Teddy had caught up with them, or they had caught up with him.

By the time I rounded the next bend in the canyon, where it began to open up, Teddy Blue was down on his knees, his horse shot from under him, struggling to rise. Blood stained his shirt—he'd been caught in a cross fire. The bastards had made a stand instead of running, instead of going back to goddamn Denver!

Teddy Blue was firing his pistol toward a rock out-crop. Then I saw Batwings rise from a rock above him, take aim with a Winchester, and blow the top of the Ranger's head off.

I jerked my own rifle, took steady aim, and killed the son of a bitch, watching him pitch from the rock and tumble to the canyon's floor. Bullets chewed up the ground around me, but I had gone into the cold-blooded state of mind of a killer—everything moved in slow motion. The remaining gunfighters were mere targets for me to calmly and efficiently knock down. Old instinct taking over, my aim steady and true, I began to kill them in the rocks until the last one threw down his rifle and ran.

I knelt beside Teddy Blue's body.

"Blue," I said. "You damn fool."

Then I searched his pockets, took his badge, his pocket watch, and a small packet wrapped in string. I opened this and found a tintype of Etta when she was young, her hair done up in reddish curls, a slight smile on her lips. Pretty and innocent. I stared at the picture for a long time, remembering the woman I'd kissed in the summer kitchen in autumn with the sweet scent of apples in the air. I realized, too, how much Teddy Blue had loved her, enough to give his life for her when he didn't have to. Also in the packet was a letter. I opened it and read it.

> *Dear Teddy, I still think of you and miss you. I wonder every day if the Comanches that you so dearly love to chase, or some outlaws, will bring you harm. I worry about you constantly. I was so in love with you when first we met, and you with me. I was just a girl but knew my own heart. How did such a heart become broken? How did our love become separated? Why wasn't I enough for you? Questions I still ask myself in my loneliest hours. But I know the answers. I know that you were born needing to do the right thing, that you were born with a sense of honor that few men have. That for you to see injustices done was simply intolerable. And your duty and your honor proved a greater power over you than did my love, though I've no doubt that you loved me. Denver is a city full of passion and life, though my own life has not been easy, my sins many—these, the price I've learned to pay for this freedom. Would that you leave your beloved Texas and join me, I would give up this life and become your wife again. But I know how utterly unhappy you would be here, just as unhappy as I'd become there on the frontier. These are matters of the heart and my heart wanted to tell your heart that I shall always love you, even though I could not love you enough, or you could not love me enough, for us to be together forever. Think of me, and never let me out of your heart for very long. Your Etta*

I placed the tintype back in the packet with the letter and slipped them into my pocket along with his watch. They didn't deserve to be lost and scattered in some lonely canyon, as lost as bones and dust.

"Dammit, Blue, why didn't you love her enough?" were the only words to express my grief at the loss of a good man, and maybe a good woman, too.

Harve saw me return without Teddy Blue in tow.

"He still up the canyon?"

I nodded.

Harve shook his head.

"Sumbitch. You get the others?"

"All but one."

He took a deep breath and let it out.

"We lost a good one," he said.

"I know."

"What now?"

"Let's saddle a horse to that hack and take Teddy to Gonazles for a proper burial."

"What about Etta?"

"I think I know where she is," I said.

"Huh?"

"Call it a feeling."

We righted the hack, cutting loose the dead horse, and hitched it to Teddy Blue's mount, then took it up the canyon and loaded his body into it.

———

The fat Mexican sheriff, Carlos Delgado, was just coming out of a café when he spotted the three of us.

"Hey, you went off to find Señor Feathers," he said, "and what you found was a Negro and a buggy. That's pretty good."

"Shut up," I said.

He blinked.

"Stay clear of me, you understand?"

He glanced at Teddy Blue's corpse in the hack.

"You kill heem?"

We continued down the street until we found a storefront advertising an undertaker.

"We'll make the arrangements," I said, "then this is where we part company, Harve."

He looked stricken.

"Why, Mac? We ain't found Etta yet."

"Because that's the way I want it, partner."

He reached in his pocket and took out his wallet, removed several bills and handed them to me.

"You'll need it—traveling expenses."

"Thanks."

"I'll see to it Blue gets a proper and fine funeral. You go on do what needs doing. Just one thing."

"What's that?"

"I'd appreciate a wire sent to me in Denver to let me know how it turned out."

We shook hands and I headed back toward San Antonio, prodded by nothing more than a feeling that was aching in my bones like a fever.

CHAPTER 31

"Vaudeville Variety Theater & Gambling Saloon is where you'll usually find him, if he ain't here," the bartender at the Golden Spur said. "Doc ain't here, he's usually there—loves the comics."

I figured anybody knew the underside of San Antonio, it was Doc Holliday and I needed to search him out.

I crossed the street, cut across Market Square, and angled my way opposite the Alamo Plaza, where some sort of festival was taking place. Dancers wearing red-trimmed skirts and peasant blouses clicked their heels to a mariachi band; the men were dressed in black with silver conchos adorning the legs of their trousers, and big sombreros. The music was lively and quickened the blood and the evening sky was streaked with crimson clouds.

I found the Vaudeville and asked the man at the ticket window if Doc Holliday was in attendance. He was a short balding man with heavy jowls shaved to a clean pink.

"Have not seen him yet," the man said. "However, I do expect him; the Rose of Cimarron is playing tonight—she's a wonderful singer, you know."

"What time do you expect him?"

The man pulled a watch from his pocket, snapped open the lid.

"He's usually here around eight—less, of course, him and Kate are getting into it."

Big Nose Kate was Doc's common-law wife. I asked the man where they resided and he said over a butcher shop on South San Saban Street.

"Which way is that?"

I followed the directions. The street was, like almost every street in San Antonio, cluttered with ox-drawn wagons. The buildings were mostly of stone or stucco, pockmarked by the weather. I found the address and climbed the outside stairs and knocked on the door.

I waited a few moments and knocked again, then the door opened and Kate stood there in a chintz robe clutched with one hand. Her hair was uncombed and it looked like she'd been crying.

"Oh," she said. "I was expecting someone else."

"Doc here?"

"He's not here," she said, her voice hoarse, the way a voice ravaged by liquor and cigars will get. "Fact, I thought you were him."

"Doc usually knock on his own door?" I said.

"Who are you?"

I told her and her eyes narrowed.

"You don't remember me, Kate. We met in Deadwood sometime back."

She was a large woman, large and sad—her love for Doc having cost her much.

"I think I remember," she said. "I can't be sure. Doc's got so many friends, so many acquaintances. . . ."

"Do you know where he is, it's important that I talk to him."

"Try the Golden Spur," she said.

"Already have."

She shrugged; her face was bloated. "Then he might be at the Vaudeville Theater."

"Tried there, too."

"Well goddamn him," she said, and began to close the door but not before I could wedge my boot in.

"I'll call the police if you try and molest me," she said.

"I'm not trying to molest you. I'm trying to find out where Doc is and I'm not leaving until you tell me."

"Well, he's not here."

I gave her a hard stare to let her know I wasn't budging.

A sob caught in her throat. "Try Fanny Porter's sporting house down the street. He has a particular little red-haired whore he enjoys there—apparently I'm not wife enough to him. Now leave me the hell alone!"

I removed my foot and she slammed the door hard and I heard the lock click from the inside. Then I heard sobs that quickly became wails.

The light of evening had gone from crimson to black silver, an almost golden dust seemed to have descended on the city and lights in windows had winked on. I descended the steps and went up the street looking for Fanny Porter's sporting house.

Hell, it could have been any number of bagnios, for I came to a block where a red light glowed in almost every window. I picked one at random and knocked and a young Oriental woman with black hair nearly to her hips answered. She was pretty and small and wore a tight-fitting blue dress.

"Yes, come in," she said.

"Is this Fanny Porter's?"

"Why you want to go there? You come in, we got everything you need right here. We got white girls and Negro girls and China girls. You don't need to go no place else. Come in, come in."

"I'm not looking for a girl," I said. "I'm looking for a man."

I realized what that sounded like the minute I'd said it. The Celestial clasped her hand to her mouth and giggled.

"Oh, we don't got no men for you. Why a nice handsome fellah like you want a man for when you can have cute girl like me?"

"No, you don't understand," I said. "Just tell me which way to Fanny Porter's."

"She got no men for you. No, no. She don't have no men like that. Come in, you see, girl be okay for you now."

I turned and left, her laughter still burning my ears.

I knocked on the next door and this time a large black man who looked like he could bend a crowbar without breaking a sweat answered and stared at me.

"You got forty dollars?" he said. "That's the price

of admission you want to come inside, sample the la-
dies. You ain't got forty dollars, keep on moving—this
ain't no crib joint like most the places up and down this
here street."

"I'm looking for Fanny Porter's," I said.

"This is Fanny Porter's. You got forty dollars or
ain't you?"

"No, I don't."

He started to close the door.

"But I got this."

He stopped when he saw the Colt Peacemaker
aimed at his nose.

"I'm looking for Doc Holliday. He around?"

He looked at the iron for another second and said,
"Please, step in, suh. I'll go fetch Doc."

The scent of lilacs and cigar smoke is a smell that
reeks of loneliness and desperation and the room was
filled with it. So, too, does the clink of whiskey glasses
and loud laughter, red drapes and wilted flowers dropping from cheap vases. I looked around, remembered a
time when a place like this was exciting, remembered
my first time in a whorehouse in Abilene not nearly this
fancy. Barely seventeen, me and some other yahoos just
off our first cattle drive. We'd been thinking about it all
the way from the Brazos and it was exciting as hell.
What it was, was just a spare room over a saloon—an
iron bed and a hollow-eyed woman wanted three dollars. But for a jug-eared, whiskey-soaked kid it was exciting. Now it simply seemed to me to be a sad place
for a man to have to find refuge in, to have to find some
sense of himself.

A woman with platinum hair and a mole on her left
cheek descended the steps leading from the upper

floor. She was barely dressed in a lavender kimono that parted at the top enough to show the mounds of her breasts. She looked to be all of maybe twenty years old unless you looked into her eyes—the eyes were a lot older.

"Howdy, slick," she said. "You come for any particular gal, or will I do?"

"I'm waiting on a friend," I said.

"Well, while you're waiting won't you buy a lady a drink, only cost you a dollar, honey."

"Dollar for cheap watered-down whiskey? I hope you got a lot of charm."

She smiled.

"I got enough," she said. "But I can see I can't fool no hardcase such as yourself, sugar. Where you hail from, somewhere in the South? I'm from Alabama."

"This what you did in Alabama?" I said.

She snorted, said, "Hell, no. I was a preacher's wife in Alabama."

"That must have been some church."

She laughed, then suddenly looked sad.

"If I could go back with my head up, I would, but I'm afraid it's too late for salvation."

"Well, salvation comes in many forms, but I'm not one," I said. "Thanks for the offer, sis."

She snorted.

"How you know what you're missing, you don't give it a try?"

"I got a feeling I know what I'm missing," I said. "Thanks anyway."

"McCannon."

I turned to the rasp of his voice.

Doc stood in a doorway in just a nightshirt and

trousers, the galluses down, stocking feet, a glass of whiskey in his hand, his arm around an ample woman with hair as red as autumn leaves. Surprisingly, except for the hair, she looked very much like Big Nose Kate.

"I need to talk to you."

"I'm in the middle of something. Henry says you pulled a pistol on him, threatened to blow out his brains, he didn't come retrieve me."

"Henry exaggerated," I said. "I only meant to shoot him in the knees, he didn't tell me where you were."

Doc smiled.

"Can it wait ten minutes?"

"If it could, I wouldn't be standing here."

"Okay, okay," he said with a wave of his glass. "Least let this poor pilgrim get dressed. I see you met Phoebe." He indicated the woman with the platinum hair.

"This poor sucker a friend of yours, Doc? Well, if I'd known, I'd 'ave thrown him a free one."

Doc shook his head.

"You'll have to excuse Phoebe," Doc said. "She's a mite loose-mouthed. Has lost all her gentility somewhere along the way."

"Hell, that and a whole lot more, Doc!" The woman's voice was full of regret.

"Be gone with you, sister, this man and I have personal business to discuss." Doc's gaze had suddenly turned serious.

I waited until Doc went back inside the room with his lady then emerged, fully dressed. He reeked of whiskey and cheap perfume.

"Let's go into the parlor, where we might have

some privacy," he said. "And where I might have a drink to settle my hash. Young Jasmine in there is enough to make a man nervous with anticipation of her comely charms. Coitus interruptus will fray a man's nerves every time."

I waited while he poured himself a drink, declining an offer to join him.

"What is it you'd have of me, sir?" he said at last.

I took out the tintype and showed it to him.

"You ever see this woman, Doc?"

He looked at it, brought it closer to the lamp, where the flame glowed white.

"Well . . . she has a certain resemblance of someone I've seen about recently," he said.

"Tell me where."

"First let me ask you why you thought I'd know her?"

"Call it a hunch, Doc."

"Because you think I'm a man who knows everyone and everything that has to do with the dark side of humanity."

"I'm interested only in finding this woman."

He looked again.

"She's a new girl—just showed up here in the district a day or two ago, recent acquisition of Madame Lu over on Water Street, near the river. Lu's a high-class Chinawoman, sells everything but herself, charges high rates. She also runs a dope den."

Something hammered my heart.

"Take a good look, Doc. Are you sure it's the same person?"

He looked again, nodded his head.

"I'm fairly sure, but not a hundred percent. The

lady in question was a bit more drawn, older, hair a bit lighter—but, she bears a strong resemblance."

"How do I find this place?"

It felt like my blood was on fire as I walked from Fanny Porter's down toward the river. A heavy fog had begun to settle over the city and the only distinct sounds were the ringing of my spurs as the fog closed in the closer to the river I got.

Somewhere in the shadowy mist a sudden burst of laughter shattered the stillness then stopped as quickly as it had begun. I was remembering the answer Teddy Blue had given me the time he had gone into the tenderloin of Ogalala looking for Etta: "I thought maybe I might find her there." Teddy Blue knew something about Etta that I hadn't until I read the letter I'd taken from his pocket—her reference to her life in Denver, the sins she'd alluded to, the loneliness. It's what gave me the hunch to come looking for her here now. That, and the feeling I'd gotten the last time I'd walked these streets. Sometimes all a man has to go on is the feeling in his gut. If Doc wasn't mistaken, then my hunch had proved right. I hurried my step.

The lights on the bridge were shrouded in fog. A set of stone steps led from the bridge to the street below— this had to be Water Street, according to Doc's directions. I reached the bottom, heard the lap of water along the banks, the splash of a fish. To my right I could barely make out the shapes of buildings, most without light, others farther down too enshrouded to see. Doc had said look for a door that had Chinese lanterns and a red dragon painted on it. That's what I was looking for when suddenly several shapes emerged from the fog.

"Where you bound to, mister?" one of them asked.

My instincts went up immediately. I was reaching for the Peacemaker when something struck me from behind, something hard that sent me reeling until a fist smashed into my ribs and another into my jaw almost simultaneously. I went down spitting blood under a rain of blows and curses, hands grabbing at my pockets while others smashed into me. The Peacemaker knocked from my hand, I reached for the Starr single-action—the one I'd taken off Batwings in the canyon fight—jerked it from where I'd positioned it at the base of my spine and shot one of the feet nearest my face. The owner screamed when I blew off his toe. I fired blindly and I heard another yelp he'd been shot, then the running of footsteps fading into the night.

I thought at first it was the fog closing in on me, then too late I realized it wasn't.

CHAPTER 32

I awoke to a dull ache, my head buzzing, went to move and everything hurt. Rolled over and sat up, found myself sitting on a hard bunk in a jail cell, the smell of human waste nearby. In the cell next to me slept a man with a long tangled beard, his mouth open in a steady snore. The smell was coming from a bucket under his cot.

My left eye was nearly closed. I could feel the lump when I went to rub it with the heel of my hand. My ribs ached every time I took a breath. Couldn't tell if it was daylight or still dark—there were no windows, just a row of cells, lanterns hung on hooks from the stamped tin ceiling.

My weapons were gone and so were the contents of my pockets. I'd been robbed and my mood was black. I thought of the letter and the tintype, how I'd hoped to return them to Etta; now they were gone.

An iron door leading back to the cells cranked open and a yahoo with a black vest, white shirt with garters on his sleeves, and trousers tucked down inside his mule deer boots came strolling down the aisle. He looked in at the man in the cell next to me and said, "Jesus, Bart, you stink worse'n a cow's butt!"

Then the man stopped in front of my cell, took a key, and turned it in the lock and jerked open the door.

"Come'n out."

I followed him into an office where three others stood or sat around—all wearing badges, two drinking coffee, one cleaning his boots.

"Have a chair, amigo," the man with the gartered sleeves said as he sat down behind a desk across from me. I saw the contents of my pockets spread on the desk—saw Teddy Blue's Ranger badge, the packet with the letter and tintype—and I was relieved they hadn't been stolen.

"You're mighty careless for a Ranger," the man said. "Letting a bunch of trash jump you down on Water Street. Lucky them boys didn't cave in your skull and throw you in the Guadalupe. Pull two or three yahoos a week out a that river."

"I shot one in the foot," I said. "Maybe shot another one, too. You find a man with his toe shot off, you'll find one of them."

The lawman looked at the other deputies then back at me.

"How come I don't know you?" he said. "I know practically every Ranger around these parts but I ain't never seen you before."

"I'm out of Houston looking for someone," I said. A lie was good only if it worked to your advantage.

"Houston, huh? I suppose you know Bob Sugar, captain with the Rangers over there."

I nodded. "Good man," I said.

"Damn got that right," the man said, and extended his hand for me to shake.

"Cal Morris," he said, "chief of police. Some of my deputies was cruising the river area, heard the gunshots, and found you coldcocked. Most get coldcocked down on Water Street ain't so fortunate, are they R. J.?" He looked at the deputy cleaning his boots who nodded.

"I've always been more lucky than smart," I said.

"You don't look so dang lucky. Who it was you say you were looking for?"

I nodded toward the tintype.

"That woman," I said.

"She commit a crime in Houston?"

"She's wanted for the investigation of a murder there," I said.

He picked up the tintype, studied it for a moment, then laid it back down.

"Jesus, pretty woman like that," he said.

"Yeah, I know."

"So you figure you'd find her down on Water Street?"

"I heard she might be in the area somewhere."

"You carrying a warrant for her arrest? 'Cause I didn't see no warrant papers among your personal effects."

"Not out to arrest her," I said. "Just want to ask her some questions. Not likely she did the killing, but she may have a handle on who was involved."

"See, the way it works, any arrests to be made in San Antone, me or one of my men make 'em. You

Rangers want 'em, you come here first, ask for my assistance—sorta what I consider professional courtesy."

"You're right," I said. "Next time I will. But like I said, I'm not wanting to arrest her, just to ask her some questions. That okay with you, I do that?"

He seemed to relax a little.

"You want us to help you find her?"

"Not yet, let me see if I can run her down. If not, I'd be grateful for the assistance. I'm sure you boys got lots better things to do than find a woman."

Some of them snorted.

"I can't think of a thing better'n finding a woman, can you, Cal?" the one cleaning his boots said.

Morris grinned, took a cigar from his waistcoat pocket, one that'd already been lit and snuffed out once, and screwed it into his mouth.

"Maybe first thing you ought to do," he said, "is find yourself a sawbones, have him look at that face."

"That bad, huh?"

"You'd scare babies and old folks. Looks like maybe those yahoos broke your nose, too."

"Thanks," I said. "You mind I gather up my things and get in the wind?"

"No, go right ahead."

"I had some weapons on me when I got jumped last night," I said. "A Colt, a Deane Adams, a Smith & Wesson, and a Winchester."

He opened a drawer, took out the Dean Adams, Smith & Wesson, and Winchester and laid them on the desk next to the tintype, badge, pocket watch, and packet that held the letter.

"Didn't find a Colt, those boys probably grabbed it

up and run off with it. Probably use it to kill or rob someone with."

"Loss of a pistol, a broken nose, cut eye—I'll settle for that," I said, and took up my belongings.

"Water Street's a bad place to go alone day or night," he said. "But I guess you already figured that out."

"Thanks, Chief, maybe sometime you ever get to Houston, I'll be able to return the favor."

He snorted, said, "Hell, don't hold your breathing waiting for me to show my face in Houston again. Last time I was there I caught the clap. You ever caught the clap, you know what I'm talking about."

"Adios."

"Take care, podner," he said.

It was good to breathe fresh air again, and in the light of day, even seeing it with only one eye, the world looked new and full of hope. I headed back to Water Street.

I was maybe two blocks from the jail when I heard someone call my name. I looked around and there, standing across the street at the edge of the plaza was Roy Bean, Cleopatra's former boss, pimp, and sweetheart. He'd asked me once whether or not he thought there was opportunity in Texas. I told him I thought there was for an enterprising man.

"Quint McCannon," he said. "I'd recognize that lanky frame of yours anywhere." He was a short, pudgy man with dark eyes and just recently it looked like he had begun growing himself a beard.

He dodged two or three mule trains crossing the street.

"Holy mother of pearl! What happened to you?" he said.

"Fell off my horse."

"Ought to learn to ride better."

"You look like you've fared well for yourself, Roy. Fancy coat and pants like that have to cost a man fifteen, twenty dollars."

He flushed with pride. "You were right about Texas. More opportunity here than lice on a dog."

He was carrying a book, a big book.

"Taken up study of the law," he said, shifting the book from under his arm to his hands. "Figured I've been on one side of the law long enough, I ought to try the other—more money in it than running whores and selling liquor to yahoos. Bought me a patch of land down along the Pecos—lawless country, the kind that needs a man of my adjudication, word I learned in this here book."

"Glad to hear things are working out for you, Roy, but I've no time to talk about it right now."

"You living in San Antone?" he said.

"No, just here to find someone."

"What about Cleo?" he said. "She still with that gamey-legged fellow she run off with?"

"He's dead. She's fixing to go East."

He shook his head, spat the chaw he'd been grinding in his cheek and said, "Fuss. I wisht she could see me now. She might not want to run off to the East, she knew I was a prosperous and righteous man."

"I'm sure. See you around, Roy."

"You need anything, I'm staying at the Alamo Hotel until tomorrow, then down to the Pecos," he shouted as I headed toward the river.

When I reached the spot where I'd been waylaid, I glanced at the ground, saw some dried blood on the rocks near the walking path, knew it was mine. I felt like I'd been leaving pieces of me all along the trail since leaving Cheyenne, but I was close to Etta now—I could feel it—and that's all that mattered.

I eventually found the place Doc had described to me the night before—Madame Lu's. Saw a door with a red dragon painted on it. I knocked, waited, knocked again. A small Oriental woman who looked as ancient as time itself opened the door and looked up at me.

"We close, you come back tonight, okay."

"I'm looking for this woman," I said, showing her the tintype.

She barely glanced at it and said, "She no here."

"Look again," I said. She started to close the door, but I held it open. She looked at me with alarm.

"You go now, I find the policeman you don't go."

"I'm looking for this woman, her name is Etta, and I know she's here. I'm not leaving until I see her."

She weighed all of seventy pounds.

"Lu, Lu!" Her voice was more like the screech of a barn owl than human. Another Oriental woman appeared, younger—a real looker.

"What is it, Nana?"

"Him," the old woman said. "He cause trouble."

"What do you want?"

I showed her the tintype. "Her," I said.

She looked at me, this beautiful Asian woman

whose skin was as smooth as ivory and eyes like black silk. She said first to the old woman, "It's okay, Nana. You go drink your tea, I take care of the gentleman." Then when the old woman left, the younger one invited me in and led me to a front parlor.

"Please, you no cause trouble."

"You go bring Etta to me and there will be no trouble," I said.

"This is very difficult, what you ask me to do," she said.

"Tell me where she is then and I'll go get her."

"You no understand."

"I've come a long way to find her, you can go get her or I will."

"She not well."

"More reason I should find her."

"Please," she said, touching my wrist as I began to move past her to go and search the house. "Let me explain something, okay?"

"You got a minute."

"This lady, she not free to go."

"Time's up, I'll find her myself."

I started to move past her again.

"You try and take her, he will kill you," she said.

"You mean Gypsy Davy?"

"Yes."

"He might not care for the results if he tries. Where is she?"

The woman wore a dress of blue silk that whispered with her every movement.

"He will kill me if you take her."

"Not my problem, lady. You should have thought of that before you got involved."

"He gave me no choice. He said he would kill me and kill my nana if I didn't take her in. He said he would cut our throats."

"What do you expect, you associate with cut-throats to begin with? Maybe you should find a new line of work."

"I can't. . . ."

"I'll find her myself," I said. "Tell me this, is he with her now?"

She shook her head.

"No, he hasn't been here for two days."

"Where is she?"

"You take her and go!" she said. "I show you her, you take her and get her out of here, as far away as you can!"

I followed her to the back of the house, past several doorways, some partly open. Inside one of the rooms I saw a woman lying on her side on a pallet on the floor, her eyes half-open, her lips wordlessly moving. The pungent odor of dope was thick in the air. When we reached the back of the house, we went out a rear door to a small building where the woman took a key from her pocket and turned it in the lock.

"You kept her locked up!"

"He tell me to. He say, 'You make sure she don't run away. You make sure nobody get to her.'"

I pushed the woman aside and stepped into the dim interior. I could smell the pungent stench of opium. Several thin blades of light pierced the cracks between the wallboards. In a matter of seconds my sight adjusted enough I could see the figure huddled in the corner of the room. My heart hammered hard.

"Etta." I whispered her name as I crossed the

room and knelt before her. In the stripes of light, I could see glimpses of her eyes. She had the frightened look of a startled animal, one that had been trapped.

"Etta, it's me, Quint."

A sob broke from her throat, an utterance of fear as I reached out and touched her arm; she shivered from the touch.

"She sick," the woman in the doorway said. "I told you, very, very sick."

I started to come closer, to draw her into me but she recoiled, murmuring words that were unintelligible, small sounds like those of a child that had been whipped. My hand struck something on the mattress beside her—a glass pipe that shattered—spilling its contents of water.

"You've got her doped!" I said over my shoulder to the woman. "No wonder she's sick. How long has she been like this?"

"Three days maybe. Not me, him. He tell me do it, so I do. He tell me make her smoke opium, so I do. He tell me I no do what he want, he kill us all."

"Jesus," I muttered, not believing what I was hearing or seeing.

"Go get me a blanket," I said to the woman. When she didn't move for a moment, I got angry. "Go get me a blanket or what he threatened to do to you will be nothing compared to what I'll do!"

She hurried away.

"Etta, it's Quint. You remember me, I know you do." I touched her hands, took them in mine as gently as I knew how and held them. She tried to resist but then let herself go limp almost as quickly. She had no real resistance left in her. I continued to say her name, telling her mine, hoping that somehow it would break through her fear and confusion. She sobbed and shook and my heart ached at the sight.

The woman returned with the blanket, tossed it to me and said, "Here, you hurry, take her and get out! He come, I tell him you here, tell him you come trying to steal her, I try and stop you. I don't care he kill you!"

I took the blanket and wrapped it around Etta and picked her up. She was frail, a quaking of bones, and I carried her out of the building and into the light. The anger in me welled up at the full sight of her. She was pale, nearly bloodless except for the darkness around her eyes. Her hair was tangled and dirty, the cotton shift she wore was stained. She was unwashed and covered her eyes quickly against the light, crying softly.

"You better hurry. He come back soon, find you with her, he kill you, kill all of us!"

I walked the six or so blocks from Water Street to the Alamo Hotel with Etta in my arms, ignoring the looks of passersby, ignoring everything but my own anger and need to protect Etta from any further depredations.

The man behind the desk of the Alamo came round and said, "Hey you can't bring her in here! Why, looks like she's in need of a doctor, this ain't no hospital!"

"Which room is Roy Bean's?"

"Pardon me, sir, but you'll have to leave."

"Mister, I set this woman down, I'm drawing my pistol and killing whatever son of a bitch happens to be in my sights. Now you tell me where Roy Bean's room is! Better still, you take me to him."

Roy Bean answered the first knock, saw me holding Etta, and stepped aside.

"Sorry for the intrusion, Mr. Bean," the desk clerk said. "But this feller insisted. Should I call the police?"

Roy Bean handed the man a pair of silver dollars and said, "No, these are friends of mine. Why don't you go down to the bar and bring us a nice bottle of whiskey. Charge it to my account. Bring up some hot water and some clean towels while you're at it."

The clerk took his leave as I was laying Etta on the bed.

"Friend of yours?" he said. "She looks in bad shape."

"She's in trouble; she'll need a doctor," I said.

"I'll go tell the boy to get one of those, too."

Roy left the room and I was alone with Etta at last, no one or nothing standing between us any longer.

She lay curled up in a ball under the blanket, still shaking, still whimpering. I stroked her hair and spoke to her, told her how sorry I was that this had happened. I wasn't sure if the words meant anything to her or not; it didn't matter—they were words I needed to say to her, words I'd been needing to say for a long time.

"Etta, I never should have left you when I did. I was a fool."

Maybe it was the words, or maybe the simple fact I'd not abused her but sat there and stroked her hair, for she calmed and lay silent beneath my hand. I had to fight back tears, seeing her like that. In that moment of peace, of her stillness, I couldn't even vow vengeance on the man who'd done this to her. All I could vow was my love for her.

"Etta, I love you. Don't leave me."

She opened her eyes once, looked at me, then closed them again.

CHAPTER 33

"How long you figure she'll be like that?" Roy Bean said.

We were sitting on the gallery of his place: a wooden courthouse, storefront, and whiskey den he'd paid Mexicans to build. It was in an empty, aimless land, except for the nearby Pecos River. A land of mesquite and Gila monsters and enough bad hombres to keep Roy Bean in business as a self-appointed judge with a handful of hired Mexican vaqueros to act as officers of his court.

There were a few other buildings nearby that comprised a village of sorts. Upon his arrival he pronounced the place Langtry after the well-known actress, Lily Langtry—a woman he adored but one he'd never met. He kept a photograph of her above his bed and another above the bar.

Etta preferred to keep to herself in a spare room the judge had fixed up for her. I'd accepted his invitation to bring her to this place of refuge.

I was torn between wanting to protect and care for her, and wanting to go find Gypsy Davy and kill him. But Roy Bean had exercised his judgment by stating that if I went after Gypsy Davy, I'd be leaving Etta alone with no one to protect her.

"That yahoo has outfoxed you before, Quint. Nothing to say he couldn't do it again. Best you and Etta come with me down to the Pecos country. Let the hand of fate take care of Gypsy Davy—sooner or later he'll come to a bad end."

It was a solid enough argument. Now here we were, nearly a month later. Roy Bean had paid a Mexican woman to feed and care for Etta's every need, and in that respect, Etta was thriving. But she continued to remain silent, refusing to talk about what had happened to her and I hadn't pushed it.

"I wish I knew," I said to the judge in answer to his question about her mental condition.

He was ciphering figures in a ledger book.

"Fines," he said, wetting the stub of his pencil before each entry. "Figure three dollars if convicted of petty theft. Five for wrongful shooting or stabbing. Ten for illegal whiskey peddling—anything that don't come through me—twenty for stealing a horse, and twenty-five for contempt of court. That should do her to begin with. Can change it around later if I need to. Now all I need is for some yahoos to break the law."

Maybe it was the sameness of the day in, day out existence we'd come to live, but I was feeling restless, worried that Etta might not ever be the same woman she had been, worried that I might not ever find out the truth of what happened to her. I needed to understand.

"I think I'll go in and check on her, Roy."

He scratched around in his beard, which by now was flourishing into a nest of gray wires. That big straw sombrero pulled down low over his eyes and the silver pistol in his belt made him look like a real bad hombre.

"Image is everything," he'd said the first time I saw him in his frontier clothes.

Etta was sitting by the window, her face to the light, when I entered the room. She didn't turn to look at me—she never did. I took a chair and pulled it close.

"How are you feeling?" I said.

"I'm okay."

"Would you like to go for a walk? We could walk down by the river."

She sat silently, her hands folded in her lap, as though she were posing for a portrait. Maybe it was the way the light caught in her hair or the way it touched her cheek or the soft curve of her neck, but I'd never seen her look more beautiful.

"We could just walk," I said. "You wouldn't have to talk, neither of us would. It might be good to get out of the room for a bit."

Still she didn't move or say anything.

I stood to leave, my hand reaching for the doorknob when she said, "Okay."

Roy Bean was telling his Mexican deputies how it was important that they not hang a suspect until *after* he'd tried them. His Spanish was poor and their English nonexistent and he was gesturing a lot with his hands. He stopped when he saw me and Etta emerge. I think he was nearly as happy as I was to see her finally leave the building.

"We're just going to take a little walk down by the river," I said.

"Do you want to take my hand, Etta?"

She didn't reach out, so I took hers into mine and she didn't resist.

We walked in silence and when a jackrabbit hopped from one mesquite bush to another, she stopped and stared at it for the longest time. Then she allowed me to walk her the rest of the way to the river.

We found a stand of cottonwoods whose leaves fluttered in the warm winds and sat on a flat rock at the river's edge. A yellow bird trilled from his perch among the reeds.

"I like it here," I said. "Quiet and peaceful. I come here when you're sleeping and think to myself this would be a good place to build a little house, raise a few kids maybe. Roy Bean may have discovered something here."

Her gaze followed the water's current. On the far bank, a large branch lay half-submerged, tickling ripples, while the dry end made a resting spot for a dozen small turtles. I saw plenty mule deer tracks near the water's edge and the sun dazzled off the river's surface like diamonds. A fish flopped downstream and Etta started and said, "Oh."

"It's okay," I said, touching the back of her hand.

She looked at me then and said my name: "Quint."

"Yes," I said.

Her eyes searched mine.

"I . . . I . . ."

"No need to talk just now, Etta. Just enjoy the peace. Listen to the river, hear how sweet."

Her fingers closed around mine.

"It will be okay, Etta. Everything will be okay."

We returned to Roy Bean's just as the shadows grew long. It never ceased to amaze me, the number of signs he'd had painted and nailed up, advertising his business, one declaring him "Law West of the Pecos"—a man whose courtroom was an upturned whiskey barrel and a folding table and if it rained hard he held court inside instead of out.

He sat there peacefully snoozing, dreaming, no doubt, about Lily Langtry; a man content in the world he'd created for himself. I realized then he was a lot smarter than most.

"Would you care to take supper with me outside this evening?" I asked Etta. "The judge would be most appreciative of the company and it looks like it's going to be a beautiful sunset." She seemed uncertain for a moment then nodded and I felt that maybe, at last, she was starting to come back from whatever dark world she'd plunged into.

We sat around the long table the judge had his deputies station in the yard while Mexican women served us tortillas, frijoles, pan-fried nopales, steaks from a young steer the judge had ordered butchered just for the occasion, and champagne from his personal stock.

He ate with his hat on but with his cuffs rolled up

and a napkin tucked in the throat of his shirt. He ate with relish and drank the same way and toasted "God and Texas" several times over.

"Why Texas is better'n ten Wyomings thrown together," Roy Bean said. "I don't know why I didn't leave that country long before now. This is what I call fat living."

Etta ate in small bites, her mood silent, as Roy Bean regaled the table guests with tales of Lily Langtry and how he planned on meeting the actress someday to personally express his affections for her beauty and talent.

"Most beautiful woman—present company excluded, Miss Etta—in the whole of the universe."

Etta smiled at this and the judge clapped his hands.

"Well you look lovely tonight, Miss Etta. As lovely as the moon and stars all rolled into one. Let's have us some music! Hector, grab up your fiddle and you and Rodrigo get to playing some."

The one took up his fiddle and the other a guitar and began to play a Mexican ballad. Etta seemed taken with the music and inclined her head on my shoulder while I held her hand. The judge lit a cigar and smoked it as nightfall descended. In the distance, the song of the river joined the music and for the first time in a long time, I felt happy and had a sense of peace.

Later I walked Etta to her room and kissed her forehead and started to leave, but this time she clung to me and said, "Not yet."

I held her close to the strains of the music coming

from the yard; several of the deputies had begun to sing in Spanish.

We stood like that, holding each other in the darkness; I could feel the ticking of her heart through my shirt as the warmth of her body pressed against me.

"Don't leave me tonight," she whispered.

"Are you sure?"

She drew me to the bed and I lay down with her and she folded herself into my arms and it was enough.

Another week passed. Etta and I took daily walks down to the river, Roy Bean always making sure that at least two or three of the Mexican deputies kept us within sight, for he was uncommonly sure that sooner or later Gypsy Davy would make an attempt to get Etta back. I was of the same mind but had asked the judge to order his men to maintain a discreet distance.

"We give her the impression we're worried about Gypsy Davy coming for her," I said, "it's likely to push her over the edge."

"Be my pleasure to try him, find him guilty, and hang him for you, Quint. First I'd fine him twenty dollars then hang him." I'd asked the judge to be cautious in his comments concerning the madman while in the presence of Etta.

Then one afternoon as we sat on the rock at the river's edge she said, "I want to talk about it, about him."

It was a moment that I'd anticipated, but now that it had arrived, I wasn't sure I wanted to hear about it.

"Are you sure?" I asked.

She nodded, stared for a time at the water, then

said, "David is my half brother and he thinks that he is in love with me."

I understood now the same last name.

"Before I came to Cheyenne," she said, "where I met you, I'd lived in Denver. I was still married to a man but had been separated from him for some time." Images of Teddy Blue floated into my mind. Should I tell her now or wait?

"I thought I could find a sense of myself," she continued. "I was foolish, of course. What I was looking for didn't exist, something I've since come to realize. My troubles have been long-standing, David and his unnatural desire for me being the source of many of my troubles. I suppose that when it didn't work out between my husband and me, it only confirmed my suspicions that I was unworthy of a decent man. Then in Denver, I fell to a new low."

She took a deep breath. This confession was difficult for her.

"I became a prostitute," she said. "I had beauty and charm but little else to sustain me. I met a rich man who introduced me to other rich men. . . ."

"You don't have to tell me this, Etta. I don't care what has happened in the past."

"Yes," she said, "I do need to talk about it."

I took her hand.

"It wasn't as bad as you might think. I lived well, was never abused, and was highly thought of by many of these men. My secret was well kept and I got invited to many parties. This life also did something else for me—it helped me forget my past, to forget my brother. The last I knew he was in the East attending medical school and I figured that whatever his childhood fantasies had been about me, he'd probably outgrown them. Anyway, it was a safe world for me, in a sense, and I wasn't terribly unhappy with it except for one thing: having left my husband."

"I know," I said.

She looked at me.

"He came to Cheyenne looking for you regarding the murder in Denver, your involvement in it. He asked me to help him find you. If it wasn't for Teddy Blue, Etta, I wouldn't be here. I wouldn't have known."

Before she could say anything further, I took the packet with the letter and the tintype I'd been carrying and handed it to her.

"I took this from him the day he was killed."

She gasped at the touch of them, held them in her hands as gently as fragile birds.

"He's dead?"

"I'm sorry I have to be the one to tell you."

Moments passed with only the sounds of the river and the occasional splash of a turtle sliding off a limb into the water.

"Should we talk about this another time?"

She shook her head.

"I won't grieve for him just yet," she said. "I'll grieve in private, not in front of you, Quint. I loved him and I love you. It wouldn't be fair to you or respectful of Teddy to grieve openly."

"I understand."

"The man I first met in Denver who introduced me around to the others was the son of a federal judge. He also introduced me to the opium dens. In a way, it was an escape from what I'd become—a high-priced whore, but a whore nonetheless."

"What happened?"

"Life soon turned into a haze for me. And then, Davy showed up in Denver insisting that he wanted to marry me, insisting that I go away with him. I refused, of course. He wormed his way into the circle I'd been involved with, his charm and wit and cleverness too much for them to resist, just as I had been too much for them to resist. He threatened to expose me, our past, if I made an effort to openly spurn him. But Tyron became jealous of Davy's attentions toward me and, of course, I could not tell him the truth, nor could I convince my half brother to leave me alone. It came to a terrible tragic end one night outside an opium den. Davy killed Tyron in a fit of rage, mutilated him."

The words broke from her as she began to weep. I held her in my arms.

"He threatened to expose me if I didn't run away with him and say that the killing was a result of an illicit love triangle, that I'd killed Tyron when he caught me with my lover—my half brother. He then fled, telling me to meet him in San Francisco. That's when I went to Cheyenne, hoping that he would not find me again."

"That's it then. He came looking for you, you got word, and asked Tom Feathers to help you escape again?"

"Yes, a wire had arrived at my aunt's house from Davy telling me that he was coming for me, that it was useless to try and hide from him. So I went to poor Tom. He was the only one I could turn to."

"Davy would have you no matter what."

She nodded, wiped the tears from her eyes.

"No matter what. Even if he had to keep me

drugged, even if he had to break my spirit by having other men violate me."

"It's over," I said. "He won't touch you again."

She looked at me with her pale green eyes, eyes that no longer trusted.

"No, he will find me again. Nothing will stop him."

"You're wrong, Etta."

"Promise me something," she said.

"What?"

"That if he comes, you will kill me, that you won't let him take me."

"I won't let him take you. I promise."

That night as I lay beside her in the bed, I wondered if I had made a promise I wouldn't be able to keep.

CHAPTER 34

Two more weeks and nothing out of the ordinary occurred, except that some of Roy Bean's Mexican deputies caught a wanted felon, a man by the name of Charlie Dick, whom the judge had a wanted poster out on for train robbery of a Union Pacific Railroad.

Roy Bean was so pleased to have his first real criminal case to preside over that he put on a fresh shirt and combed his hair.

The deputies had hog-tied Charlie Dick and had to crow-hop him up the steps to the gallery of the Jersey Lilly.

One of the deputies who could speak the best English told the judge they'd caught the man trying to steal a horse, but once Roy Bean took a good look at him, he remembered the wanted flyer and charged the man with his rightful crime of train robbing.

Charlie Dick was a large, dark-eyed man with black brushy eyebrows and he stared defiantly at the judge.

"You ain't got no legal right to try me!" he said.

"That train I's supposed to rob was in Kansas; this here's Texas!"

"I reckon a tallywhacker like you would know the law," Roy Bean said. "I reckon you studied *Blackstone*, read his book and all, and know all there is to know about the legal system, jurisprudence and all that."

"Huh?" Charlie Dick said.

"I reckon 'cause you're so goldang smart, you got caught trying to steal Hector's horse whilst he was inside a whorehouse, not knowing of course that Hector's horse is stone-blind and that he'd walk you around in circles."

"He was a goldanged hammerhead, or I'd got clean away!"

"Well, I want to abide by the law," Roy Bean said, "and see you get a free trial, so I'm appointing you defense counsel before we get started."

"Defense counsel?"

"Hector," the judge said to his Mexican deputy, the one that could speak English the best. "Since it was your horse this man tried to steal and you're the only one speaks a lick of Americano around here besides myself, I appoint you to defend this yahoo in my court. You got the floor first."

Hector Gutierrez was a slender man of some fifty or sixty years of age who had met enough gringos in his time to have picked up a working language.

"Sí, Señor Bean."

Then Hector looked at Charlie Dick as if to say, "I'm sorry, señor, but I don't understand too very much about the law."

"This is a joke!" Charlie Dick said. "Might just as

well take me out and hang me as to have this goldang greaser sumbitch be my lawyer."

"I fine you five dollars for use of abusive language in my courtroom," Roy Bean said, and hammered the folding table with the butt of his pistol. "Any more outbursts in my court by the defendant will result in . . ." He paused and thumbed through his law book then said, "Contempt of this court, which will cost you another five dollars."

"Well, you just as well might fine me a thousand dollars!" Charlie Dick said disgustedly, " 'Cause I ain't got a red cent!"

"A thousand it is," Roy Bean said, rapping his table twice more with his pistol. "And in lieu of cash payment, the court shall confiscate those fancy spurs you're wearing. Where'd you get 'em—off the heels of a dead man's boots?"

It went like that for as long as Roy Bean could stretch it out. He didn't want his first court case to end too soon, not knowing when his deputies might catch another lawbreaker. Finally, however, Roy Bean pronounced the man guilty of robbing the Union Pacific and trying to steal Hector's blind horse. He ordered his deputies to deliver the man to the jail in Del Rio along with a request for the reward money.

"I think the judge's bark is worse than his bite," Etta said, having witnessed the "trial."

Roy Bean's spirits were high, having presided over his first real case, and he announced at the supper table that evening that he had decided to go to Chicago to see Lily Langtry perform on stage.

"It's a dream come true," he announced, his eyes

misting over at the very mention of her name. "Miss Etta, you and Quint are invited to join me."

She looked at me.

"Would you like to go?" I said.

"No." Then turning her attention to Roy Bean, who was seated at his customary position at the head of the table, she said, "I think that you should go alone and see her." And he knew exactly what she meant and was grateful for the encouragement.

Later, while Etta was inside, Roy Bean and I sat on the gallery and smoked.

"I'll make sure there's enough deputies to keep an eye on your back," he said. "I sent half with Charlie Dick, and Ramon has to go down across the border because his mother is dying, but that still leaves Juan, Rodrigo, Hector, and Xavier. All good men who can shoot."

"Thanks," I said. "But if Gypsy Davy hasn't shown himself by now, I doubt that he will. I expected him last week, the week before that, but who knows? Maybe he's dead, maybe in jail somewhere."

"My thinking, too," Roy Bean said. "I expected to see him long before now. Say the sumbitch has long dark hair?"

"That's the description I have of him. I've never met him."

"Well, I told my boys they see any yahoo with long dark hair to shoot first and take depositions later."

"You looking forward to Chicago, seeing Lily Langtry?" I said.

He sat there, his legs crossed at the ankles, holding the stub of a cigar between his teeth.

"In a way I am and in another way I ain't. You

know how it is, you had this dream all your life, then you get a chance for it to come true. Part of you wants it, but part of you don't, because once it comes true, it ain't a dream anymore."

"I understand that," I said.

"Just thinking about it makes me breathe hard."

Roy Bean left early the next morning for San Antonio, where he would catch a train to Chicago. Once he'd gone, the whole place seemed quiet as a stone. He'd ordered the bar closed because none of the remaining deputies knew how to make change in case anyone stopped by for an "ice beer" or cigars. The four deputies drew straws to see which went fishing and which stayed behind to keep an eye on things, meaning— according to the judge's orders—Etta and me.

Etta said, "Let's pack a picnic lunch and go down to the river and watch the men fish."

I think she knew the reason all of the deputies hadn't gone fishing and wanted to give them an opportunity to enjoy themselves while the judge was away.

We made sandwiches and took some ice beer, enough for everyone, and walked to the river, the deputies trailing behind, with their rifles and fishing poles.

The sky was as blue as I've ever seen it and Etta seemed happy and held my hand and it was as though none of the past had ever happened, as though we were just a couple who were beginning to fall in love.

We spread a blanket beneath the cottonwood trees and had our picnic while the deputies fished.

"Look," she said, "Hector has caught a catfish."

It seemed to delight her as much as it had Hector.

Then his head exploded in a bloody spray and he pitched into the river, the catfish still flopping from the end of his line.

"Run!" I said, but Etta seemed paralyzed.

The other three deputies dropped their fishing poles and scrambled for their rifles but Rodrigo was cut down by a bullet to his spine. I pulled Etta to cover behind one of the cottonwoods as I watched Xavier and Juan snatch up their Winchesters and take a kneeling position of defense.

Across the river from a crop of rocks, I saw the glint of a rifle barrel, then it was gone.

I called to the deputies in Spanish to lay down a line of fire toward the rocks while I took Etta out of harm's way and back to the house. They took aim and began firing.

"We have to make the house," I said. She looked at me. "Etta, he won't get to you, I promise."

She nodded and I took her wrist and told her to move ahead of me and run as fast as she could. I shouted for the deputies to do a slow retreat but to keep up enough firepower to protect themselves. Part of me felt like I was running out on a fight, but Etta's safety was more important to me than my sense of pride and duty. I had only one duty and that was to her.

We reached the house and I gave her one of my pistols and told her to go inside her room, lock the door, and stay there.

"Quint . . ."

"He won't get to you."

She looked at the pistol I'd placed in her hand.

"If he does, I know what to do," she said.

I kissed her and went back outside, running toward the river. But halfway there I met Juan and Xavier who were doing a quick retreat.

"He quit shooting," Juan said.

"I think maybe we killed him or something," Xavier said.

"What you want us to do, boss?"

"Get to the house, one in front, one in back and keep an eye out."

"What about you, boss?"

I looked at them, saw the earnest loyal eyes of men who Roy Bean was probably paying too little to risk their lives.

"The woman," I said. "If he gets past me, don't let him get to her. You can't kill him, you kill her."

They exchanged looks, then nodded.

"We won't let him get her, boss."

"Good, get going."

I made my way to the river and took up a position behind one of the thick cottonwoods where I could take clear aim at the rock outcropping. Hector's body had already floated downstream and Rodrigo lay facedown as though he were taking a siesta there on the warm banks.

I waited for any sign of movement from the rocks and asked myself after an hour what the hell was going on until I realized that Gypsy Davy wouldn't still be there. He was too crafty for that. He'd eliminated two of us, then in the confusion had made his escape. I cursed myself for not having figured his next move and retreated back to the house.

That's where I found them, Juan and Xavier, their throats slit, and my heart sank.

Then the door of the courthouse flew open and Gypsy Davy stepped out onto the gallery, one arm around Etta's waist, a small but deadly looking blade pressed to the side of her neck.

"Don't be foolish," he said. "Throw down that rifle and rid yourself of those pistols."

Etta looked at me, her eyes reflecting utter despair. I'd failed her again.

"Seems we all want her," Gypsy Davy said. "Enough that we're willing to die for her. Are you willing to die for her, sir? Better yet, is she willing to die for you?"

"What sort of man would kill the woman he supposedly loves?" I said.

His face flashed anger, then amusement.

"Love? What would you know about it? Love is not wanting to live without the object of your affection. If I cannot have Etta, then nobody will."

"You're a coward," I said. My anger boiling as much at him as it was at myself.

He laughed.

"Do you think by calling me names that will somehow save your life or hers? Honestly, Etta, what sort of rustic have you taken up with? A man who can't even protect you, just as the last one and the one before that weren't able to protect you. Only I can do that, my darling. You should know—"

It was as though his knife-hand simply exploded, followed by the sound of rolling thunder. The blood splatter covered Etta and instinctively she screamed as Gypsy Davy was knocked backward, releasing his grip on her. I was on him in an instant, hammering his face, the bloody stump of his hand flailing wildly, trying to hold me off.

Whether from pain or fear or both, he drove his full weight against me in one mad charge and we went over the railing and landed hard on the ground with him atop me. The force knocked the wind from my lungs and in that instant he grabbed a derringer from his pocket and stuck it to my face. I slapped his hand hard just as he pulled one of the triggers, the shot grazing my cheek. His strength, however badly wounded he was, was unbelievable.

I struck him twice in the jaw, knocking him off me, and scrambled to my feet. He was coming up with the pistol when I slammed a forearm to the side of his head at the same time I drove a knee into his face. He flopped on his back and lay still.

I staggered to Etta's side.

"Are you alright?" I asked. She was desperately wiping the blood from the side of her face.

"Yes, yes!" Her voice was filled with terror. "What happened . . . ?"

I didn't know. Then I heard the sound of a rider, the soft clop of hooves on the hardpan and looked around.

Sweet Jesus, it was Harve Sweetwater!

He dismounted, carrying a Winchester.

"Hell of a shot for a one-armed man," I said.

"Not such a good shot, considering I was aiming to blow off his pumpkin," Harve said. He looked at me, then at Etta. We both knew the risk he'd taken. An inch or two off the mark, she would have been dead. I tried not to think about it, because I knew that sooner or later Gypsy Davy would have killed Etta—if not with a knife, then some other way not as kind.

And as though he had read my mind, Harve said to Etta, "I didn't have a choice, I hope you know that."

She gave him a knowing look and he said, "Well, I guess we're done here. I guess we can all go home now—"

A bang like the slap of a screen door, and Harve spun sideways, sank to the ground.

I came around instinctively, drawing the Deane Adams, and shot Gypsy Davy, the little pearl-handled derringer clutched in his fist. His body jerked once, then lay still.

Harve sat there in the dust clutching his hip, blood trickling through his fingers.

"Damn it to hell and gone!" he moaned. "He's as bad a shot as me."

"Why'd you come back?" I asked, kneeling beside him, stuffing his fancy red kerchief in the wound in his hip.

"Aw, hell, Quint. When'd I ever listen to anybody?"

"Maybe you will now."

He looked at the patch job, grinned weakly, and said, "You think Cleo would cotton to a one-armed man got himself a limp?"

"It's what's in here, partner," I said, tapping his

shirt pocket. "I think she'll like you clear down to her shoes."

"Well, maybe I'll stop in Cheyenne on my way back to Denver and see does she like soirees."

CHAPTER 35

Roy Bean said, "Where's all my deputies?"

I told him what had happened and he sat down on the top step of the gallery and said, "Holy Jesus—they're all dead?"

"They didn't have to die," I said. "They stayed because they were loyal and good men."

He removed his top hat, the one he'd worn to Chicago with the fancy suit, and fanned air on himself.

"Hector was the only one could speak any English," he said. "I'll miss him something terrible. The others, too. They might not have spoke English, but they played dominoes good and knew how to catch fat catfish."

"I hope you'll see if they got families, they're taken care of, Roy."

"Not to worry, we're all like family here. Got to be, we're all we got—just each other."

"I didn't mean to visit harm on you or your men," I said.

He shook his head. "I invited you, remember?"

We sat there for a few moments, then he said, "Etta, she okay?"

"She'll make it, Judge."

"She inside?"

"No. She went back to Nebraska. She had an aunt who lived there. Has an empty home waiting for her. Someplace peaceful."

"What about you?" he said. "You going to join her?"

"Maybe someday, Judge. She needs time to bury the dead."

He took a deep breath, let it out, said, "Damn if I couldn't stand a drink. You?"

We drank liquor on his gallery and watched the first rain in weeks drip off the eaves.

"I never got to see Lily," he said. His cravat was twisted, his fancy shirt dusty. "She'd gotten ill and the performance got canceled. I paid a stagehand to let me sit in the theater even though I knew she wasn't coming. In my mind I could see her up on the stage singing a song just for me. Later I'd take her flowers and ask her to escort me to dinner where we'd eat oysters and drink fine champagne and laugh and talk the night away."

"I'm sorry you didn't get to see Lily," I said.

"I am, too, in a way. Thing is, I still got her here," he said, tapping a stubby finger to his heart. "She'll always be there. I don't suppose you can probably understand that, a man foolish as me?"

"I understand what you mean, Judge."

"What's your immediate plans?"

"Hadn't thought about it, Roy. Why do you ask?"

"Well," he said, "it'd be nice to have a deputy that spoke some Americano, somebody I could play dominoes with whilst waiting for lawbreakers."

"You offering me a job?"

"You needing one?"